One Last Gift

a Novel

by

Sherry Ann Miller

Published and Distributed by:

PUBLISHING & DISTRIBUTION

Granite Publishing and Distribution, L.L.C.
868 North 1430 West • Orem, UT 84057
(801) 229-9023 • Toll Free (800) 574-5779
FAX (801) 229-1924

First Printing: July 2000

Cover Photograph: Allen Fife
Cover Design: Tamara Ingram
Page Layout and Design: Sunrise Publishing, Orem, Utah

ISBN: 1-930980-01-9
Library of Congress Card Number: 00-106752

Dedication

This book is dedicated to three very special men in my life:

First, to my father, Burke George Stone, Senior, who taught me well and often that I have the agency to choose the way my life will turn out, and from whom I inherited whatever talent I may have as a writer;

Second, to my eternal companion, Frank D. Miller, for his tireless support and dedication, not only as husband and sweetheart, but as confidante, sounding board, editor and personal manager;

Third, but by no means least, to Apostle Russell M. Nelson, who gave me the confidence to continue in my chosen path.

Hearts Anchored
with Love

Preface

Each person must learn about the reality of God at their own pace, in their own time, and through their own experiences. For most of us, these moments of learning arrive as tiny bursts of illumination to our heart and soul, without fanfare or special effects. However, when one has truly strayed from the Gospel's path, and upon a journey that may never bring their heart home to God, it is sometimes necessary to endow that person with an extraordinary experience that will change their life forever. Such is the case with Kayla Dawn Allen, who left the Gospel ten years earlier to pursue another pathway. She is about to discover what it means to come face to face with her own mortality and what the word "eternal" really means. Join her now, and watch her miraculous story unfold...

Chapter One

"Hard port tack!" Kayla yelled aft as she whisked the stray ends of her honey blonde hair behind her ears. Simultaneously, she held up her left arm to illustrate her instructions.

Josh turned the wheel counterclockwise, the bronzed muscles in his arms barely flexing with the effort.

Lady Dawn, a beautiful Ericson 38, responded with the grace and refinement of royalty, slipping through the December wind in a hasty left, narrowly missing the stern of Tenacious, another sailboat that had been in the lead only moments before. Lady Dawn passed Tenacious by a scant few meters on her starboard beam.

The Saturday afternoon Cruiser's Regatta, a spur of the moment race in International waters outside San Diego Bay, conjured up during the only storm free weekend of the Christmas Season, had turned into a healthy race.

The wind freshened on their starboard beam, the mainsail filled rapidly and hugged to port. Kayla tugged on the boom vang sheet, tweaking the mainsail until it no longer fluttered along the leach.

Meanwhile, Josh released the starboard jib sheet and the Genoa did a lofty curl around the mast forward, then filled with air from starboard as Kayla pulled the port jib sheet tightly through the self-tailing winch. Lady Dawn heeled hard to port as Joshua eased the wheel an inch back to starboard. The sailboat picked up speed, the rails only a few inches above the water, white spray misting their wet passage. Kayla stepped across the cockpit to the starboard bench. Then she pressed all her weight against the starboard gunwale. Quickly they gained a lead on Tenacious.

"Four hundred meters and closing," Kayla yelled. The wind carried her voice everywhere but aft, as she raised her left hand, four fingers exposed. She tucked another finger down against her palm at three hundred meters.

Tenacious held its pace, giving fair tribute to its name. Lady Dawn and Tenacious were the only contenders for first place, the other sailboats having fallen behind several tacks ago.

If Lady Dawn could only keep her speed another three hundred meters, Kayla thought wildly, but Tenacious was bearing down and would soon retake her wind. The situation warranted a desperate measure and as that thought formed in her mind, so did the solution.

"Hard Starboard Tack!" she screamed back at Josh. Her right arm went up simultaneously, but she kept her middle finger crossed over her index finger as she did so, hoping that her soul mate would understand the hidden message. She looked back and saw Josh wink at her.

Running his hands around the wheel clockwise without touching the wheel gave the appearance that he was beginning a starboard tack.

Ruth Broadman, navigator on Tenacious, screamed to her husband, "She's tacking to starboard!" At the same time Ruth raised her right arm and pointed for direction.

"Not this time!" yelled Captain Bill. "I'll not be outrun by that little lady!" Immediately he turned Tenacious' wheel to starboard, realizing halfway into the turn that Lady Dawn was not changing course. His starboard tack gave Lady Dawn the advantage she needed. He threw his hat upon the deck and swore a stream of profanities, to no avail.

Lady Dawn whisked forward, taking full advantage of the prevailing wind. Tenacious could never recover and pass her now. Within moments she passed the final marker. The commodore's gun gave an enormous bang, signaling Lady Dawn's complete victory.

Kayla yelled joyfully, jumped down from the cockpit bench and into Josh's waiting arms. They kissed and embraced as they listened to radio chatter filling the cabin with congratulations for them!

"Lady Dawn, you've never failed me!" shouted Kayla.

"She's a beauty!" Josh agreed.

Kayla smiled as she remembered a day last summer when Josh raced against Lady Dawn in his Cabo Rico 38 and lost the race three boats behind.

After performing their obligatory salute to the crew aboard the commodore's boat, they headed toward Shelter Island.

Kayla maneuvered Lady Dawn with as much skill around the harbor as had Joshua out in the race. Funny, she mused silently, I never thought sailing would thrill me this much.

Her thoughts wandered back to a time, seven years ago, when she was engaged to marry Ed Sparkleman, Junior, a man who worked on her father's Utah ranch. She had grown up in the same mountain valley with Ed Junior and his three brothers. They were sons of her father's best friend, Ed Sparkleman, Senior, who was always called Sparky by everyone who knew him, to avoid confusion. She and Ed Junior had planned to live on her father's ranch and have a house full of children. At that time she had no hope of sailing the sea and she thought she would spend the rest of her life on the Bar M Ranch.

Now her dreams had become reality: Kayla was actively participating in ocean sports that, as a child, she'd only read about. Sailing, sea shell gathering, fishing, marine biology and navigation consumed her free time. In addition, she was a successful corporate officer in a government funded, civilian operation, doing research in marine sciences and climatology, fields that had captivated her interest and fired her imagination. She owned her own sailboat and would soon have her condominium free and clear of all encumbrances. Best of all, she had met and fallen in love with Joshua Bridger Clark.

She looked at the engagement ring on her left ring finger and delighted in the way it sparkled as the sunlight reflected off it. Thoughts of sailing with Josh for three full months this coming June thrilled her beyond all expectations. They would then be on their honeymoon together, Kayla and her husband, Josh.

Her fiancé juggled his life between many roles: meteorologist, marine scientist, Lieutenant Commander in the United States Navy, world navigator, and Captain of his own impressive cutter-rigged sailboat, a Cabo Rico 38 named Bridger's Child. Soon he would begin his most challenging role of all, that of husband. Somewhere in their promising future, Kayla hoped, he would also be known as Father.

Kayla shivered in anticipation and looked down in the cabin at her fiance.

Joshua gathered up the bright work covers. He tossed the blue canvas pieces out onto the cockpit cushions, then followed them out through the companionway. He spread the mainsail cover first, fastening the canvas at the bottom of the boom, his muscles flexing in the afternoon sun.

Just looking at his bronze skin and hair-dappled chest, visible beneath his unbuttoned shirt, gave Kayla goose bumps. He was trim and well muscled in all the right places. His handsome face was both rugged and tender. She could spend hours just staring into his soft blue eyes and running her fingers through his thick, chestnut hair.

More important to her than his outward appearance was his gentle nature, regardless the strict, military upbringing in which his father had raised him. Josh was the kind of man who could be a perfectionist if there was a reason for it, yet he could also bend, be forgiving and compassionate when the situation arose. One of the things she loved about him was his spontaneity and his willingness to make changes whenever warranted.

Why he loved Kayla, on the other hand, she simply could not understand. Yes, she admitted to herself. She was somewhat pretty, with long, honey blonde hair and dark, sparkling brown eyes. Her slim body was endowed in abundance where feminine curves were important. Regardless of her womanly beauty, Joshua knew her to be stubborn and unyielding unless it could be proven, by some scientific basis, that she was wrong.

When men think of wives, thought Kayla, they want women who are gourmet chefs, fastidious housekeepers, great mothers and erotic lovers. So far Kayla felt she had failed in at least three areas. She could neither cook nor bake; unless one considered canned soup and deli-style sandwiches a gourmet meal, her cooking skills were less than basic. Her condo was never what she would term "military clean." Third, although she loved children, childhood development was not on her priority list in college. As for being an erotic lover, she studied Joshua's male form in his docker pants and open shirt as he placed a cover on the forward port. She felt her body heating up with an insatiable desire that surged through her. Sometimes she felt the game of waiting until their wedding day was not worth playing. She wanted him! Now!

"What?" he asked as he gave her a quizzical grin.

"What back?" she answered, somewhat embarrassed.

"It looked like you were about to ask me something," he explained.

"No," she lied. Then she amended, "Not yet, anyway." She blushed as she realized he had almost read her thoughts.

"Hmm," he mused. "Maybe later?"

"Absolutely," she agreed, knowing in her heart it would be much later... on their honeymoon.

He smiled. "You can release the tension on the jib sheets now," he said, as he hung a fender forward on the starboard side.

"Aye, aye, Captain," she grinned. She released the jib sheet from the port cleat, let it go slack and recoiled it, then did the same to the starboard jib sheet.

Swinging into slip 16A, they were greeted by many of the Cruiser Regatta members. Some of them assisted Joshua with docking lines as the boat slipped gracefully next to the dock. Congratulations became the mainstay of conversation from them all.

Kayla stepped down to the dock as Tenacious' captain, Bill Broadman, reached forward and shook her hand. "Smooth trick, little lady," drawled Bill.

She punched him in the arm playfully. "I thought everyone had seen the movie, Wind," she responded.

"I must have missed that part," Bill admitted sheepishly. "Why don't you and Josh join us for dinner up at the Bay Club?"

"We'll have to take a rain check on that, Bill," said Josh, jumping down from the starboard side to the dock. "The Navy's got me clocking in at 0400 hours. I've got another week ship side doing the El Nino study. Then we're both at the labs until Christmas, analyzing data."

"Speaking of Christmas, are you two putting your boats in the Float Parade this year?" asked Bill.

Josh winked at Kayla. "I'm still hoping to talk Kayla into it, Bill."

"By the looks of that ring on her finger, you're good at sweet-talking Kayla into anything, Josh!" Bill exclaimed as he slapped Josh on the back and raised an eyebrow.

Bill's wife rushed over to Kayla's side. "He finally got around to proposing!" Ruth gushed. "Look, everyone! Kayla's sporting an engagement ring!" Cheers from the crowd came in response.

Kayla blushed, Josh beamed.

"When's the wedding?" asked the Commodore.

"The end of May," said Josh.

"May?" Bill put his arm around Kayla's shoulder. "That's almost six months away," he protested. "Now, listen up, little lady. If that slow poke wants to make you wait six months before he'll marry you, I've got two brothers who'd give their eye teeth to do the job next week. You just let me know if you change your mind."

Kayla smiled demurely. "Somehow I think he's worth waiting for."

"Did you hear that?" Bill bellowed. "She thinks Josh is worth waiting for!" Bill began singing and gyrating his hips at the same time. "Girl, he's got a hold on you!"

Ruth elbowed Bill in the ribs. "Leave them be, you drunken old sailor."

"I'm not drunk, Ruthie," Bill complained. "I'm imitating you!" He let out an animalistic laugh.

"That's what I thought," said Ruth. "And it ends here." She grabbed him by the ears playfully and kissed his forehead. Bill settled down immediately.

Everyone laughed. Then "Goodbye," "Congratulations," "Catch you later," came from the throng and within moments the welcoming committee vanished.

Kayla helped Josh unload her personal gear to the car.

"You don't mind skipping supper with Bill and Ruth, do you?" Josh asked as he stowed their belongings in the trunk.

Kayla smiled. "No, I wanted to get home early tonight. Dad said he might call."

They got into the white Toyota and Josh started the engine.

"You spoke to him?" he asked quietly.

"No. He e-mailed me, but I didn't pick it up until last night."

"Then you haven't told him about our engagement yet?" Josh steered the car out of the parking lot and onto Shelter Island Drive.

"No. That's why I wanted to get home early," Kayla sighed. "I know he's going to be happy for us, Josh."

"I wish we could tell him in person, Kayla," he complained. "It's impersonal announcing it over the phone."

"I probably won't see him until Christmas," she explained, "if he comes to San Diego at all. Besides, he told me last August that you'd make a great catch."

"Yes, but that was BEFORE you caught me," he reminded.

The drive along Rosecrans into La Playa became a nerve-wracking jumble of narrowly missed accidents, screeching brakes, honking horns and holiday shoppers annoyed at the heavy traffic. "Welcome to the Christmas rush," Josh mused aloud.

"Can you believe we have less than two weeks?" she asked.

"Which reminds me, Mother and Father are having a dinner party the night before Christmas Eve with family and some of their friends. They want to make it a formal announcement party."

"That sounds interesting," Kayla hedged. "How many friends?"

"Knowing Mother, ten or twenty."

"But—?" she asked, sensing the hesitation in his voice.

"But Father is obliged to invite his former officers from the base, as well as mine. We can expect no less than fifty or sixty guests."

"That's a mob, not a gathering!" she exclaimed. "Will she need me to help her with that many coming?"

He shook his head. "I'm sure JonPaul and his staff will manage fine, but I'll tell her you offered. It will give her one more reason to elaborate on why she thinks so highly of you."

The Toyota turned left on Nichols, toward the bay, where Shelter View Condominiums overlook Shelter Island with San Diego in the background. The modern two-story building had sold out quickly and Kayla was one of the lucky few to get a bid in on the top floor before the prices skyrocketed. She had purchased a three-bedroom condo on the southeast corner, which suited her lifestyle perfectly. The white stucco building was framed handsomely with sandstone red tile roof, giving a definite Spanish flavor. Fringed palms and red ginger plants lined every pathway. The gardens were well-maintained. Kayla felt her investment was worth the initial risk she'd taken.

Josh maneuvered the Toyota into an underground, secured area where he parked in a vacant spot next to Kayla's aquamarine Oldsmobile. "When we're married, your two parking spaces should work out well for us," he observed casually.

This was the first time he'd ever spoken of their living arrangements since they began dating almost eighteen months ago, Kayla was surprised, but she tried to keep her response as unconcerned as his observation. "We're going to live here afterward?" she asked, hoping she sounded more delighted than relieved.

"Yes, I thought that was understood."

"Of course," she answered. "I hadn't given it much thought, but it would be rather awkward for me to live aboard full time like you do. I have too many books and furniture. I need more space than that."

"Listen, Kayla, I realize you probably want a home after we marry, but until our children start coming along, I don't see any reason to sell your condo. Besides, I have a notion that you're going to want to build a house to suit your own design." A frown wrinkled his forehead as he worried whether or not he had overstepped his bounds.

Kayla turned to him and wiped the wrinkle away with her thumb as she gently caressed his rugged face. "I am, Josh. I was just surprised that you had mentioned it. We've spent a year and a half together yet we've never discussed anything personal, including financial matters and housing issues," she said. "I was beginning to think we were always going to live on the edge."

He kissed her fingers tenderly. "We have a lot more going for us than money, Kayla," he persuaded. "We have quite a number of common interests."

"Like sailing," she agreed, interrupting him, "and fishing and marine sciences and the theater."

"Strawberries," he teased. "Walks on the beach, research, writing, jogging, computers, dancing."

"There's one thing you haven't mentioned," she mused aloud with a delicious grin.

"Oh?" He raised an eyebrow.

"I absolutely adore you!" Kayla exclaimed.

Josh gave her a long and lingering kiss in response. His voice was husky and needful when he said, "And I adore you, darling Kayla, but I also feel much more than whatever is found wrapped up in simple words like 'love' and 'adore.' I doubt there is a word in the English language quite strong enough to describe how I feel!" Then he kissed her again.

When he finally let her up for air Kayla decided that she needn't worry whether or not she could be an erotic lover. She felt confident that was one role she could manage far beyond the call of duty.

After saying goodnight at her condominium door, Josh kissed her one more time and headed down the hall. She hoped he felt as frustrated as she did, but she was also grateful that he could control his own needs and desires. That, too, was one of the things she loved about him. He guarded her feelings carefully, rarely intruding on what she considered important. Even when they disagreed he respected her right to her own opinions.

Inside her condominium Kayla had excelled in her goal of creating an environment straight from the ocean floor, with splashes of coral and aquamarine giving color to the basic sandstone interior. Kayla also loved botanical gardens and had formed several tropical plants into groupings to give her condo a more casual feeling.

Glancing at the clock, Kayla hoped she would have time for a bath before her father telephoned. She ran a warm bubble bath while she watered her plants, then returned to her bedroom where she stripped off her clothing and unceremoniously dumped them into a hamper.

She returned to the bathroom where she reclined in the hot, bubbly water. Almost immediately she felt her body relax and her neck muscles ease. The water soothed and comforted her and took away some of her longing for Josh. She had never imagined she could want someone to the extent that her whole body would physically ache.

The telephone rang, interrupting her thoughts and jarring her out of her reverie. She wrapped a towel around her soapy body and rushed down the hall to her bedroom where the phone rested on a night stand by the bed.

"Hello," she answered breathlessly.

"How's my little princess?" came a deep voice from the receiver.

"I'm fine, Dad. And you?"

"I wasn't sure I'd make it in time to call you tonight. I had to help Sparky find a stray that wandered off."

"Were you successful?"

"Found her keeping warm up in Sutter's Cave, after we'd spent three hours of saddle time searching in a blizzard. It took another three hours to get her back on the winter range."

"How is old Sparky?"

"Aw, his rheumatism acts up every time a storm blows through, but other than that, he's the meanest, scrawniest, stubbornest ranch hand this side of Texas."

Kayla could easily picture old Sparky with his stubbly silver whiskers and receding hairline. She knew that her father's description of him was made in jest. The two men shared a friendship that had strengthened both of them over the past three decades, and Mont would readily give his life to his best friend, if it were needed. "Give him my best, Dad. I miss my childhood pal sometimes."

"How about your Dad? Don't you miss him sometimes, too?" came the complaint.

"That goes without saying, Dad. You know that."

"A Father knows a lot of things, Kayla, but sometimes he just likes to hear the words."

"I love you, Dad. You're the best."

He only hesitated a moment before he asked, "Then why am I the last one to get the news?"

"What?" she asked in surprise.

"I heard about your engagement through the grapevine, Kayla. When were you thinking on telling me?"

Was that a hint of disappointment she heard in his voice? Kayla felt she had violated their sacred trust. "Who told you?"

"Sparky's youngest son, Abbot, goes to the University down in Salt Lake City. His mentor is Hans Bridger Clark. Need I say more?"

"Josh's brother? Oh, Dad, I didn't dream word would get back to you so fast. I'm sorry."

"It's okay, Princess. An oversight, I figured."

"No, Dad, it's not like that at all. Josh proposed two days ago. We told his parents the same day. Then we telephoned you several times, but you were out. That was when I e-mailed you that I needed to talk to you."

"I hoped it was something like that, Princess. Now don't you worry about your old Dad. I'm tickled as punch about you marrying Josh. I told you he'd be quite a catch and it looks like I was right."

"Yes, Dad. You're always right."

"So when's the big day? And don't tell me it's a Christmas wedding. That's too soon."

"The last Saturday in May, Dad. Will you be able to come?"

"Wild horses couldn't drag me away, little princess. Me and your mother, we'll both be there."

The mention of her mother gave Kayla a start. Then she realized what her father meant. She smiled to herself and acquiesced. "You might have something there, Dad."

"KayDawn is never far from me, Princess, you know that."

"I know, Dad. Listen, I'm still dripping, I was in the tub. Do you mind if I call you back later?"

"If you'd like, Princess, but I can't guarantee I'll hear the phone. I'm plum tuckered out, think I'll hit the hay right after dinner. It's been a long day in the saddle. I'll be home tomorrow after Church. Will you call me then?"

"Oh, Dad, I have to work tomorrow. Josh is going ship side and he's sending some critical data to me via satellite. You understand, don't you?"

"When will you get home?"

"The download will probably take at least four or five hours. That will put me back here around 2100 hours, at the earliest."

"In layman's terms, Princess."

"I probably won't get home until nine or later, Dad."

"That will make it ten o'clock here."

Kayla realized the problem immediately. Mont's normal schedule was precise and predictable, dictated by the needs of his own physical limitations. If he didn't eat by 5:00 P.M., his stomach protested all night long. Bedtime, too, was predictably by 9:00 P.M. "What about Monday, Dad? I have Monday off."

"Yep, that'll work," he drawled. "I'll call you right after supper, around 5:30."

"Fine. I'll be waiting for your call and I won't be in the tub," she giggled. "Bye, Dad. I love you."

"Bye, Princess. Talk to you on Monday."

Kayla replaced the receiver and scurried down the hall to the bathroom. She ran more hot water to adjust the temperature back up where she liked it, then sank once again beneath the bubbles.

That went well, she thought to herself, even if her Dad had learned about the wedding from someone else. She felt an immediate sense of gratitude that he could forgive easily.

His comment about her mother still bothered her, however, and she found herself going back to it repeatedly. His words echoed around in her mind until she felt nauseous with them: "Me and your mother, we'll both be there."

Lamont Allen, better known as Mont among his peers and family, could be tenaciously stubborn when it came to Kayla's mother. He believed KayDawn's spirit still lingered near him whenever he needed her guidance or influence. Mont was a deeply religious man who believed completely in what he called "spiritual manifestations." Kayla couldn't blame her father for clinging to his dreams, but to her that's all KayDawn was, a dream in a lonely man's heart, a hope in an otherwise empty void. She couldn't fault him for wanting to hang onto her mother.

KayDawn Murray had married Mont Allen after a whirlwind courtship. Within nine months she'd presented the rancher with his only child, whom he affectionately named Kayla Dawn Allen.

Kayla didn't remember her mother. The bits and pieces her father told her had failed to make the woman seem real to Kayla. Mont blamed KayDawn's death on himself. He'd wanted another child, a son, and had pressed her into agreement shortly after Kayla was a year old. Unfortunately, KayDawn hemorrhaged when the embryo implanted in one of her fallopian tubes and the doctors could do nothing to save her.

These memories brought moisture to Kayla's brown eyes. It had been a long time since she had allowed herself to think about her mother. She had seen photographs of KayDawn, a striking beauty with deep brown eyes and auburn hair.

Mont often told Kayla that her mother had a quick mind and a gentle manner that few women could equal. She used to rock their infant daughter to sleep every night while singing a little tune to her, one that Mont taught Kayla when she was still a child. What was that song? Kayla tried to remember it, but she couldn't. The realization forced a single tear to slip silently down her cheek.

Chapter Two

After leaving Kayla at her condominium, Josh headed the Toyota back to Shelter Island, to the Bay Club Marina where his Cabo Rico 38, a fine, classic sailboat named Bridger's Child, waited at slip 18A. He had been living aboard for two years, ever since the El Nino Project (ENP) was initiated between the United States Navy and the Oceanic and Atmospheric Laboratories, Inc. (OAL), a government-funded, civilian corporation actively engaged in a study about the effect of ocean temperatures on atmospheric changes, among myriads of other projects.

Kayla, who had been working for OAL for four years as a climatologist and marine scientist, had moved up the ranks to Executive Officer over the civilian portion of the El Nino Project. Josh met Kayla two years earlier when he was assigned to act as liaison between the OAL and the U.S. Navy, during all military involvement in the ENP.

At the Bay Club Marina, twelve of the two hundred boats moored there were owned by people who lived aboard. Josh had become personally acquainted with each of them and felt that he belonged to a peculiar, yet considerate and neighborly community. The "live aboards," as they were affectionately called, performed a great service at the Bay Club Marina, and as such, were treated by BCM management like royalty. Each live aboard knew the owners of every boat on their dock and made it their personal duty to keep an eye open for strangers, vandals and the occasional misfit. Fortunately, these were few and far between because the BCM was a locked facility with security guards who patrolled day and night. Without a pass key for the gate, the only access to the marina was by boat.

Josh slipped his key back into his pocket, after passing through the security gate, and headed down to A Dock where Bridger's Child waited for him. The classic sailboat scarcely budged in the water when

Josh stepped on board, indicative of the stiffness engineered into the design of the sailing craft.

Josh's mind wandered in all directions as he unlocked the padlock at the companionway and entered the cabin below. The finely detailed teak interior of the well-appointed salon escaped his attention as he reflected back in time and considered his life before and after meeting Kayla, in almost a complete review, pausing when he pondered over the last two years.

He sank down onto the port settee and flipped on a light, then spread a newspaper out on his knees, but he couldn't concentrate enough to read it. Instead his thoughts focused on other things.

Josh had enjoyed his military career following graduation from the University of Southern California. He had always been able to do basically as he pleased. Since he'd grown up in a military family, he was well adapted to schedules, goals and achievements. Much to his mother's dismay, he'd had little interest in settling down, marrying or raising a family. He supposed it was because he had such a full and engaging career. He had to admit to himself that he hadn't met anyone with whom he had wanted to share his life.

The feeling that he had the world by the tail came to a complete and screeching halt two years earlier when he met Kayla. Thoughts of Kayla had imbedded so deeply inside Josh that he doubted he would ever be the same. Intuitively he knew that he loved her from the moment his eyes rested upon her.

His entire lifestyle unraveled before him and he wandered around in a stupor for several weeks. In the very beginning of their relationship he felt clumsy, he could hardly communicate with her until they had worked side by side for almost three months. During that time period he had suffered terribly. He couldn't eat or sleep well. His concentration on the El Nino Project was sadly lacking. His mother even noticed the changes and "hovered," as most mothers do.

During the first three months of their acquaintance he analyzed the situation in its entirety. His first consideration regarded Kayla's undeniably beautiful countenance. Her frame and gentle features excelled far above every woman he'd ever seen or met. Positive that physical attraction was his first downfall, he discounted Kayla's beauty as unimportant altogether.

Secondly, he hoped to discover why her personality and character traits had so totally enraptured him. He considered her professional demeanor and her ability to completely control her staff without seeming the least bit domineering. She was also capable of performing any scientific function pertinent to the El Nino Project without discipline, explanation or instructions.

Josh started listing other things he noticed about her, from which he could gain more insight into her personality. He noticed she had an adorable smile that melted his knees and spine, realizing this was not in his best interest. She liked to laugh and he learned quickly that she could tease when she felt a joke was warranted.

He reviewed her credentials, learning that she had received her masters degrees from Brigham Young University in Climatology and Meteorology in only four years, an outstanding feat. Three years later, she received her Ph.D. in Marine Biology and Oceanography from the University of Southern California. She had been a prominent member of OAL for four years, having excelled in every position in which the company had advanced her.

It took him three months to analyze his own heart and feelings and build a composite list of all Kayla's attributes. When he had completed that, he knew he was in a serious predicament. He already loved her with every fiber of his being, but he had no idea how she felt about him.

For the next three months he fumbled around her like a school boy trying to decide on the most appropriate way to ask her out. Fortunately for him, he heard through one of her co-workers that she was interested in purchasing a used sailboat and he happened to own Bridger's Child, which gave him a leading edge. He mentioned casually, or at least he hoped it had been casually, that he knew a little about sailboats and would welcome the opportunity to assist in her search. It took them most of that first summer to find the Ericson 38 that she "fell in love with," and he hoped and prayed, once Lady Dawn had been duly christened, that Kayla would "fall in love with" him, as well.

That Fall Kayla had invited him to fly to Utah with her, to help her father for a week on his ranch, rounding up stray cattle and getting ready to move the herd south to the winter range. He jumped at the chance and appreciated the opportunity to see a side of Kayla he never knew existed. She could ride horses like the wind, rope and brand a calf with an ease she'd grown adapted to, while being raised high in the Uintah Mountains.

Her father, Mont Allen, was just as rough and rugged as the land he loved and lived for, yet he was tender and empathetic for Kayla's needs and desires. Mont's entire life had been devoted to Kayla. Josh realized it would take a special man to earn the respect and trust of Mont where his daughter was concerned. Fortunately for Josh they already had one strong connection in the field of religion. The two men had discussed ethereal theories and concluded that their religious beliefs were similar and compatible. Although Josh did not belong to any formal religious group, as did Mont, their basic beliefs were almost identical.

Kayla had never shared her religious opinions with him. She had been raised under her father's standards and respected them, but Josh had never heard her say that she believed the same as Mont.

After the trip to the ranch he felt more secure in their relationship and they spent nearly every waking moment together when they weren't knee deep in work. They attended the theater, enjoyed dancing and formal military functions, went sailing, fishing and snorkeling together. Nearly every day they jogged together after work.

He found there was nothing that he couldn't enjoy doing with her and she seemed to enjoy everything that interested him. Josh didn't have a single memory of her that he couldn't savor.

The only trait that worried him, he had discovered early in their relationship, was Kayla's rigid stubbornness, which he blamed on her having been raised by Mont, who radiated tenacity at every turn. Josh hadn't yet decided if this was a fault or an attribute, but he was positive it wouldn't matter in the long run.

His blue eyes softened as he recalled the past eighteen months of dating, the pleasure and joyfulness that permeated his life for loving Kayla. They seemed to fit together companionably. They rarely quarreled and when they did Kayla was usually right. He smiled. He felt divinely blessed for having found Kayla after thirty years of living without her. He remembered all their activities over those months of dating and wondered if she loved him earlier on than he'd thought.

Reaching for the telephone, Josh dialed Kayla's number. She answered on the third ring. Just hearing her voice made him feel whole and complete.

"Hello."

"Were you sleeping?" he asked, realizing he'd spent more than two hours deep in thought regarding her.

"No," she answered. "I was just, well, to tell the truth, Josh, I was just thinking about you."

"I'm glad," he smiled to himself. "I was doing the same, only about you."

"What did you decide?" she asked. "Am I worth it?"

"Of course!" He was surprised by her question. "You're worth more than anything in the world to me."

"But you're giving up so much to marry me," she protested. "Your naval career can't possibly mean less to you than I do."

"Without you, nothing else matters," he admitted. "You know that I have a promising career teaching marine science at the University, beginning in September. That will give us plenty of free time in the summer to spend together. You and our life together are the only things of any importance to me. I've known that for more than two years now."

"Two years? We've only been dating for eighteen months," she responded.

"But I knew that I loved you from the moment I first met you, two years and two days ago," explained Josh.

"You proposed on the second anniversary from when we first met?" she asked in surprise.

"I'm fairly sentimental," he apologized. "I couldn't stand the thought of another day going by without you knowing how much I care about you. I feel like I've loved you forever, Kayla."

"Oh, Josh," she sighed, "I hope now that we're engaged we'll keep sharing our feelings openly. I love to hear you say you love me. I've waited a long time."

"You have?" he questioned.

"Of course," she explained. "Before you put this ring on my finger, I didn't have a clue as to how you really felt about me."

Josh laughed. "You don't know how much I've needed to share my feelings with you. The first moment I met you my heart melted and poured into yours," he confided. "I've been caught between longing and fear ever since."

"Longing and fear?" she asked in surprise.

"Longing for you to return my love and fearing it would never happen," he admitted.

"Has it been that bad?" she wondered aloud.

"You have no idea!" The relief she heard in his voice said more than any words could have.

"I'm sorry, Josh. I had no idea love could be so painful for you."

"Wasn't it ever painful for you?" he asked.

"For me," she confessed, "loving you is the best thing I've ever done for myself."

"I feel much better hearing you say that!" exclaimed Josh. "Kayla, I have to confess that I don't think I could go on living if I didn't have you beside me."

"You have nothing to fear on that score. When you put this ring on my finger I knew it would stay there forever," she admitted. "But I'd better let you get your rest or you won't be able to get up on time tomorrow."

"You're probably right," he conceded. "I'll try to make a computer connection by 1500 hours tomorrow. You'll be ready?"

"Of course."

"I'll be back late Thursday. Oh! I forgot to tell you that Mother and Dad want us to have dinner with them Friday evening. My mother is dying to start planning our wedding for us."

"She is?" Kayla laughed. "That's so like her."

"Did your dad call?" he asked.

"Yes, but your brother beat us to the punch line."

"Hans?"

"Yes, he knows Sparky's son, Abbot."

"It doesn't take a marine scientist to figure out who told Hans," he admitted. "Was Mont disappointed to hear the news second hand?"

"I think so, but he didn't make anything of it."

"At least one of us has a parent who understands," said Josh.

"Your parents do, too," she encouraged, "just not all the time."

Josh laughed. "On that note, I'll say goodbye."

"Bye, Josh. I love you with all my heart."

"I love you back," he said, emotion evident in his voice.

Josh replaced the receiver and walked forward to the head. Studying his face in the mirror, he smiled, "You are the luckiest man alive," he told himself, "but maybe it's not luck at all, maybe someone upstairs *IS* watching over you." Satisfied with his second guess, he nodded, turned out the lights and went to bed.

Mont Allen, owner of the Bar M Ranch, slept fitfully. Ever since Sparky told him that Kayla would be marrying Joshua Bridger Clark, Mont had been uneasy. He hoped it had nothing to do with his daughter's wedding plans.

He rolled out of bed and went down on his knees, once again, unable to control the unsettled feeling in the pit of his stomach. He felt empty inside, as though even KayDawn, his beloved, departed wife, had left him alone for a season. After a long and hearty prayer he stood and put on a plaid flannel robe and soft wool slippers.

He wandered through the old log lodge that had been his home for more than sixty years without turning on the lights. He knew every inch of it by heart, down to the last knothole. His father had built the lodge before Mont arrived in the Allen family.

He stepped down the hand-hewn log staircase to the large Gathering Room, where country dances had livened the household on many occasions, where ranch hand and ranch owner shared space on the leather furniture, and swapped stories near the huge rock fireplace. He smiled to himself as he thought about the Gathering Room. In his youth, the massive room had been called the "Living Room," since the family did most of their 'living' there, but ever since he married KayDawn, it had been dubbed the "Gathering Room." She insisted it could not possibly be a Living Room. As she put it, "A crowd could gather here!" Even now, twenty-seven years after her death, Gathering Room remained the name by which the place was known.

In this home they affectionately called "The Lodge," Mont had bid farewell to both his parents and three older brothers, himself being the only one of four sons who lived long enough to inherit it.

Out past the front door he walked, and onto the wide covered porch, where he sat down in an antique rocking chair made by his grandfather more than eighty years previous.

Here is history, he thought to himself, where the West was tamed through the blood and the sweat and the tears of the rancher, where herds of cattle had grazed and grown season after season, since before Mont was a child. Owner of the Bar M Ranch, more than a thousand acres of grazing land and the only privately owned property of its kind within the boundaries of Ashley National Forest, Mont realized that time would never change the beauty of the scene before him. It remained perpetually the same.

Across the small meadow below him stood blue spruce and native fir trees tall as sky scrapers, each tree striving to reach higher toward the heavens than the others. A cozy cabin, tucked among the pine trees on the other side of the meadow, puffed a light and airy smoke from its chimney. The smoke drifted skyward, lifted by a fresh breeze, and danced among the incoming snowflakes. The snowfall had eased considerably and he knew, from experience, that the storm had almost died.

How he wished the fire within his soul could be extinguished so easily. The almost physical discomfort first settled in his belly, like a rough boulder with sharp edges. If the weight didn't injure him, the edges surely would, he decided.

He felt as though his own life had become a fragile sort of existence. Not that he was ailing. With exception of an irritable gut and a grumpy disposition, Mont felt he was the picture of health. Of course, there was the fainting spell two months ago, but the new medication took care of that. Lately, however, he felt life slipping away from him and he couldn't explain why. He even wondered if he would soon follow the path his wife had taken so many years ago when she left her body here and walked in spirit back to God.

Was his uneasiness because Kayla was finally going to marry? Was it because his little Princess would now become someone's Queen? He shook his head with that thought. He was genuinely happy for Kayla and he liked Josh well enough. Josh wasn't of the same faith, but he had the same insight and that was equally important in the scheme of life.

Mont had already looked into Josh's background and he was satisfied that Josh could support his daughter, had good ideals and standards and a healthy upbringing.

What was really troubling him? His thoughts went back to the past several months and the request from Sparky's boys. They wanted him to sell the ranch. He still had to give them an answer, but as he looked out over the valley he wondered if the disposition of the ranch was the real reason he couldn't sleep tonight. No, he decided at last. Sparky had been like one of the family all these years and some provisions must be made for him, but could Mont ever sell the ranch to please Sparky's boys? He'd hoped for something better than seeing the ranch run into the ground by a herd of ambitious developers. Oh, he knew the boys meant well, but he also knew they'd been talking to that lady investor who'd tried to sweet talk Mont into selling it to her a year ago.

Concern about who Kayla planned to marry bothered him a little. He wasn't totally convinced that she loved Josh more than she loved Ed, but like so many other parents, hand picking his child's spouse was not an option he'd been given. He didn't know how he would settle that question so he buried it for the moment.

Mont finally decided that most of his uneasiness came from within himself. He wondered if he was still in good standing with God, whom he affectionately referred to as "the man upstairs." Like most people when they reach their fifties or sixties, he began analyzing his life's purpose. He asked himself whether or not he'd made a difference to anyone along the way.

There comes a time when every person has to meet head on with the limits of their own mortality and Mont had reached his time. He supposed it would come sooner or later, but he'd always hoped it would be later. The past few weeks he found himself keeping a score of the good and the not so good about his daily life, and to his dismay, he occasionally found a deficit in his account at the end of the day.

What he felt particularly sad about was that Kayla didn't seem to attach any importance to the spiritual side of life, although he'd invested most of her lifetime trying to teach her about what's really important. He felt that somewhere along the way he'd failed her.

The other thing that bothered him was the last promise he made to his wife, KayDawn, the day she passed away. He had given his word of honor that he would give Kayla the trunk with the memories of KayDawn that he'd held in privacy all these years. He hadn't shared them with Kayla, not even after making KayDawn the promise. He lowered his head in shame. "I'm sorry, KayDawn. I failed you, too, honey," he whispered.

It was then that all the memories came flooding back and he thought on something he'd tried to bury for twenty-seven years. The images were so real and startling that he found his eyes filling up with tears, regardless of his effort to control them. First he saw, in the back of his mind, the truck racing down the mountain road at break neck speed. It seemed so real he could even smell the leather upholstery and the dust choking his lungs. Then he could see himself driving the truck like a mad man down to the hospital at Vernal.

His wife, KayDawn, bled beside him on the seat. She was pale and calm yet her voice was urgent. "Mont, you have to promise me one thing," she pleaded as the truck bumped off the dirt and onto the hard pavement. "I don't want Kayla to grow up without knowing her own mother."

"KayDawn, honey, you ain't gonna die. I'll get you to the doctor in plenty of time," he had scolded. "I don't want you talking like that."

"Promise me, Mont," she clutched at him and Mont put his hand over his right arm, just where she'd touched it so many years ago. "Promise me, Mont. You give her my hope chest and all my memories. Don't let her forget about me, Mont."

"You ain't—" he began once again, but her fingers dug into the flesh on his arm and he realized her pain must be unbearable.

"Promise!" she demanded, cutting off his protest.

"I promise, KayDawn, but you're gonna feel silly about this tomorrow when I take you home. You can give Kayla the trunk yourself."

"It's a hope chest, Mont. You tell her it was her mama's hope chest."

"Okay, honey, but here's the hospital," he said as he squealed the tires into a sharp turn toward the emergency room entrance. "You're gonna be fine now."

Mont parked the truck near the emergency room and hurried around to the passenger side where he scooped KayDawn up and carried her into the hospital. After that everything happened so fast he hadn't even noticed the blood that had soaked through his sleeve. It even ran down the front of his shirt and onto his jeans.

The doctors rushed KayDawn behind a curtain while a nurse asked him to wait in another room. It seemed like he'd paced the floor only ten or twelve minutes, at most, when the doctor came in and said simply, "I'm sorry, Mont. We couldn't save her."

Mont's mouth dropped open as he gasped in shock. He felt as though he'd been kicked by a mule and all the wind was knocked out of him. It took several moments before he finally asked, "Are you telling me my KayDawn is dead, Doc?"

When the doctor nodded, that was the last thing Mont ever remembered about KayDawn dying.

The next thing Mont knew six months had passed. Kayla was walking and chattering. Winter had come and gone without him ever realizing it.

Sparky filled in the gaps in Mont's memory. He said Mont walked around in a daze so long that Sparky had taken to sleeping at the ranch half the time to keep an eye on him. He'd had to hire a young Navajo girl from the reservation to come in and keep house for Mont and take care of Kayla. Sparky also said that Mont had spent at least five of those six months in bed, refusing to get up or even bathe. The only time he ate was when Kayla put food in his mouth and that was how he stayed alive. The doctor suggested they encourage Kayla to make a game out of it, so they gave her cookies and fruit and whatever else they could to help her persuade her daddy to eat. She'd literally saved Mont's life.

Later Sparky learned for himself what it was like to lose his wife and Mont was able to repay Sparky in kind for some of what Sparky had done for him.

Mont sighed with the memories. He shivered, realizing how cold the weather had turned. Then he wiped the tears from his face with his hands, and afterward, wiped his moist hands on his robe. The snowstorm had left more than four feet of fresh snow on the ground and he was glad they'd gotten the cattle down to the winter range before the worst of it hit them. It had been an unseasonably dry fall and they were beginning to wonder if winter was going to come at all this year.

It seemed hard to believe Christmas would be here in less than two weeks, yet this was the first snow fall of the season. Still, it'd give the cross country skiers something to do between Christmas and the New Year.

Then the idea struck him. He knew exactly what he could do to make it up to KayDawn for not keeping his promise. It would take some planning and a heap of persuasion, but Mont snapped his fingers and stood up, anxious to begin.

Chapter Three

Sunday traffic seemed unusually light as Kayla drove northeast on Rosecrans to Interstate 5, then south until she connected up with State 75 across San Diego Bay. An unusual red-orange glow seemed to accompany the morning smog and the San Diego-Coronado Toll Bridge was the perfect place from which to view it. Yet Kayla did not take much notice as she drove across the bridge to Coronado and straight on fourth street until she made a right turn onto Alameda.

The barrenness of the Coronado peninsula always captured Kayla's imagination and she wondered if it had always been so desolate. Perhaps man had desecrated it enough that it simply could never recover. If she didn't know there was ocean on all four points of the compass, she would have thought she had wandered into some desolate desert country where military housing ruled the neighborhood. She also wondered why the military had no imagination when it came to color schemes. Nearly all their buildings were painted a drab sandy yellow.

At the end of the block she parked the aquamarine Oldsmobile in front of a row of military buildings one story tall that looked like squat, fat caterpillars across the desert sand. Each building, or pod, as it was called by the U.S. Navy, housed various divisions of civilian and military operations linked closely to one another for the purpose of research. Inside the building that housed the Oceanic and Atmospheric Laboratories, Inc. (OAL) stood a security desk and a small main lobby, with offices and labs leading off, via doors around the perimeter. This arrangement saved a great deal of space and provided easy access to security from nearly any anteroom.

Not that security had ever been a problem, Kayla thought to herself as she signed in at the front desk and picked up her identity badge. Who would want to steal "secrets" about El Nino and its relationship to temperature increases near the equator?

She smiled as the security guard, a Corporal in the U.S. Marines, assigned to secure the OAL site, per Navy request, recognized her. "Seems a little formal making the Commander's XO sign in, doesn't it, Miss Allen?"

"Excuse me?" she asked, uncertain of the Corporal's question.

"Word travels fast on base, Ma'am." He grinned and tapped her ring finger lightly while arching an eyebrow in approval.

"I guess it does, Corporal," she said, admiring the engagement ring in question. "Although this diamond could have been from anyone other than Commander Clark, don't you think?"

"I don't think so, Ma'am. We received a memo from retired Admiral Bridger Clark to take good care of his daughter to be," he explained.

"I see," she nodded. "Were there any other instructions?"

"No, Ma'am," he answered, "but the Admiral is a man of few words, don't you think?"

"Yes, I do," she laughed. "Well, turn the power on for the main computers, Corporal Edwards."

"Yes, Ma'am," he said as he turned, opened a power box behind the desk and flipped several switches.

"And set up the emergency generators," she continued. "We can't risk a brown out today."

"No, Ma'am, we can't."

"Thank you," she responded then turned to enter her office.

Each room in the building was sadly lacking in style and modernization, but Kayla had been able to place a few tropical plants in one corner to take the edge off the severity of the place. Where creature comforts were lacking, however, the company made up for everything in the choice of their electronic equipment, which was state of the art from the ground up. Kayla went to one panel along the south wall and flipped on a switch. An almost inaudible humming sound tuned up instantly. Small lights of various shapes and colors lit up a switchboard and Kayla noted the readings for each and every one of them, logging them down in a notebook. Within moments a huge antenna on the roof began to rotate in alignment with specified satellites as they passed by in the atmosphere miles above the earth's surface. Three computer screens, mounted on a shelf to the right of her large desk, hummed into action. Kayla sat at the desk and studied each one of them. She could network from one computer to another with a button on the keyboard and she now did so, her fingers flying over the keys with skill and ease.

The day passed quickly, and when a flashing window appeared on the main screen, Kayla realized she had been so involved in her own work she'd failed to notice that Josh's window of opportunity had arrived. She made a few keystrokes and the computers began downloading information that Josh sent to her via Satellite from somewhere in the Pacific between Cocos Island and the Galapagos.

While she waited, she pinpointed his location from the satellite transmission exactly, then studied a detailed chart of the Pacific Ocean that filled an entire wall in her office. She marked the spot with a push pin and labeled it, then opened a laptop computer and began entering data pertinent to the download in order to file the incoming information categorically into sections, once she received it.

The download took more than six hours with only a few hesitations as one satellite went out of range and another picked up again. Kayla kept busy with other studies until she could finally type in the words, "Transmission ended, 973.2 megabytes stored. Out." Kayla backed up the computer system on three separate one-gig disks, locked all three in separate vaults, then turned off the computers.

When she stepped out into the lobby, the security guard handed her three pieces of paper. "Base headquarters hand-delivered these messages for you during the download, Miss Allen. A Mr. Lamont Allen wanted you to return his call right away."

"Thank you," she said, taking the papers from him. "I'll do it in my office." She turned and re-entered the office where she placed a briefcase on the desk, took a cellular phone out of her purse and turned it on, then dialed the number and waited for her father to answer. She was concerned about calling so late, but she felt it must be urgent for Mont to call her at work on a Sunday three separate times. How she wished Corporal Edwards had told her earlier, but from past experience, she knew that telephone use within the main pods was strictly off limits, especially during satellite transmissions to prevent contamination or theft.

After only two rings she heard Mont's gruff voice, "Hello."

"Dad, it's Kayla. Is something wrong?" She tried to keep her voice calm.

"It's about my coming to San Diego for Christmas, Kayla," he explained with a hint of urgency in his voice that put her on edge. "I won't be able to make it and I was hoping you'd agree to come home. I have some loose ends I need to tie up. Do you think you can do that?"

"I don't see why not, Dad," she answered, certain that something was terribly wrong with Mont. "I can get away most anytime with a few days notice. Would you like me to come right away?"

"I know you're busy, Kayla, and Christmas is getting close. Could you come for two weeks? How does this Saturday sound?" he asked. He seemed tense and anxious. Kayla felt a lump of fear rising in her throat.

"Dad, is everything all right?" she asked.

"Kayla, everything will be all right if I can get you home for a little while. I've gotta go, Princess," he said, cutting their conversation short.

The line went dead before Kayla could respond any further. Immediately she dialed a travel agent and made her request: an open-ended round trip ticket to Salt Lake City International Airport, and a one-way flight to Vernal, Utah, via private charter.

Kayla returned to the lobby. Corporal Edwards was getting ready to transfer his shift to another Marine Corporal. Kayla approached the desk and signed out. As she did so, she questioned, "Do you know where those calls from Lamont Allen originated?"

"No, Ma'am," said Corporal Edwards, "but I know how to find out."

"Will you do that for me, Corporal?" she asked.

"Yes, Ma'am." Immediately the Corporal dialed a number and spoke with someone on the other end. While he did so, Kayla returned to her office to pick up the briefcase she had left on the desk and forgotten in her concern about Mont. By the time she arrived back at the front desk, Corporal Edwards had a piece of paper for her.

"Thank you. I won't forget this," she promised. She looked down at the paper and read Corporal Edwards' crisp block letters:

CALL # 1, BAR M RANCH, 435-789-BAR-M

CALL # 2, BAR M RANCH, 435-789-BAR-M
CALL # 3, ASHLEY VALLEY MEDICAL CENTER,
435-789-9999

Kayla sighed in dismay and stuffed the paper into her purse. Then she rushed out to the car and began the drive home. Her mind raced with concern for Mont. What was he doing at the Medical Center, which, to her way of thinking, was just a glorified title for the local hospital in Vernal, Utah? Every conceivable reason why he would have telephoned her from there left her feeling more uneasy with each passing moment.

By the time she reached the condominium it was well after 9:00 P.M., yet she had no idea how she'd driven home. Her hands were shaking and she had trouble getting her key in the condo door. Finally she forced herself to calm down. Within moments she stopped trembling and turned the key.

Once inside she dropped the briefcase on the floor and latched the door locks tight. She rushed down the hall to the bathroom where she studied her face in the mirror. The woman staring back at her was pale and distraught.

How she hated this game Mont played with her. Why can't he speak what's on his mind? His preconceived notion of tact and diplomacy had always been a nugget of contention between them. In fact, it had become one of her most annoying pet peeves.

Why must we always stop and think about what we say so that we don't worry or upset someone else? Why do we dance around the issues without getting our toes near the surface, all for the sake of protocol?

She shook her head, thinking how Josh had said only the night before that he had loved her from the moment he first met her. Yet he'd tortured himself for two full years before he'd ever told her.

Kayla was just as guilty. Because she'd been raised to use tact and discipline in conversations, she had not been able to share her feelings with Josh, either. Strong emotions built up inside her. She felt weary at keeping restraint a viable, almost tangible exercise so as not to expose feelings to anyone other than self.

Suddenly she realized she was very angry. She was angry with Josh for not telling her he loved her early on and angry with Mont for not explaining what was wrong with him.

Most of all Kayla was angry with herself. She had no idea how to get that private part of herself out, the part that whispered, "Keep it in! Don't let it out or someone will be unhappy."

If Mont was sick or dying she wanted to know about it.

The moment of anger passed and Kayla wandered into the kitchen where she tossed a quick salmon salad together, then took her plate out onto the deck to watch the city lights beyond Shelter Island and the marinas.

Dark clouds had come in during the day and now the first drops of rain began falling. Their two-day reprieve from El Nino had passed and San Diego was in for a long siege of rain, according to the weather charts.

For a moment she wished she had gone with Josh down to the Naval Carrier. That moment slipped by quickly, and she realized it was a relief that the new data had arrived. Although she wasn't required to go into work the following day, she decided to anyway. It would give her one extra day to begin, with her staff, to sort all the information out, and decipher what it meant. That was the challenge she enjoyed, and she had to admit, she was quite good at it.

She decided the best solution to the problem with her father would be to throw herself into her work until it was time to leave for Utah.

In the meantime, Kayla would have to figure out how she could let Josh's parents down without hurting their feelings. Though retired from military duties, Admiral Clark still maintained a close relationship as an advisor to the U.S. Navy, and had little patience for any alterations in his strict schedule. Josh's mother, Sarah, took a more relaxed and negotiating stance in family affairs. Sarah would understand, but that still left the Admiral to contend with. After some analyzing, she finally concluded that Admiral Bridger Clark was Josh's problem, not hers. He would have to deal with his father.

That left only one fly in the ointment, how to tell Josh. He had planned on her spending Christmas week with him and his parents at their La Jolla home, beginning Christmas Eve Day, a week from Thursday.

Kayla sighed wearily and wandered back to the kitchen where she rinsed off her plate and put the dishes in the dishwasher. Then she brushed her teeth and went to bed.

On Monday Kayla went into work, regardless that it was her day off. This kept her mind busy and unoccupied with worry about Mont and eased, somewhat, the aching she felt while missing Josh. The week passed quickly. Kayla was up by six and at the office by eight. She worked her staff tirelessly, resisting the temptation to go home by five each night as she watched them depart one by one. If she arrived home by 10:00 P.M. it was an early night for her. In that time she got more accomplished than she could have if Josh had been around.

When Thursday night finally arrived she went home early enough to be there for his call, which she expected around 11:00 P.M. She stood at the sliding glass door and watched the rain splatter against the deck incessantly, as it had done nonstop since Sunday night.

True to his promise, Josh telephoned at 10:59 P.M. and she smiled at his punctuality.

"Hello," she answered quickly.

"Did you miss me?" he asked.

"Yes, but the question could be reversed."

"My worse times without you were after hours when life calmed down on board."

Kayla smiled. "I'm glad to hear it." Then changing the subject, she said, "We've been analyzing the data you sent, we've even come up with a new hypothesis," she announced. "But it can wait until morning."

"As long as you're not ready to hang up," he responded. "I need to hear your voice. Talk to me."

Kayla took a deep breath. "First," she began, "there are going to be some changes in our Christmas plans."

"Oh?" he asked.

Kayla explained her feelings regarding her father's phone calls and Josh seemed genuinely concerned and interested in what was going on in Mont's life.

Then Josh explained about life at sea, and on board the carrier. He described, in detail, his duties and responsibilities. He also shared some jokes he'd heard that weren't too off color for her.

She laughed and snuggled up to a big pillow on her bed.

Before they realized, it was 2:00 A.M. and they finally said good-bye. Kayla hung up and sank back into her cozy bed, but she couldn't sleep. She tossed and turned for almost two hours. Finally she decided around 4:00 A.M. to get up and go to work.

Traffic was refreshingly light that time of day and the rain had finally stopped. She wondered how long this reprieve would last as she whisked over the freeway in record time.

When she arrived at OAL, she was surprised to find Josh's white Toyota in the parking lot. She checked in at the front desk then walked over to Josh's office and knocked on the door.

"Come in." His voice seemed tired.

Kayla opened the door, walked in, then closed the door behind her.

"If that's the coffee, Corporal, just set it on my desk," said Josh, not taking his eyes from a map of the Pacific Ocean on the wall. From his standing position he couldn't see that it was Kayla so she walked up behind him and wrapped her arms around his waist. "Say," he started to complain. Then he put his hands on her wrists and realized immediately who it was. "Say!" he exclaimed, this time with no irritation in his voice whatsoever. He turned around and took Kayla in his arms where he kissed her soundly.

Out at the front desk the Corporal on duty watched them eagerly on a television monitor. Josh drew back for a moment, looked straight at the camera above the door and asked, "Are you getting all this Corporal Lauer?"

The Corporal pressed a button on his desk and said, "Yes, sir!"

"Then switch the camera off, Corporal Lauer," said Josh.

"Yes, sir!"

A small red light on the camera face blinked off and Josh was satisfied that the Corporal had responded to his order. He looked down into Kayla's sparkling brown eyes and said, "Now, where were we?"

She snuggled even closer and whispered, "I think we were right about here . . ." She placed her hands on the sides of his face and brought him nearer until his breath mixed with hers. Then she kissed him more thoroughly than she'd ever done before.

When she finally let him up for air, he said, "Whew! If this is why my parents felt a shorter engagement might be more appropriate, they were right. I'll never make it until May!" And he kissed her soundly as punishment.

The rest of the day Kayla and Josh were both miserable. They wanted only to snuggle up in each other's arms and forget the world, but they did their best to maintain an orderly work environment for their staff. Josh was particularly impressed with the conclusions Kayla had drawn from some unexpected data he had sent to her. It warranted further investigation and would take weeks to sort out, but Kayla and her work force had catalogued and filed nearly every piece of data in a concise format that would make investigation time run much more smoothly.

The employees at OAL were not surprised to see that Kayla and Josh both quit work at precisely 5:00 P.M. that evening. They gossiped among themselves as to the reasons why Kayla had plunged herself into work so hard while Josh was away, and everyone commented about the size of the diamond Kayla wore.

Kayla drove to her condominium, took a quick shower and dressed in a casual aquamarine dress that floated about her like she was made for it. She brushed her blonde hair until it sparkled and fell about her shoulders in soft waves, then put on a matching sweater and a touch of perfume.

Joshua arrived a few moments later. He looked dashing in his military whites, everything "spit and polish," as he called it. Josh always wore his best military uniforms when around his father as a symbol of respect towards Admiral Clark. He certainly had no passion for wearing them, otherwise. He had confessed this much to her early on in their relationship. It was the first hint Kayla had that Josh was ready to retire from military life.

As Kayla contemplated on their relationship, she realized that Josh had shared more of his feelings with her than she had thought last Sunday evening. It was just his affection for her that he had guarded so carefully. She felt immediately grateful that those days were behind them now. As if to emphasize the fact, Josh approached her with a subject that had evidently been bothering him all day long as they boarded the elevator and pressed the down button.

On their way down to the parking garage, Josh prefaced his request with a confession: "I don't think I can endure Christmas without you,

Kayla. This past week has shown me that much. Do you suppose Mont would mind if I come with you?"

She hesitated. "I don't know, Josh, but I'll ask him. It's a little late to take the same flight, since I leave tomorrow at noon."

"I know, but I didn't mean tomorrow. I meant in time for Christmas." He paused. He didn't want to make her feel pressured, but on the other hand, he didn't want her to underestimate his affections for her, either.

"Let's go back up and call him before we go over to your parents," she suggested with a broad smile.

The elevator doors whisked open and Josh pressed the "up" button. The doors closed and they started up again.

Kayla was secretly delighted that Josh cared so much about her. It was obvious to her that their week apart was just as miserable for him.

Her silence made Josh a little nervous. He felt like he was intruding on something sacred and private between Kayla and her father.

Within moments they were back in the apartment where Kayla walked to the telephone in the kitchen and dialed a number.

Mont answered immediately. "Hello."

"Dad," Kayla smiled. "Were you in bed?"

"Nope," Mont drawled. "I'm reading the evening paper."

"Dad, I have a question," she began.

"You're still coming, aren't you Princess?" There was a note of concern in his voice.

"Of course, Dad, but Christmas is an important event for Josh and me this year. We really want to be together. What do you think we should do?"

Josh smiled at her choice of words, grateful that she wanted his company as well.

Kayla smiled as she heard Mont's response: "Tell Josh that if he'll give me from tomorrow night to Christmas Eve Day alone with you, he can come up Christmas Eve and spend the rest of the week. Tell him to bring his family, too. There's always plenty of room up here. I need to talk over some things with you alone for the first few days, Princess, you understand."

"Yes, Dad. And I think you're wonderful for being willing to share," said Kayla with fervor. "I'll see you tomorrow night then."

"I'll be waiting for you, Princess," Mont responded. "I'm happy about you coming, Kayla. I hope you know that."

"You knew I would come, Dad," she teased. "Admit it."

"Well, now that you've got Josh to be your knight in shining armor, I wondered how much pull your old dad would have," Mont chuckled.

"Tomorrow night," Kayla reminded him. "I love you. Bye."

She turned to study Josh's expression. He was grinning from ear to ear. "I guess you heard, hmm?"

"Not all of it," he said.

"He wants you to come up Christmas Eve and bring your whole family with you," she told him. She wrapped her arms around his waist. "I'm not nearly so worried now as I was earlier. He sounds so good, so healthy. Surely I've blown everything out of proportion."

"Probably," said Josh. "I wonder if my parents would go," he mused aloud. "It would take some talking, but I'm sure you can handle it."

"Me?" she punched him playfully in the arm. "They're your parents!"

"They're almost your parents, as well," he reminded.

"Hmm," she said with a mock pout, "I never considered that. If I marry you, I have to accept your parents as part of my family."

"And I have to put up with Mont and Sparky," he bantered back. "Think about that!"

"Oh, I've got it much easier than you," she agreed.

"That's what I was afraid of," he said dryly

She looked up into his soft blue eyes and studied his face for a moment, as if wanting to memorize every feature.

"What?" he asked.

"What back?" She gave him a delicious smile and pulled him down to kiss him, much like she'd done earlier that morning at the office.

After a few moments he pushed her away gently. "If you keep that up we'll never get to my parents' home in time for dinner!"

"Okay," she agreed heartily. "I won't ever do it again."

"Hey!" he complained. "Don't say that!"

"Then what's more important? Kissing me or going over to La Jolla for dinner?"

"Hmm, let me think," he teased, stroking his chin. "Dinner or kissing? Hmm . . ."

"Joshua!" she protested.

"No contest!" he announced. He pulled her as close as he could get, leaned against her warm, trembling body and kissed her mightily.

Chapter Four

On a cliff a few miles north of La Jolla stood a capacious villa constructed of cobblestone, brick and tile, surrounded on three sides by meticulously groomed tropical gardens. The southwest side, facing the ocean, held an Olympic size swimming pool, jacuzzi and covered patios with open lawn gently sloping downward for more than two hundred feet, all the way to the cliff. The perimeter of the property was fenced with a solid brick wall ten feet tall on three sides, with black wrought-iron gates and a circular cobblestone driveway. The brick wall at the cliff's edge, by sharp contrast, was less than three feet tall and afforded a spacious view of the ocean and La Jolla beach to the south.

The home itself was built to resemble a French villa, with a wide, formal, covered entry and lots of southwest facing sliding glass doors that opened onto several covered patio areas. The center half of the home, designed mainly for entertaining, was open and expansive, with a great room large enough to hold a hundred guests comfortably. It had a distinct Mediterranean flavor in the decor and furnishings. The dining room held one long olive wood table hand made in Italy with capacity for sixty guests. A gourmet kitchen, opposite the dining room, was separated by a swinging door. One end of the villa housed the master suites, with den, media room, sewing and craft room, spacious bedroom and living room, while the opposite end housed the guests' bedrooms, eight of them, a reminder of the hope Sarah's father had that his daughter would have many children. A short distance from the house stood a four-car garage and beyond that, the delightfully well kept servants' quarters.

Kayla couldn't help feeling a bit uncomfortable as they drove past the gate and into the estate. Granted, her father's ranch house exceeded all expectations of size from a child's standpoint, but she worried their future children would get lost at Grandma Clark's house.

Sarah Hansen Clark came from wealthy stock. The entire Clark Estate had been a wedding present from her parents on the day Sarah married the Admiral, as Bridger Clark was often called, even by lay-men. Grandpa Johannes Joshua Hansen, known as Hans, had hoped Sarah would give him "a half dozen grandchildren," since he and his wife had only been able to have Sarah. Unfortunately for all their wishes, Sarah remained barren for many years. Then a mighty miracle fell upon them when Sarah gave birth to her only children, twin boys. Naming the two came easy for all of them. Hans and the Admiral went to work immediately persuading the women in the family to agree: Hans Bridger Clark for the first born twin and Joshua Bridger Clark for the younger.

When Grandpa Hans died of causes incident to age a few years past, Grandma Hannah came to live with her daughter, Sarah, and the Admiral. Mother and daughter had always been dear friends and Sarah couldn't allow her mother to live in a house full of servants without any family around her. The Hansen family mansion was sold, and all the family investments were consolidated. Grandma Hannah, her weary body now showing the heavy toll time had taken, held a wealth of knowledge and memory in her finely tuned mind. Hidden beneath her silver hair and wrinkled skin were priceless memoirs she now hoped to record, with Sarah acting as scribe and confidante.

Along the formal driveway Kayla saw evidence of the gardener's magic touch. A tropical array of winter flowering shrubs and groups of palm trees varying from short and stout, to tall and towering, greeted them. A gentle rain fell peacefully, yet nothing so beautiful as the scene before her could ease the discomfort within.

How would the Admiral react to news she would not attend the upcoming dinner party, held exclusively in their honor as a formal way to announce their intended wedding? She sighed as the Toyota drew nearer the French villa.

Joshua parked the car near the front door and walked around to help Kayla out. "You're quiet tonight," he mused aloud, taking her hand and holding the umbrella for her at the same time.

She stood and straightened her dress. "I was thinking about your family," she confessed.

"Did you come to any conclusions about us?" he asked.

Kayla smiled. "The contrast between us is rather startling, Josh. It must be true that opposites attract."

"Meaning?"

"When I went to girls camp as a teenager we used to sing a silly song about mountain girls," she explained. "I couldn't help wondering what a mountain girl is doing marrying into such a civilized and wealthy family."

"Hopefully she's doing it because she loves the guy she's marrying," he suggested.

She wrapped an arm around his waist and turned toward the front door. He put his arm about her shoulder. "I'm marrying you because I want to go on loving you for a lifetime," she answered. "But I was thinking about our children on the way over and I wondered if they might be as intimidated as I am about coming over to Grandma Clark's house."

"Grandma Clark," he rolled the name around on his tongue. "I like the sound of that. How many children do you suppose we'll have?"

"Unlike our grandparents, Josh," she explained, "we usually get to choose."

"Good! Shall we have a son first or a daughter?" she could hear the bantering in his voice.

She chose her answer carefully. "That may be a viable choice in the future. Right now I think I might be able to adjust to one of each."

"Adjust?" came his quick response.

"I worry what kind of a mother I will be."

"Are you serious?" he asked in surprise.

She nodded. "I know it's silly, but I don't have one positive childhood memory of my mother," she answered. "I hardly know more than her name and what she looked like from photographs. So how am I supposed to know how a mother relates to her children?"

He frowned and was about to answer, but the front door opened. Grandmother Hannah hobbled toward them using a cane. Her silver hair sparkled in the light beneath the formal awning. "Will you be joining us for dinner or standing out here in the rain, admiring each other all night?" Hannah asked with a twinkle in her eyes.

"Grandma!" Josh beamed. He folded the umbrella and stepped forward onto the covered entry where he gave his grandmother a big hug.

Kayla joined him and offered Hannah her hand. "Good evening, Hannah."

The older woman brushed the gesture aside and wrapped her wrinkled arms around Kayla, squeezing her tightly. "You call me Grandma now, Kayla. You're the granddaughter I never got to have until now and I'm going to enjoy every minute of it!"

Kayla laughed as Hannah stepped between her and Josh, took both of their arms and allowed them to escort her through the great room, past the glass sliding doors and out onto a covered patio where Sarah was lighting candles at a beautifully decorated glass table. Gentle rain splattered the cobblestone beyond the drip line where the tiled roof ended.

"Oh! You made it," Sarah smiled, giving Kayla and Josh a kiss on the cheek and a warm hug. "I thought we'd dine out here this evening. The rain has been so refreshing and JonPaul turned on the patio heaters so we won't get chilled."

"It looks delightful," said Kayla. "You've gone to so much trouble."

"No," Sarah disagreed. "All I did was light the candles. JonPaul did everything else."

The man in question slipped out through the kitchen door. "Five more minutes, Madam," he intoned. His black hair was tipped with a faint sprinkling of silver. He had been a member of the family's staff for years and had more than earned his place in their private gatherings. His wife, Jeanette, a superb chef, preferred to remain in the background while JonPaul served as secretary, procurer, waiter, butler, and chauffeur, depending on the needs of the family. Besides JonPaul and Jeanette, there were two housemaids, one grounds keeper and one gardener, but it was obvious by his manner that JonPaul was the man in charge. If anything went wrong, JonPaul took full responsibility. At the opposite end of that spectrum, if anything went right, JonPaul accepted the credit, then distributed proper proportions to all those assisting him.

"Thank you, JonPaul," said Sarah. "Will you inform the Admiral that his son and daughter have arrived?"

JonPaul winked at Kayla. "Yes, Madam. Straight away." And with that he vanished through the kitchen doors more quietly than when he'd arrived.

"How is your biography coming, Grandma?" asked Joshua.

Hannah fairly beamed. She loved it when someone besides Sarah took an interest in her memoirs. "We're working on the final chapter now," she confessed. "I must admit my Sarah has been indefatigable! Nearly every day she sits four hours taking dictation, then another few hours at the computer, entering all my words."

"Every day?" asked Kayla, intrigued.

"Oh, no," explained Hannah. "On Mondays and Fridays we both work at the hospital. The hospital administrator gave me permission, regardless of my cane, to do volunteer work as many hours as Sarah does. She delivers incoming flowers, packages and letters to patients, but that's too difficult for me. I get to sit at a big desk in the lobby and when someone wants to know where a patient is, I look it up on a computer and I tell them where to go."

"It doesn't sound too difficult, Mother. You've been telling me where to go for forty years now," Admiral Bridger Clark stepped onto the patio from the great room.

"Bridge!" Sarah exclaimed.

"I'm sure Hannah knows that I'm teasing her, Sarah dear," said Bridger.

"I do?" asked Hannah playfully.

"Yes," said Bridger, giving Hannah a quick kiss on the cheek. "You only say you moved in here to be near Sarah, when in fact, you couldn't live without me!"

Hannah blushed. "You always get the better of me, don't you Admiral?"

"That's why I'm the XO in this family," he agreed. Then he turned his attention to Josh and Kayla. "Son, Daughter," he said, shaking Josh's hand and giving Kayla a brief kiss on her cheek. "I suppose you won't mind me calling you 'Daughter' on occasion," he hoped. "I've been waiting a long time for this opportunity."

"Of course not," Kayla agreed, "as long as you allow me to call you both 'Dad' and 'Mom'."

"We'd be delighted," he agreed. Sarah nodded. Bridger assisted Sarah onto her chair and slid it in for her. While Josh assisted Hannah to a chair, the Admiral outmaneuvered him in doing the same for Kayla.

Josh smiled and let any protests remain unsaid, knowing it unwise to argue with the Admiral.

When Bridger took his place at the head of the table, he motioned for Joshua to sit beside him. "Son," said Bridger. "Your mother and I were talking," he looked across at Sarah.

She shook her head faintly.

JonPaul whisked into the room with the first course, a delightful shrimp salad with home-baked crackers, French style. After he'd placed a healthy portion in front of each person he left them and returned to the kitchen.

Bridger continued, "Your mother and I were talking about Bridger's Child. Had you thought about selling? Or will you remain a two-boat family?"

Sarah nodded ever so briefly. Kayla was probably the only one who noticed. She wondered what those two were conniving about as the conversation continued.

"We haven't made any decisions yet, Sir. In fact, we haven't even discussed it. We felt it a bit premature," answered Josh respectfully.

Bridger nodded, "I ask because I wanted to offer you permanent mooring up at Friday Harbor in the San Juans. I happened to run across a fairly new boat slip up there. I know how much you love the area and I had planned to give it to you for a Christmas gift this year, but your mother thinks it would serve better as an early wedding present."

Josh beamed. "That's great!" he responded. Then he said playfully. "But you're not going to buy me a mansion overlooking the ocean, are you, Dad? Kayla and I plan to live in her condo at La Playa for a while and build our own dream house later on."

Bridger laughed. "You know me too well, son. You will accept the boat slip, right?"

"Against my better judgement. Yes, Sir!" Josh smiled and rubbed his father's shoulder for a moment.

"I can hardly buy my son a thing without offending him," Bridger explained to Kayla. "He has some fool hardy notion that he should earn his way in the world."

"Which is how it should be," Kayla smiled. "However, the boat slip will be great this summer while we're honeymooning up there. Thank you, Dad and Mom. It was a very thoughtful gift."

"Josh mentioned that he was searching for mooring sites for your honeymoon trip," added Sarah. "When he said you were going to the Northwest, we knew we should give this present early, save you both some docking fees and long distance phone calls."

Hannah spoke up, "It would break my heart if you sold Bridger's Child. Your grandpa loved that boat!"

"I would never sell Bridger's Child," Josh assured her. "I'm fairly sentimental about it, just like Grandpa. And the mooring will solve our two boat dilemma," Josh continued. "We can moor Bridger's Child in the San Juans and keep Lady Dawn here in San Diego. Then we'll have inexpensive housing in the Northwest for vacations and such, while still being able to sail down here. It'll be like having 2 cabins on the water!"

Hannah smiled so wide her whole face lit up, wrinkles and all. "That's exactly what your grandpa would have wanted!"

The main course, chicken medallions with asparagus in cream sauce and wild rice, tasted exceptionally good. Jeanette had a remarkable talent and the Clarks felt particularly fortunate that she used that talent for their benefit.

Conversation ranged from the El Nino Project to the various duties of a volunteer at the hospital; from the price of Hummel figurines, a favorite collector's item for Sarah, to some unusual stories Hannah told about her youth in the roaring twenties, which kept them laughing through the meal.

By the time dessert arrived, Kayla felt she could scarcely eat another bite. Jeanette had prepared miniature Baked Alaska for each of them and Kayla felt obligated to try it. To her amazement she found it settled well with the dinner, yet didn't seem overly sweet or rich.

After supper they retired to the Great Room where a cozy fire took the chill off them. They gathered around the fireplace in overstuffed furnishings of Mediterranean blends and mahogany accents. Hannah sat on a dark, cherry wood rocker and nodded off to sleep as the others visited.

"I hope you'll let me help you with your wedding plans, Kayla," suggested Sarah. "Anything I can do, I'd be honored."

"We haven't had time to discuss it, yet," said Kayla. "I'd like my dad to be included in the planning, as well."

"He must get lonely," offered Sarah, "with you living here while he's back in Utah."

"He's always got Sparky," said Kayla.

"Sparky?" Sarah asked.

Josh cleared his throat. "Sparky is a nickname for Ed Sparkleman, Senior. He's the lead ranch hand at the Bar M. After Kayla's mother died, Sparky took it upon himself to help Mont raise her. He's lived on the ranch in a cabin they built ever since Sparky's wife passed on. He and Mont are almost inseparable."

"Sparky's lucky to have your father for a friend," observed Bridger.

"And vice versa," said Josh. "From what Sparky told me, Mont had quite a rough time after Kayla's mother died."

Kayla's mind wandered back in time to the days of her childhood. She'd never noticed Mont having a 'rough time' about anything. His rugged exterior and occasional gruff manner gave her the impression that little could phase him. On the other hand, he'd never remarried after KayDawn passed away. In her childhood she hadn't thought about it. Now that she was older, the thought bothered her a great deal.

"Kayla," said Bridger, breaking into her thoughts. "You've been unusually quiet tonight. Is anything bothering you?"

Kayla gulped as she realized the moment had arrived. "Actually," she said timidly, trying to gather courage. After a brief moment of hesitation, she added, "I've been trying to think of some way to approach this without seeming ungrateful." She studied their expressions carefully. Josh nodded in her direction and it reassured her. "I know you've gone to an enormous amount of bother in our behalf for the announcement party on the twenty-third, but something's going on at the ranch. I don't know what it is for certain, but my father made three urgent telephone calls to me last Sunday while Josh was at sea. When I returned the calls he said he needed me to come home for at least a week or two. I'm leaving tomorrow."

Sarah reached out and touched Kayla lightly on the arm. "Is he ill?"

Kayla paled a little at the thought. "I hope not. The problem is, he's a private man and whatever is bothering him, he won't tell me until he feels comfortable about it. I did learn that one of the calls he made was from the medical center at Vernal."

"Then he is ill!" said Bridger.

Kayla didn't want to believe it. "Whatever is wrong is private. I know that much. I spoke with him just before we came this evening and he sounded fine."

"Either he's ill or he's not," said Bridger, a slight edge to his voice. "Which is it?"

"I don't know," she confessed. "I wish he'd told me more, but the telephone isn't where he 'airs his laundry,' so to speak."

"A simple solution," Bridger suggested, taking command. "You fly out tomorrow as planned, then come on back in time for our little announcement party. If you need to, you can always fly back the next day."

"No," said Kayla firmly. She noticed the frown wrinkling Bridger's forehead. "He asked me to come for two weeks, and I told him I would."

Bridger's jaw line tightened noticeably. He nodded, though Kayla sensed his restraint.

Joshua noticed also and came to her aid immediately by saying, "On the other side of the coin, whatever it is that Mont needs to tell Kayla, he evidently plans to get it taken care of by Thursday because he's invited all of us to fly out to the ranch for Christmas Eve to spend a week with him. It'd be a good opportunity for the three of you to get acquainted, take in some cross country skiing and do some preliminary planning for the wedding."

Bridger did not soften. "I see," he said wearily. "Your mother and I will discuss it and let you know." He stood and shuffled softly across the great room's expansive floor, failing to say good night at all.

Kayla's eyes filled with moisture and she quickly blinked the tears back while turning her head so Sarah wouldn't notice. Josh put his arm around her shoulder. "He'll get over it, honey. The Admiral has a difficult time understanding when the campaign doesn't work out to his every expectation."

She smiled as though nothing had happened. "I know," she said lightly.

Sarah, more astute than she had imagined, asked gently, "When did you say you were leaving?"

"My plane leaves tomorrow at noon," Kayla answered. "I'm terribly sorry, Sarah."

"If we accomplish nothing else this evening," said Sarah, "then let me remind you that you will soon be our daughter. We'd prefer that you call us Mom and Dad."

Kayla grinned, then hugged Sarah unexpectedly. "Thanks, Mom," she said. "That means everything to me."

Chapter Five

Saying their goodbyes to Sarah and Hannah, Joshua held open the Toyota passenger door for Kayla. Then he got in and turned on the key. The Toyota purred to life and he drove the car down the driveway and out onto the street. Driving through La Jolla, he remained on Coast Highway 101 southbound to Mission Bay. Although it was dark, the rain had finally given up.

Joshua parked the car near Mission Bay Marina and took Kayla's hand. "I understand there's a new boat out here, a real beauty. Are you game?" he asked.

Kayla looked quizzically at Joshua. "I'd love to," she agreed. "But something you said earlier tonight is bothering me."

"Oh?" he asked. "What is it?"

"How many children do YOU want to have, Josh?"

"Me?" he questioned. "I'm easy, Kayla. I'd like a large family if that's what would make you happy. On the other hand, if we have two children and you feel that's enough for you, don't expect an argument from me."

"So you're letting me make the decision in this?" she wondered.

"No," he disagreed. "I'm telling you that I want a large family, but I love you more than anything or anyone. I'll not jeopardize that love for all the children in the world." He stroked her cheek tenderly. Then he opened the car door and stepped out onto the pavement. When he helped Kayla out of the car, he removed his military white jacket and wrapped it around her shoulders.

It had stopped raining, but there was a chill to the night air.

"Thank you," she accepted. "It is a little cool tonight."

"Come on," he said. "You've got to see this boat." He reached inside the car and grabbed his cellular phone. After dialing a number, he said, "Commander Clark here." A pause, then, "Great! We'll be right down."

They walked down the dock to the gate where a young Marine greeted them. "Good evening, Sir," said Corporal Dunbar, a freckled face, red-haired throw back from the Viking era. He saluted Josh.

"At ease, Corporal," said Josh. "As you can see, my fiance is wearing my stripes right now."

"Sir. Yes, sir." Corporal Dunbar winked. "I heard you'd proposed to her and might I say, sir, she's a beautiful catch."

"I'll agree with that," Josh smiled. "Now, where's this ketch I heard about?"

"Straight this way, sir," he said, leading the way down the docks to the last one and all the way to the end. "We don't see too many Hallberg-Rassys in our neck of the woods. They're made in Sweden, you know, in a little town named Ellos. My dad visited there once during shore leave when his Fleet was in that area. He says Ellos is the most beautiful setting for a boat yard in the world."

When they neared the forty-nine-foot ketch Kayla held her breath. The semi-flush deck was entirely laid out with teak. The workmanship was exceedingly fine. The clean lines and details to hardware specifications were amazing.

"She's a beauty, all right," said Josh, exhaling sharply.

"I'll bet she costs a pretty fortune, too," said Kayla. "Oh, I love teak decks, don't you?"

"You couldn't touch this boat for less than half a million," said Corporal Dunbar. "Believe me, this baby is the top of the line."

"I wish we could see inside," mused Kayla.

"We can," Josh told her. "Dunbar."

The Corporal took a key out of his pants pocket. "Yes, sir!" He unlocked the companionway gate and removed it for them.

"Oh, this is too sneaky," said Kayla. "We could get in big trouble doing this."

"I don't think so," smiled Josh. "It was shipped over here by the Admiral. Corporal Dunbar agreed to maintain it."

"Oh, you're kidding!" exclaimed Kayla.

Josh shook his head. "It's a Graduation Present for Hans so don't say anything!"

"That's right!" she remembered.

To Corporal Dunbar, Josh explained. "My brother finally earned his fourth doctorate and now he's been offered a great job down here at USC. Dad likes to spoil us and Hans enjoys letting him."

"It must be nice," said the Corporal. "I'm just happy to live aboard a boat that can get close to this one."

"So you're a live aboard?" asked Kayla.

"Yes, Ma'am. I've got a dandy Westsail 32. She may not win any races, but she'll go anywhere!" he said proudly.

Below decks the Hallberg-Rassy exceeded every dream a man would ever want in a boat, from the well-appointed salon and galley to the two custom state rooms. Rather than using a teak interior, the Hallberg-Rassy's cabin was almost entirely mahogany, which is the standard for boats in Sweden.

"Someday," said Josh, "I'd like to restore a boat like this and sail around the world."

"Someday," Kayla agreed, wrapping both arms about his waist, "I'll join you."

"You mean that?" Josh asked her quizzically.

"If that's what you want," she agreed. "To quote a recent phrase, I'm telling you that I love you more than anything or anyone. I won't jeopardize that love."

Back at the condo later that night, Josh stretched out on the sofa and Kayla snuggled up to him. "I'm sorry my dad upset you," said Josh, stroking her long, blonde hair.

"I wasn't expecting that kind of reaction," Kayla responded. "Mont would have shrugged and said something like, 'that's too bad, little Princess. I guess we'll have to put our plans on hold.' Then he would have asked me to kneel with him while he offered a prayer." She sighed.

"Was that last sigh because of my father or yours?" he questioned.

She smiled. "A little of both, I guess."

"Care to elaborate," he suggested.

Kayla nodded. "You know my father is spiritually inclined," she paused and studied his expression carefully. She couldn't tell how he would interpret her comments. She continued carefully, "I've not heard you say much about it since last year, when you and Dad were comparing notes at the ranch that September. Remember?"

"Yes," he agreed. "He's got fairly sound doctrines, don't you think?"

"I don't know," she smiled. "I was raised with a religious background and I thought I believed, at one time, like he does."

"And now?" he asked cautiously.

"He scares me," she confessed. "He thinks my mother hovers around him. He says he's seen her and that she's his guardian angel."

"What's wrong with that?"

Kayla sighed. "I don't know that anything's wrong with it. It's just that it doesn't feel right to me."

Josh nodded. "I see."

"No, let me explain," she continued. "If I learned one thing from my father, it was that I should question everything. He always said that nature lived by its own set of rules and man would get farther ahead by trying to understand nature than by struggling against it. By his own reckoning, the laws of nature decreed that his wife should die. I'm sure it wasn't easy for him. I know it was painful, yet in all these years he's never explained it to me in any detail. My mother is dead. I've never seen her since she died, regardless what my father says he's seen. I don't cling to some dream or hope about her because I know she's not coming back."

"I'm sure your father understands that, Kayla," Josh offered.

"I know he accepts that her body died," Kayla elaborated. "Somehow he thinks the laws of nature don't apply to my mother. He believes that her spirit lives on, but don't you see? Within the confines of those very laws by which he lives, Mom is dead. How could she possibly come to see him or give him guidance or whatever it is that she feels happens between them? By all the laws of nature, she's gone."

Joshua nodded. "Kayla," he began. "Do you believe in God?"

"I was taught to believe," she answered. "Yet in my heart I just don't know."

Joshua sat up and held her for a long while, neither of them speaking. Finally he sighed. "It's unimportant right now whether or not you believe in God, Kayla. However, I do have inclinations toward the spiritual side as well as the natural side of life. Someday our children are going to come to you with questions about God. When that time comes, you're going to need some answers for them."

She stood and pulled him to his feet. "Will you help me?" she asked. "With my scientific mind, I have to question everything."

"Sometimes we become attached so much to the natural order of life that we fail to realize that everything has a spiritual side."

Kayla smiled. "You have strong feelings about God, haven't you, Joshua?"

"I have," he agreed.

"Of all people," she sighed and wrapped her arms around him. "I never dreamed a scientist could also have religious convictions."

"Perhaps being a scientist has strengthened me where God is concerned," he offered.

"How so?" questioned Kayla. She failed to comprehend what he meant by the expression.

"Consider the theory of evolution," he explained. "I can understand it and teach it and even believe it, up to a point."

"Which is?" she asked.

He put his hands on her shoulders and studied her dark brown eyes. "The theory of evolution begins with a single cell that multiplied and divided until it became the first life form on our planet."

"I know," she agreed.

"Being a scientist, I have to carry the theory one step farther. What or who gave that first cell 'life' so that it could divide?"

"It had life to begin with," she responded.

"No," he shook his head. "If it had life to start with, it would have divided billions of years earlier, whenever it first received 'life.' Whatever time frame in which that first cell divided, something or someone had to place 'life' into it first. I choose to believe that someone is God."

"It sounds easy enough from your point of view," she confessed. "Still, it takes more than a simple explanation to convince me. I have to analyze everything down in minute detail."

"You're a hard case," he agreed. "Perhaps that's one of the things I love about you." He kissed her lightly on the nose. "But if you're going to get any rest between packing and leaving tomorrow, I'd better go. I'll pick you up around 10:30 for the airport."

"All right," she nodded.

Long after Josh left, Kayla pondered on the evening's events and conversations. He wanted to sail around the world AND have a house full of children. Somehow she didn't think the two goals were compatible.

The thing that disturbed her the most was his conviction about God. Josh's faith came easily for him, it seemed. She knew that she would have to struggle for every ounce of faith that she could find.

Too, she regretted having offended Bridger Clark by announcing her intention to travel to Utah at her father's request. While she packed an adequate amount of clothing, three suitcases full, she went over and over in her mind all that was said, all that could have been said, and what she should have said to remedy the situation. Still, she couldn't imagine how any Christmas party could possibly be construed as more important than an anxious request from her father.

After packing she started cleaning the condo, washing everything down, dusting, vacuuming, scrubbing. She emptied the refrigerator and hauled a load of trash down to the main dumpster. Then she gave her plants a healthy drink.

By the time she felt ready to travel on an extended trip, it was nearly three in the morning. She took a quick shower and hopped into bed, falling asleep almost immediately.

The telephone ringing awakened her. She rolled over and reached for the phone before she opened her eyes. "Hello," she mumbled sleepily.

"Are you still in bed, Kayla?" asked Josh from the other end of the telephone line.

"What time is it?" she asked, opening her eyes.

Bright sun filtered into her room from the living room. She glanced at her watch at the same moment Josh said, "Fifteen minutes before I pick you up for the airport."

"I'll hurry," she gulped and hung up the phone before saying goodbye.

Kayla dressed quickly, threw her bedding back on the bed and fluffed up the pillows, then dashed to the bathroom where she brushed her teeth and combed her hair, putting a bow at the crown of her head.

By the time she was putting on her shoes, the doorbell rang. Josh let himself in with the key when he heard her yell to come in.

"Don't say it," she encouraged. "I know I overslept. I didn't get to bed until 3:00 A.M."

"What were you doing up until then?" he wanted to know. Then, "You cleaned the condo!"

"It was that bad before that you noticed?" she asked with a frown as she slipped on her shoes.

"No, it wasn't bad at all," he explained. "It's just that this morning I can see the vacuum cleaner marks on the carpet." He grinned.

"Aha!" she exclaimed. "How do you vacuum without leaving marks?"

"You'll have to ask someone more professional at that than me," he responded. "My condo is a boat, my cabin floor is teak and all I do is wipe it down with a damp cloth and oil it once in a while. I don't think you'd want me to do that to your carpet."

"Maybe when we're married you can experiment with the vacuum until you get it perfected," she suggested. "Shall we go?"

He picked up two suitcases and complained mightily. "What are you taking with you, lead?"

"Heavy clothes," she grumbled playfully, picking up the third suitcase. "And Christmas presents." Almost as an after thought she said, "Please don't forget to water my plants every other day."

"Got it," he agreed.

The Christmas traffic, terrible as it was, could not compare to the airport crowd. Inside, people anxious to get home for the holidays thronged the corridors. Josh had to park the car quite a distance from the main terminal. By the time they checked Kayla's bags and had passed security, they only had fifteen minutes until boarding. Standing room only became the order of the day so they found a semi-private corner in which to wait. Children squalled, parents scolded, grandmothers smiled. A huge bouquet of balloons came bouncing down the terminal toward them.

"There they are," a familiar voice penetrated through the crowd.

Kayla glanced around Joshua to see who it was. To her surprise, Bridger and Sarah rushed toward them, planted them both with kisses and hugs. Bridger gave the balloon bouquet to Kayla apologetically. "I know they won't let you take these on the plane," he explained, "but maybe Josh will put them in your condominium for you."

"You didn't need to do this," she exclaimed taking them from him.

"Yes, I did," said the Admiral. "I was rude last evening and my wife reminded me this morning that your father's concerns are far more important than a dinner party."

"It's all right, really, Dad," she said, giving him a hug.

"Anyway, I'm sorry. Will you keep on calling me Dad?" he asked. Kayla nodded.

"I hope that if I should ever need you, the way your father needs you right now, you'll be there for me, as well." He gave her a crooked grin.

"I will," she affirmed. "Thank you so much for coming, Dad." She gave him a big hug which he returned eagerly. Then she turned to Sarah. "Thank you," she said again, hugging Sarah as well.

"Would you tell your father we'd be delighted to accept his invitation?" Sarah asked, giving Kayla a warm smile.

"Really?" Kayla laughed aloud.

"Really!" said Bridger.

Sarah explained, "We'll arrive on Christmas Eve, probably around six in the evening, according to JonPaul's calculations."

"How many will there be?" Kayla asked. "We'll need to make up the guest rooms."

"Grandma will be staying here, she thinks she's too fragile to go with us. Hans is flying in tomorrow and he'll stay with her. It will be Dad and I. And Josh of course," Sarah winked. "We'll only be able to stay a few days. Bridger has some other commitments. We'll leave the Sunday after Christmas, but Josh will probably stay longer."

"Of course I will," he agreed heartily. "I won't be leaving the Bar M Ranch without Kayla."

"You're all so good to me," Kayla said to them. "I don't know how I can ever thank you!"

"Marry my son!" announced Bridger. "That would repay us handsomely."

"Plan on it!" Kayla affirmed. She gave the balloon bouquet to Josh and asked, "Did I tell you to water my plants?"

He nodded. "Every other day."

The announcement came over the intercom system. Her flight was boarding. "Use the distilled water under the sink. Tap water is too contaminated," she explained.

"We drink it," he offered.

"I know, but we're used to chlorine and fluoride. Plants are more fragile."

"Do I water them today or tomorrow?"

"Tomorrow. Will you still love me by Christmas Eve?"

"Kayla!" he protested at once.

"Gotcha!" she laughed.

He pulled her close and kissed her vigorously in response.

When he finally released her, Kayla gave Sarah and Bridger a hug and kiss. "Bye, Dad. Bye, Mom."

"Goodbye, darling Daughter," said Sarah. "May God's blessings be with you."

"Thank you," said Kayla, almost cringing from Sarah's expression. Fortunately, Joshua was the only one who picked up on her reaction.

"Take good care of your father," said Bridger. "We'll see you Thursday night."

Joshua swept her into his arms and kissed her soundly one more time. When he released her, he grinned. "Will that keep the fire burning until I get there?"

"And then some," she blushed.

"I love you!" he yelled happily.

"And I love you!" she affirmed with a broad smile.

She waved and turned to hurry down the boarding tunnel. As she did so, she heard Sarah say to Joshua, "She's a keeper!"

He responded with, "Don't I know it!"

A warm sense of happiness settled over her that had far more importance than all the Christmas cheer around her. She felt exhilarated with the love she had found among the Clark family.

Chapter Six

Kayla reclined the back rest on the airplane seat just as soon as the plane glided through the first layer of clouds. Another El Nino storm for the San Diego area, she thought wearily, noticing how the cumulonimbus layers had formed dark anvil shapes on the horizon. Fortunately for her, she would arrive in western Utah long before this storm, which would give her and Mont a chance to do some cross country skiing before new snow arrived.

She changed planes in Salt Lake City from the large jet on which she'd arrived to a small, privately chartered Cessna for the rest of her journey. Ordinarily she would have asked her father or Sparky to meet her in Salt Lake then drive the three hours to Vernal. Under the circumstances, she wanted to arrive at the earliest possible moment. Flying over the Wasatch Mountain Range, and then the Uintahs, brought back a million memories. The rugged landscape below her looked almost inviting right now, as though someone had scooped whipped cream into steep mounds then scratched the surface with a fork. Occasionally she saw a few glimpses of forest pines, but most of the trees were covered with white frosting snow.

When she finally reached the small airstrip at Vernal, she realized the rain storm that had swept through San Diego earlier in the week had arrived before her, this time dumping snow three feet deep in places. The temperatures dropped to a chattering 18 degrees.

Stepping from the plane, she took a deep breath and felt the cold bite into her lungs and nostrils. Yet it did not surprise nor bother her. She'd grown up in this country and knew full well the temperamental weather conditions. She knew it would be even colder at the Bar M Ranch, if she could get there by road at all. Looking at a helicopter on the helipad, she recognized it as the one Ed Sparkleman called his "Li'l

Posse." Suddenly she doubted that the roads would be cleared as far up as the ranch, if at all.

As if to answer her question, a slim, tall man stepped outside the control house and walked toward her with a familiar gait. Edward Sparkleman, Junior, her former fiance, stepped lively across the plowed airfield.

"Ain't you a picture for sore eyes," he drawled as he approached and gave her a thorough look. "You haven't changed a lick, girl. You're still the prettiest thing this county's ever seen."

"Hello, Ed," she smiled. "Did my father send you?"

"Since I'm the only one who knows how to fly the Li'l Posse, what do you think?" he winked.

"The roads are closed, then?" she asked.

He held out his hand and escorted her across the air field to the shelter. "Been closed for two days now. We're supposed to get a break in the weather until Christmas Eve Day, then it's supposed to snow like the dickens again."

"Lovely!" she exclaimed with enthusiasm. "It'll give Dad and me a chance to do some cross country skiing."

He opened the door of a small block building and let her inside. A propane furnace warmed up one corner of the small room. Behind a desk Ed flipped a few switches on a radio. "Bar M Ranch, this is Li'l Posse. Come back." He received a fair amount of static in return so he repeated the phrase twice more.

Then a light meter blinked on and a gravelly voice said, "Li'l Posse, this is the Bar M Ranch, over."

"Is that you, Mont? I can barely hear you, come back." He only had to wait a moment for Mont to adjust the receiver before Mont's voice came over the air waves loud and clear.

"It's Mont all right. Is my little Princess there yet?"

"Your special delivery has arrived and is ready for transport," drawled Ed. He winked at Kayla.

"Are the skies down south cleared up?" came Mont's response.

"That's affirmative, Mont."

"Then bring her on home, Ed. The pot's on the stove. Bar M Ranch out."

"Will do, Mont. Li'l Posse out." He flipped off a switch and turned around to face Kayla. "Sounds like he's chomping at the bit to get you home, Kayla Dawn. You ready?"

His calling Kayla by both of her given names unsettled her. Ed was the only person to ever do that. She hadn't expected it. Hearing his familiar voice, addressing her as Kayla Dawn, brought back a flood of memories.

Before she could respond, the door whisked open and Corky McCall poked his head inside. "I put your luggage in Li'l Posse's belly, Kayla. You're ready."

"Thank you, Corky. It's nice to see you again," she said to the stout, cherubic man in dark blue coveralls and grease stained face. At least his hands were clean. She smiled to herself.

"You, too, Kayla. And congratulations on your engagement," Corky added, almost as an after thought.

She raised an eyebrow quickly and he smiled and shrugged in response. "Word travels fast in this neck of the woods, Kayla. Well, I got work to do. Merry Christmas!"

"To you and yours," she agreed.

Corky nodded, then left as quickly as he'd come.

Just hearing the words, Merry Christmas, brightened her spirits. Kayla looked at Ed who was watching her every move as if memorizing. "What?" she found herself asking, then realized immediately that the question was something Josh would have asked her.

"Aw, nothing," he mused. "I was just wishing time had been as kind to me as it has to you." He took her elbow gently and helped her out to the helicopter.

Kayla couldn't help wondering what Ed meant by his wish, but she wasn't going to ask. She didn't want to stir up old fires for fear they weren't fully dead yet.

Once she was strapped securely inside the helicopter, he entered from the other side and turned on a small heater.

After switching a myriad of toggles and buttons, the helicopter roared into life, it's blades rotating faster and faster until they almost disappeared from view. It was already dark and the moon, a sliver in the eastern sky, was faintly covered by a thin layer of cirrus clouds.

Ed put ear phones on, as did Kayla. Each had a voice transmitter, allowing them to converse over the roar of the propellers. After Ed monitored for air traffic, he asked, "Have you ever seen Christmas in Vernal from the sky?"

"No," she responded quickly. She almost added that the city lights were not in a direct line between them and the Bar M Ranch, but she bit back the retort.

"It's a little out of the way," he said as though agreeing to her line of thought. "But worth it," he quipped.

"Then by all means," she agreed, glad that she hadn't said anything. Ed couldn't possibly know how anxious she was to see her father. If Mont was ill, Ed would not be the first person he would tell. More likely it would be Sparky or herself.

As the helicopter lifted up into the air, she felt a momentary thrill in the pit of her stomach. Contrary to female stereotypes, she was one woman who loved adventure and new experiences. She hadn't ridden in a helicopter for several years and she planned to enjoy every moment.

Ed piloted the helicopter eastward for a short distance until the city lights came into full view. With Christmas lights making the scene more spectacular than ever, Kayla gasped in amazement at how truly beautiful Vernal could be. A Christmas Tree was lit up right in the middle of town, and blinking lights of red, green, yellow and blue, flashed out merrily below them. Even the dinosaurs in the outdoor museum were decorated with tiny white Christmas lights.

They came upon a building Kayla almost didn't recognize. It had been remodeled extensively and now had an ethereal appeal to it that had been lacking in years past, at least to Kayla's way of thinking. When she finally recognized the building, she questioned Ed, pointing it out to him. "What have they done to the tabernacle?" She remembered the tabernacle specifically because she had sung in a church choir there many times in her youth.

"They made it into a Temple," Ed answered. "I thought everyone knew that."

The surprise in Ed's voice made Kayla cringe.

"Guess Utah news doesn't travel as far as California," he offered.

"No," she agreed lamely. "It doesn't." At least not the news I listen to, she thought to herself. She brushed the incident aside and thought no more regarding it.

"Vernal got a bid from a new industrial company that makes computer components. They're building a new plant southeast of town. It will open up at least a hundred new jobs," Ed explained as they flew toward it and Ed pointed out the site. "We've had at least fifty new houses built and several new businesses." He piloted the helicopter around the perimeter of the city. "Well," he drawled, "that concludes the tour of the city. Shall we take you home, Kayla Dawn?"

"Yes, thank you," she agreed heartily.

Ed maneuvered the helicopter northwest, past the outskirts of Vernal and toward the Bar M Ranch located up in the heart of Ashley National Forest and the Uintah Mountain range.

Soon they flew above the thick forest, but it was too dark to see much of anything from their position. Pinion pine trees and Blue Spruce don't come with built in Christmas lights, Kayla thought wistfully to herself, smiling as she did so.

Kayla glanced over at Ed sitting beside her as he piloted the helicopter with skill that amazed her. His face was illuminated by the cockpit lights and she could see that he hadn't changed much in seven years.

He had Sparky's lean, tall, almost gaunt look about him, but that's where the resemblance ended. His hair, though less blonde than hers, still sparkled from beneath his Stetson hat, which he always wore. His eyes, gray green in color, changed depending on his mood. Happy times found his eyes bright green, like emeralds. Somber, angry feelings changed his eyes to steel gray. The feature usually made him readable, like a book. Somehow he had learned to control those emotions because Kayla could not interpret his mood right now.

Dragging her heart back to a time more than seven years ago, Kayla focused on the events that led to the dissolution of the relationship between them, as well as their wedding plans.

Ed and Kayla had grown up together. When she was born, he was already a toddler. They played cowboys down in the meadow in front of the lodge. When his three brothers came along they became known among the locals as the "Dreadful Five," the meanest, toughest posse any rustlers would ever want to meet up with. They were each given a share of the herd and they saw to it that no rustlers ever attempted to steal from them. The fact that the oldest was only eight and the youngest, Abbot, a mere four years old, had nothing to do with the fact that these cowboys ("and cowgirl!" she recalled adding vehemently back when she was still a child), struck fear in the hearts of make believe rustlers everywhere. She'd forgotten about the Dreadful Five and all the fun she'd had growing up in the Uintah Mountains.

Kayla smiled with the memory. Then came those teenage years when she thought she would absolutely die if Ed didn't fall madly in love with her and carry her off on his white charger. Which is exactly what he tried to do until her father insisted she go to Brigham Young University for a well-rounded education. He'd promised her that she could marry Ed after she graduated, if that was still what she wanted to do.

How grateful she was for the wisdom of her father, wisdom she hoped she would have for her children. Little did she know, back then, that learning and studying would become second nature to her. In her wildest dreams she could not have conceived that such ingeniously devised tools had been given to her: a discerning mind and an insatiable thirst for knowledge.

Yet when she returned to the Bar M Ranch after graduation, she knew that Ed would still expect her to marry him. Somehow she'd confused loyalty with love. Within a few days of returning home from BYU, she told Ed that she was ready to become Mrs. Edward Davis Sparkleman Junior, wife and mother to his little brood of ranch hands.

As the time for the Wedding approached, Kayla grew restless and uneasy. Unable to focus on anything, not even mounting a horse, she had locked herself in her bedroom and wept silently, fearing her chances to increase her learning and further all future hopes of becoming a marine scientist were fading into the distance.

Mont had picked up on her signals even though she'd been entirely unaware that she had given them. He started by talking about Ed's strengths and qualities.

There wasn't much that Ed couldn't do, when he put his mind to it. He more than proved his ability at the ranch, not only in the everyday chores, but in field skills as well. He could rope and brand a calf quicker than anyone she knew, with exception of Mont. Kayla had no doubt that Ed would be a kind husband and a thoughtful father. He had several important qualifications.

However, Kayla really wanted to further her education. BYU classes had enlivened her and set her on a journey from which there could be no turning back.

Ultimately it was Mont who advised her to follow her heart above all else. Even though she thought she still loved Ed, in time she realized her feelings were more familial than romantic. Her loyalty would end where her heart could begin. Mont agreed to break the news to Ed first, to soften the blow, she hoped.

Mont gave Ed the disturbing news the very next day. Immediately Ed stormed into the Gathering Room and confronted her. It was plainly evident that there was no softening anything where Ed's heart was concerned. She told Ed about the scholarship she'd been offered and she planned to pursue a career in marine science at the University of Southern California. He pursed his lips together tightly. His fists clenched around the brim of his Stetson. He shoved the hat back on his head and nodded his consent. Then he turned on one heel and shuffled out the door like a whipped mountain lion.

Their relationship had been strained afterward for a number of years. During vacations and visits home, Kayla faced the same situations. Ed would avoid her at every turn, speaking to her only in clipped sentences. About two years ago he lightened up and she finally felt that he had reconciled his emotions to what had happened to their relationship.

After they broke up, he spent his time shuffled between working and pilot school. He learned to fly helicopters. Now he worked the ranch with his dad, Sparky, whenever he could, but his main occupation was flying Li'l Posse for Sky Patrol.

They were civil to one another now, sometimes they were almost friends again, though the days of the Dreadful Five were gone forever.

Breaking into her reverie, Ed began a subject that had been bothering him all the way up to the Bar M Ranch: "Kayla Dawn, I don't mean to concern you, but your Dad's getting on in years."

"He's 56," Kayla responded. "Statistically speaking, he should have a good twenty years ahead of him."

"I don't mean to offend you, Kayla. He's well enough, I suppose, for now." Ed gave her a quick glance. Her face looked soft and delicate from the pale, diffused, interior lights. "Dang, you're a beauty, Kayla Dawn!" he exclaimed unexpectedly. "A fellow hardly knows how to approach someone like you."

"With both eyes open, I suppose," she teased. Then she wondered about his motives. "Is there a point to all this?" she asked.

"Only that the boys and I have been talking about the ranch, Kayla," he confided at last. "We've been talking to Pa and to Mont. Those two are worse than a couple of old women when it comes to the Bar M."

"Oh?" she asked, wondering what Ed planned now. She frowned

Ed had more to explain, but didn't know quite how to begin. Finally he said, "Times are changing. Your dad's got a gold mine under his feet and he doesn't even know it. Why, he could get millions for his spread without batting an eye. He could retire and move on out to California near you. What does he want to hang onto it for?"

So that's it, she thought angrily. The boys, meaning Ed, Tom, William and Abbot, all Sparky's sons, want the ranch.

"Have you talked to Dad about this?" she asked.

"Sure have. He always says he'll think on it a spell, but that's as far as it goes," Ed complained. "All you'd have to do is say the word, Kayla Dawn. You could have your dad out there where you could keep an eye on him and take care of him in his old age."

"I would never move him off the Bar M, Ed. It's been in his family for eight decades, ever since his Grandpa Moulton homesteaded there. His father built the Lodge more than seventy years ago. All Dad knows is the ranch. I could never move him away from it," She tried to keep her voice even and unhurried, regardless of the knot at the pit of her stomach.

"I'm not asking you to, Kayla Dawn," he continued. "But his health isn't getting any better and it won't be long before you'll have to step in and take protective measures. Wouldn't it be better to work out an agreement with him now, rather than when you're forced into it? At least he could enjoy retirement. He could live nearby you, fish in the ocean every day. You know how he loves fishing."

"I know he loves the ranch," she targeted the conversation back to Mont's best interest. "He loves riding horses and roping calves and branding steers. He loves the mountains and the meadows and the whole outdoors as pictured from his bedroom window. He doesn't want the ocean and salt water fishing. He loves rainbow trout. He once told me that catching a wild rainbow was one of the greatest pleasures a man can have."

"All I'm asking, Kayla Dawn, is that you think about what I'm saying. We've seen signs of him slowing down lately. He gets winded easily, sometimes his lips get a little blue," Ed proceeded, hoping to play on sympathy. "Just last Fall he had a little spell. I was standing right beside him in the meadow when he suddenly fell like a limp rag upon the ground. Doc said he was wearing himself out, said his ticker was acting up some."

"Dad never told me this," she responded.

"That old polecat ain't gonna tell his baby girl that he's sickly," reasoned Ed. "He'd sooner die as have you thinking less of him."

"That's true enough," she agreed. "Maybe I can speak with Doctor Brown."

"You been gone too long, Kayla Dawn. Doc Brown retired two years ago. Mike Nillson took over Doc's practice about the same time."

Kayla shook her head. "Not that bully, Mike Nillson, who liked to push me in the creek?"

"One and the same," drawled Ed. "He married up with Sally Peterson."

"That was a foregone conclusion," she said. "He always was sweet on Sally." Then she shook her head again. "But he's a doctor now," she mused aloud.

Ed doggedly returned to his former topic. "Think about what I've said, Kayla, for your father's sake. I'm worried that one of these days you'll get a phone call from Pa saying it's too late." His voice held a fatalistic tone.

Bright lights from the Bar M Ranch swept into full view and Kayla pointed, hoping to change the subject. "Look," she exclaimed. "There's the Bar M."

Even at night the Bar M Ranch held a certain charm and beauty all its own. The Allens had owned it since before World War I. Her grandfather, James Moulton Allen, began homesteading more than a thousand acres nearly eighty years ago. He built the lodge before Mont was ever born.

Mont had all the lights on in the lodge, a two-story log structure made entirely of Douglas Fir. A wide porch on the main level was protected from rain storms by a deck off the second level. A country kitchen, dining room, laundry room, den, Gathering Room and bathroom were all located on the first level. A spiral staircase made from hand-hewn logs swept up to the second level. Upstairs were six large bedrooms and three more bathrooms.

An oversized generator in a shed behind the lodge provided emergency electricity for the ranch. The small power plant was fed by a fuel storage tank built into the mountain side in a hand-dug cave lined with concrete. Mont, always thinking ahead, had planned the storage facility with every consideration for environmental safety. In addition to exceeding fuel storage safety standards, the storage tank was large enough to hold six months of fuel for the generator. Fuel oil tanks also enclosed within the cave provided convenient heating for both the lodge and a smaller cabin just across the meadow. These few modern conveniences, so far away from civilization, had been a great help to them over the years.

In front of the lodge lay an open expanse of meadow, fenced only around the perimeter, with a corral in one corner of the area. A small stream ran diagonally across the meadow. A spring house, built by Grandpa Allen, lay hidden in the trees behind the lodge. The spring provided clean water year round. In the summer time, fresh watercress grew along the edges of a small creek that had formed where the excess spring water was diverted down the mountain to the meadow stream.

Beyond the meadow, Spruce and Pine stretched toward the sky like taut, thin soldiers in lackadaisical formation. West of the meadow stood the remains of a summer garden, now buried in several feet of snow. Not far from the smaller cabin stood a large old barn and a row of sheds connected together. Mont generally wintered over enough livestock to keep them fed through the cold season: a jersey cow, two beef cattle, two pigs, a dozen chickens and two fat turkeys. In addition to ranching, Mont made it a habit to raise all that he needed for food, whenever possible.

To the east side of the lodge a large helipad had been cleared of snow. A wide path had been plowed through the white mounds, leading from the lodge and across the meadow, over a small bridge, to the smaller cabin, as well as to the helipad, which was located about half way between the lodge and the barns to the east. Another path had been plowed to the barn. Wide, deep tracks from a tractor snow plow were evident within the pathways.

Bright lights focused on the helipad where a red 'X' had been painted on the concrete.

Ed exhaled in frustration, realizing that talking to Kayla was about as easy as talking to Mont. "Yep, there she is," he agreed as he maneuvered the helicopter for a soft landing.

Within moments Kayla was wrapped up warmly in her father's arms as he escorted her to the house. Kayla radiated with the warm glow that coming home brings to those who love it.

Chapter Seven

Arms gathered around her and lips were pressed against her cheeks, beginning with Kayla's dad and ending with Morning Sun, the Navajo woman who'd helped Mont and Sparky raise her. Two of Ed's brothers, Tom and William, were on hand to welcome her home. The group was so busy welcoming Kayla they failed to notice Ed unloading her three suitcases from the helicopter.

Tom, who was especially boisterous, scooped Kayla up into his strong arms and carried her up the front steps and through the front door way. He placed her down by the hearth in the Gathering Room as everyone crowded around her. Kayla smelled liquor on his breath and this worried her, but she shrugged if off and reached out to hug Tom's father, Sparky.

"The only one missing is Abbot," she said, giving Sparky a pinch on his cheek, "the little snitch."

Sparky grinned. "It was just as much my fault as his, I reckon," admitted Sparky playfully. "News about our baby girl getting married couldn't keep itself tucked behind my tongue, Kayla. I just up and spit it out the moment I heard it."

She gave him another hug. "Oh, it's okay, Sparky. Dad wasn't too mad, was he?"

Sparky stuffed his oversize hands into his jeans pockets. "Naw, not too much!"

"He just turned purple in the face and dang near turned over dead is all," Tom piped up quickly, laughing hard as the liquor controlled him.

William playfully smacked Tom over the head with his hat. "Did not! Kayla, you know Tom's just spoofing you."

"I know," laughed Kayla. "Tom, do you take anything in life seriously?"

"Just one thing, Kayla darling," said Tom, curling his soft leather hat up in his big hands.

"What's that?" she wanted to know.

"I just wanted to know," he paused. Then he looked around at all of them, realizing he had their undivided attention. "I just wanted to know," Tom said, bending down on one knee unsteadily. He looked up into Kayla's eyes, took her small hand in his oversized one and pleaded, "How come you're gonna marry a navy man when you coulda' had any one of us four cowpokes?"

"Hey!" yelped William. "Speak for yourself, Tom. What if Melanie hears you talking like that?"

Tom, quick on the draw, said, "She'll snap you up much quicker if word gets out that she's got competition, Will!"

"Maybe we should phone Charlene and see what she has to say," offered Ed dryly, removing his hat as he walked through the open door way. He placed one of Kayla's heavy suitcases by the sofa.

"Melanie? Charlene?" Kayla questioned. "You boys have been holding out on me. What's going on?"

Tom stood up and made a gesture as though he'd been pierced through the heart. "She got me, Kayla, straight through to the core!" He spun around and fell over backwards in a true faint. Fortunately, William caught him before he hit the floor.

"Sorry, Kayla," explained William. "Tom's been drinking again. I don't know what we're going to do with him."

Ed sighed and looked at Sparky. "Sorry, Pa. Tom's about trashed Kayla's homecoming party. I'll take him back to the cabin."

Sparky gave Mont a sheepish glance and frowned. "It woulda' been easier raising girls, I think!" he snapped. "I'll get the rest of your suitcases, Kayla."

Ed threw Tom over his shoulder. "I'll help you, Ed," offered William. Ed nodded and left quickly, carrying Tom with him. Sparky followed his three sons outside and pulled the door shut.

Morning Sun clapped her hands. "We're so happy you come," she announced. "I bake your favorite apple pie for you."

"That's sweet, Morning Sun," thanked Kayla. "You needn't have bothered. I'm happy just being home."

Mont kept his mouth shut, but it seemed obvious to Kayla that her father wanted to say something about Tom's behavior. She disregarded it by linking her arm in his and taking Morning Sun's hand. She walked them over to the sofa. "Sit down now, both of you, and tell me how you've been."

Kayla sat beside Morning Sun and studied the Navajo woman's round bronze features, more particularly her well-rounded belly. Kayla hoped the surprise in her mind and heart hadn't revealed itself on her face as quickly. The woman had formed a special place in Kayla's heart many years earlier.

Morning Sun folded her hands quietly and said, pointing to her rounded belly. "The time of Morning Sun's joy has been planted."

"You're going to have a baby?" asked Kayla, hoping the incredulous tone of her voice hadn't been noticed.

Morning Sun gave her a crooked grin and shrugged. "For twenty years now we ask the God of Heaven many times to give us a child. He is slow to answer."

Mont used the time to study his daughter and commit every expression from her sparkling brown eyes to her active hands to memory. She often used her hands to explain or express a point. Feeling that Morning Sun needed some assistance, he told Kayla, "She and her husband are excited to be first time parents. Doc Nillson says she's the picture of health. He sees no reason why she can't have this child safely and live long enough to raise it."

"Yes," said Morning Sun. "You like?" She took Kayla's hand and placed it on her growing belly.

Kayla rubbed the spot gently until she felt a tiny little bump beneath Morning Sun's dress. "I think it moved! It moved, Morning Sun! Did you feel it?"

Morning Sun smiled. "A busy child, this baby."

"Do you know what sex it is?" she asked.

Morning Sun shook her head. "The God of Heaven will show us soon enough."

Sparky tapped on the door and opened it. "Here are your other suitcases, Kayla. I... I'm sorry about Tom and all."

"Don't worry," insisted Kayla. "He'll be okay, you'll see."

"Ed is ready to take you home, Morning Sun," said Sparky. "If you're ready."

Kayla looked at her father who explained, "Morning Sun no longer works for me. Her baby has to come first, you know."

"Of course," said Kayla. "It's been so good to see you, Morning Sun."

"Morning Sun always has special place here for Kayla," she responded as she placed her hand over her heart.

Kayla embraced her and bid her farewell. Sparky escorted Morning Sun out to the helicopter. Mont and Kayla followed them and watched from the porch. After Ed had piloted the helicopter into the air and far off in the distance, Sparky turned to face them.

"Think I'll turn in, Mont," said Sparky. "There'll be plenty of time for me to talk to Kayla tomorrow after Church."

"Sure," said Mont, nodding.

Sparky turned and walked down the cleared path toward the cabin across the meadow. Kayla noticed immediately the spunk had gone out of his long familiar gait.

Mont turned Kayla about and pointed her toward the front door. "Nothing like throwing you right in the thick of things, is there?" he asked.

"Why don't you tell me these things on the phone, Dad?" Kayla asked him as she pushed the heavy door open and walked into the Gathering Room. "You could have e-mailed me or written a note."

"What would you have done about Tom if you'd known?" he asked gently.

"If he'd shown up on the job plastered like tonight I'd have fired him on the spot," she announced.

"And hurt Sparky in the process?"

"You think what Tom's doing doesn't hurt Sparky?" she demanded a bit too sharply.

"Where did you get your temper?" he wondered aloud, smiling down at her like she was still a little girl.

"Dad?! I'm trying to be serious here," she snapped.

"Do I bring out the anger in you, Kayla? Because I don't remember this side of you the last time you were here." He rubbed her shoulders and gave her a coaxing smile.

She softened. "Less than two minutes alone with you and I have to get testy," she complained. "I'm sorry."

"It's all right. If you can't yell at your dad, who can you yell at?" he asked, giving her a quizzical grin.

"Certainly not anyone else," she agreed. "No one else loves me enough to put up with my yelling at them."

"Not even Josh?" he teased.

"We've never had occasion to yell at one another," she told him. "However, last Saturday I yelled TO him, does that count?"

"I don't think so," he answered, kissing her lightly on the forehead. "Now, are you hungry?"

"Starving," she agreed. "I slept through breakfast, skipped lunch because I was late getting up, ate some stale peanuts and soda pop on the plane, and— No wonder I'm starving!"

"Come on," he offered. "I've got hot soup on the stove, Morning Sun's apple pie, and if that's not enough, I'll fix you a sandwich that will fill you up clean down to your toes."

They went into the kitchen where Mont pulled cheese, turkey, roast beef and sprouts out of the refrigerator. He plastered slices of rye bread with mayonnaise and mustard, then layered the sandwich stuffing thickly between them. Within a few moments he'd sliced them diagonally on plates and ladled a bowl of hot bean soup for her. He cut them both a slice of apple pie and poured some fresh, raw milk to complete the meal.

While he worked, Mont talked about the recent snowfall and its inherent threat. "So it sets us up for perfect avalanche conditions," Mont said, explaining how a prior snow storm melted slightly, then froze hard again just before this last snow fall. "The stuff's up there just waiting for a good warm day to come crashing down."

"Just like every year," she agreed, "except during the drought."

He nodded. "I suppose we do get ripe avalanche conditions a good share of the winter, don't we?"

"Yes, but fortunately, we're much higher up the mountain than most people."

He pushed a plate across the counter to her. "You want to say it or shall I?"

Instantly realizing he was referring to the blessing on the food, she said, "You go ahead."

He bowed his head and offered a prayer as sweet as any she'd ever heard from him. When he was finished, he picked up half a sandwich and started eating it.

"I'm surprised to see you eat this late, Dad," Kayla told him.

"I couldn't eat all day. My belly's been powerful upset lately," he explained. As an after thought he amended by saying, "Guess I've been too excited about having you come home. Do you realize it's been fifteen months since you've been here?"

"But not fifteen months since I've seen you," she reminded. "Or did you forget our sail last August?"

"That was surely great," he agreed. "Who would have thought my little Princess could drive a boat?"

"It's pilot, Dad." She smiled.

"That, too," he agreed, taking another bite.

Kayla ate as she studied the man before her. Except for all the streaks of silver where blonde hair used to be, she almost couldn't tell that her father had aged at all.

Mont had broad shoulders, slim hips and a strong set of muscles from years of hard labor. Doc Brown had once said Mont had the strongest pair of lungs this side of the Mississippi and Mont claimed it was from breathing clean mountain air all his life. He'd never smoked a single cigarette, he boasted, and had rarely spent time indoors except to sleep.

Yet beneath that rugged exterior lay the heart of a gentle giant, Kayla knew, especially where she was concerned. He'd been her guardian angel all her life, the kind of angel she liked best, the kind you can see and touch and smell and hug.

Kayla helped with the dishes after supper. It seemed strange to her, washing dishes while Mont rinsed and stacked them in a drainer by the sink. She wondered how Sarah and Bridger would react to something like that. Well, they would soon find out.

"Did I tell you that Josh's parents are coming with him Christmas Eve?" she asked absently, drying her hands on a towel.

"Good!" He led her into the Gathering Room where he sat her down on the long, overstuffed, leather sofa. Then he sat on the floor and slipped off her shoes. He started rubbing and bending her feet in all directions, gently yet firmly.

"Do you know how long it's been since anyone massaged my feet?" she asked.

"I'd say since August," he nodded, continuing this labor of love.

"I can't remember a single time after school when I came home that you didn't rub my feet before I went to bed," Kayla observed.

"My dad used to rub our feet," he explained. "I've always thought that was one way a parent could get his child to hold still long enough to talk and listen to her."

"Maybe," she agreed. "You don't suppose that's why we always had such a good relationship when I was growing up?"

"There you are," said Mont. "I wonder how many generations of massage therapists there are in my family."

"Dad," she said, timidly at first, then a little more bold. "Are you all right?"

"Same as always, Princess," he answered. "Why?"

"Last Sunday on the phone, you seemed so distressed," she told him, "that afterward I had the numbers looked up at the base switchboard. You'd called from home twice, but the third call came from Ashley Valley Medical Center."

Mont shook his head in bewilderment. "Sparky got called in to bring Tom home. Doc Nillson said he'd been drinking again and had been in an accident. I went on down with him to make sure the boy didn't give Sparky any trouble," he explained. "When we got down there, I remembered that I'd left a couple messages for you and I didn't want you to return my calls only to find me gone. I telephoned again from the waiting room, hoping to catch you."

"So, you didn't want me to come home because you wanted to tell me you had cancer or heart disease, right?" she asked.

He smiled. "No, but I can't tell you yet what's going on yet, Kayla. You'll know soon enough what this is all about," he told her.

By this time he'd rubbed her feet so thoroughly her whole body relaxed. "I think I died and went to heaven," she murmured, laying back on the sofa.

He covered her up with a quilt and sat opposite her on an easy chair. She yawned sleepily as he talked and her eyelids grew heavy.

"I remember a thousand such nights, Kayla, when I massaged your feet so well, you fell asleep on that very sofa. Remember?" he asked.

"Mmm hmm," she agreed, her eyes closing wearily.

He reached over to the lamp and turned it down. "Dad," she said, rolling over.

"Yes, Princess," he answered.

"We have to go cross country skiing while I'm here. I haven't been in years."

"We will," he agreed. "But let's not worry about that tonight."

"All right," she agreed. "But tomorrow we'll plan for it." And with those words, Kayla fell sound asleep.

Mont picked up his bible and read for a while, but he didn't feel the least bit sleepy. His daughter was home, his Princess, and as he had always done, he would watch over her for just a little longer. After all, his time to be her protector was almost over. Soon enough he would place her hand in the hand of another man who would take over the position that Mont had cherished these many years. Gentle father that he was, he left his chair a moment, bent over and kissed her lightly on the cheek. "Goodnight, little Princess," he whispered.

Returning to his chair, he allowed his mind to wander back seven years when he did the hardest thing he'd ever done in his entire life as her father.

When Kayla first announced, right after high school graduation, that she planned to marry Ed Sparkleman, Mont knew she was too young. Somehow he'd convinced her to go to college first and round out her education. If she still wanted to marry Ed when she returned, he promised he'd throw her the biggest wedding reception Vernal had ever seen.

Kayla could see wisdom in attending BYU. While she was there, Mont sent Ed to Arizona State University at Phoenix, giving Ed the same rash promise he'd given Kayla.

Mont loved Ed like he was his own son. Indeed, he felt the same way about all four Sparkleman boys. He'd helped Sparky raise those four boys just as surely as Sparky had helped Mont raise Kayla. The seven of them were just one big happy family, with a Navajo nanny split amongst them to temper them with her womanly skills.

It hadn't been fair to Kayla, raising her without a mother. After loving and losing KayDawn, Mont just didn't have the courage to try again. Besides, he had to admit, he still loved KayDawn as if it were twenty-eight years ago. Time had not diminished one ounce of the love he had for that woman, not one ounce. If anything, he mused to himself, he loved her more now than he did then.

Mont never did tell Kayla about sending the boys to college. That's why Abbot was at the University of Utah right that moment, because Mont put him there. Out of respect for him, the boys had each agreed not to mention it to Kayla. Not that she would have minded, he didn't think. He just didn't want her thinking those four boys had ever replaced the son that cost her mother's life. Which they couldn't, he realized immediately. Still, they were Sparky's sons, and he and Sparky went back a long time. It wouldn't be right if he didn't help out where he could.

When Kayla received her master's degree in four years and countless hours of hard work and dedication, graduating at the top of her class, he couldn't have been more proud. The same day she came home from graduation, she walked through the front door and announced, "I'm going to marry Ed Sparkleman, Father, and I expect you to live up to your promise."

He'd been proud as punch to agree with her, especially since Ed had returned a week earlier with an almost identical announcement. Mont loved to watch Ed and Kayla go walking down in the meadow. Sometimes they'd sit on the bridge and toss pebbles into the stream. Sometimes they'd hold hands and dance around like they used to when they were children, but after about three weeks of this, Kayla began to get restless. She couldn't sleep and she started losing weight. That was when Morning Sun found the letter pressed between the mattress and box springs of Kayla's bed. The poor woman could read English, albeit brokenly. She took the letter straight away to Mont, knowing that to do so risked her losing the trust of her beloved Kayla, the child she never could have, the woman she'd helped raise.

Kayla had been offered a full scholarship at the University of Southern California to begin studying for her doctorate in one of the marine sciences. One of Kayla's professors from BYU had recommended her, sent in her transcript without her knowing about it, and if she wanted, she could start classes in September that same year. It was evident from the letter that Kayla read it over and over. Her tear stains had splattered the paper.

Mont asked Morning Sun to return the letter to exactly the same position she had found it. Kayla would never know they had invaded her privacy. At least Mont could now put a reason to Kayla's mood swings and changes in her temperament.

He made a hasty trip to Provo, Utah, the very next day. Looking up Kayla's professor took more time than he'd wanted and he found himself staying in Provo a few days trying to connect up with the man, who was extremely busy, but managed to fit Mont in his schedule.

Professor Parker had nothing but praise for Kayla. He went so far as to say that Kayla was probably the finest candidate he'd ever recommended for a full scholarship. He felt inclined to believe that she had wanted the scholarship, but he hadn't heard from her yet . He had no idea whether or not she planned to accept it.

When Mont drove home a few days later, he did so with tears in his eyes and a heavy heart. He had wanted Kayla and Ed to marry. He loved Ed and knew that it would break his heart to lose Kayla one more time. As for Kayla, if she truly loved Ed, he figured the scholarship issue would have to be worked out. He knew what love was all about, having loved KayDawn with all his heart and soul. If she'd had a chance at a scholarship and she truly wanted it, together they would have moved heaven and earth to get her through.

It all boiled down to one thing: the scholarship. Kayla could have Ed and the scholarship if she chose, or she could have one or the other, but she would have to make a choice. He felt reasonably certain that Kayla would choose both.

The following day he asked her to ride horses with him, take a picnic lunch, pick berries and spend a day with her dad. After all, he reasoned, three more weeks and she'd be married. There would be little time for her father afterward, he'd teased.

So far the plan was working. What he hadn't expected, when he finally pried open the lid on her feelings, was that she felt it was her duty to marry Ed. She had promised Ed and her father that she would marry the man. Out of her misplaced sense of loyalty she was going to tie herself to a man she did not really love.

His entire plan backfired in his face.

There comes a time in every parent's life when they have to weigh what is better for the child, completely disregarding their own churning emotions or considering what is good for the parent. He hadn't expected it and the moment hit him full on like a freight train. The air was knocked out of him and he sat down on a large boulder to keep from falling down.

Finally, Mont did what he had to do, regardless how much it hurt him. He told her two sentences that cost him the son he'd always wanted and the daughter he'd always cherish. The words echoed around in his head so loudly he felt paralyzed by them. "Follow your heart above all else," he had encouraged her. "Loyalty should end where your heart begins."

Yes, that was the darkest day he'd ever experienced as a father. And the second darkest moment came the very next day when he had to take Ed aside to explain why he shouldn't mail out the wedding invitations.

Chapter Eight

When Mont could not awaken Kayla for Sunday Services, he left a note for her on the coffee table.

> "Kayla, I've gone to Church. I tried to wake you, but was unsuccessful. I'll be home by 1:30 P.M. There's Pompanoosuc Porridge in the fridge.
>
> Love, Dad"

Kayla groaned and rolled over, crushing the note in her hands. She hadn't even heard the helicopter! 'You're home for one night, Kayla, and you turn back into a little girl!' she said to herself. 'Grow up!'

She rolled off the sofa onto a bear skin rug and luxuriated in the warm sunshine pouring through the front windows. From her vantage point she could see the log beams across the ceiling two stories tall. She studied them with great detail, finally concluding that the only things holding them in place were leather straps a half inch thick.

"That's odd," she began. Then in her mind, 'Oh, Kayla! You're talking to yourself again.'

After a while she stood up and wandered into the kitchen where she opened the refrigerator. On the top shelf sat a bowl of pompanoosuc porridge, an old favorite that Morning Sun used to make for them. Evidently Mont now had the recipe. She placed the bowl in the microwave and turned it on. Rich cream, recently skimmed from fresh, raw milk, Kayla poured from a small pitcher. She stirred a spoon of honey into the bowl, then enjoyed one of the heartiest breakfasts she'd had in a long time.

Glancing at the clock Kayla realized she must have just missed Mont leaving, it was only 10:30 A.M.

When Kayla had washed the bowl and spoon and placed them in the dish drainer, she decided to make herself useful. She carried her three suitcases, one at a time, upstairs.

Mont had left her bedroom just the way it was when she was a teenager, with the exception of new bedding and curtains. Otherwise, the shelves were the same, the knickknacks and collectibles exactly as she had left them so many years before. The main difference she could find was that everything was clean! Mont must have had someone in here sprucing up the place, she decided. She didn't know how long Morning Sun had been out of commission, but she did know how well Mont liked house keeping. She was sure he'd rather go in for a root canal.

Quickly she unpacked her suitcases and put the clothing neatly in the dresser drawers. A few things still needed to be hung up and she looked inside the closet. Hanging just where she'd left them was her heavy winter clothing freshly laundered or dry cleaned. She hadn't taken these to California with her, knowing she would never get an opportunity to wear them in the sun belt of the West Coast. Even her ski bibs and parka had been cleaned and hung up in almost perfect condition.

Stripping her clothing from her body, she put on a plush terry robe and carried her soiled clothing out to the laundry chute where she dumped them. Then she headed toward the bathroom. Within minutes she felt the invigorating spray of a hot shower pouring down her nakedness. She washed her hair and used a puff ball bursting with bubbles for her skin. After conditioning her hair she rinsed and turned the water off.

Suddenly she heard someone calling her name. "Kayla Dawn!"

"Up here," she answered in her loudest voice. She knew how little sound traveled at the lodge. The massive logs used in the construction of it didn't give sound a chance.

She heard footsteps coming down the hall and then someone tapped on the bathroom door.

"Yes?" she asked timidly.

"Kayla Dawn!" Ed Sparkleman's frustrated voice came from the other side of the door. "Your dad sent me back for you. He was hoping you'd get up in time for the last meeting."

"I'll hurry," she agreed. "Why don't you wait downstairs?"

"I'd rather wait up here and watch," he drawled with a laugh. "But under the circumstances I'd better yield to your suggestion."

Kayla listened long enough to hear his footsteps go back down the hall. She wrapped a towel around her head, slipped the robe back over her shoulders and knotted it at her waist. Then she opened the bathroom door and headed toward her bedroom.

"Dang!" came Ed's disappointed voice. He was perched on the railing at the top of the stairs. "I was hoping you'd come through in the buff."

"Ed!" she complained. "What's going around in that devious mind of yours?"

"Nothing that ain't been there for more than a decade, Kayla Dawn," he drawled. "Unfortunately for me, that's as far as it ever goes." He gave her a crooked grin and laughed. "Aw, don't worry about me, Kayla Dawn. *I'm* not going to attack you!"

"I didn't think you were," she responded. "I hope I know you better than that!"

"I just thought maybe you were thinking about Morning Sun—" He stopped short.

Kayla's mouth dropped open and she stared at him. When she finally regained her composure, she asked, "What about Morning Sun?"

He headed on down the stairs in full retreat. "Hurry up. I'll wait for you in the Gathering Room."

She stomped down the hall to the overlook. "What about Morning Sun?" she demanded.

"Kayla Dawn," he said, shaking his head. "I thought you already knew or I wouldn't have said one word."

"You've already started it," she accused, "so tell me what you know about Morning Sun."

"Sorry, Kayla Dawn, I've got too much respect for your daddy to even go there." He slumped into the easy chair, grabbed a magazine from a stand beside it and opened it up, covering his face so he wouldn't have to look at her. He pretended to read it.

Kayla could plainly see that he was not going to talk to her about Morning Sun. In frustration she squinted at Ed angrily and snapped at him, "You're reading that upside down!"

He looked up at her over the edge of the magazine. "Oops!" he exclaimed then turned the magazine right side up and resumed his reading position.

Furious with both Ed and her father, she spun around and rushed back down the hall. In her bedroom she put on underclothing, a forest green velvet dress, black slip and a pair of nylons then went back to the bathroom to roll her beautiful blonde hair into a french twist. She curled tiny ringlets in the front and sides, put on a splash of makeup, then slipped into her black pumps. Searching through her closet she located a suitable wrap and put it over her shoulders. She was still seething when she stepped down the stairs and snapped, "Let's go!"

If she thought she'd get out to the helicopter with her dignity in tact, she was mistaken. Her black pumps simply made any progress futile as she slipped and slid all over the walkway. Ed tried to prevent her falling by supporting her by an elbow.

"I'll go back and get your boots, Kayla Dawn," observed Ed as she slipped once again. "That'll help."

"No!" she protested. "I'm not going to arrive at Church like some mountaineer fresh out of manure training."

"Kayla Dawn, if you ain't the most persnickety woman I ever met!" he exclaimed boldly.

"And you can keep your opinions to yourself!" she snapped.

"There's no sense punishing me for something Mont should have told you last August," he accused.

She went to take another step and slid once more. Ed barely caught her in time before she went sprawling all over the walkway.

"Enough of this!" Ed growled. He lifted her up onto her feet, turned her around to face him, bent over and placed his right shoulder against her belly. "Hmm," he observed casually. "Why didn't I think of this to begin with?"

"You wouldn't dare!" she demanded, but before she could say anything more she found herself slung over his shoulder like a sack of flour as he carried her to the helipad. She protested the entire way, but it was a futile effort. When he had her securely belted inside the helicopter, he took his position as pilot, and they both put on their ear phones with the voice transmitters.

"Sorry," he said, "but even on the Sabbath Day a decent Christian has to get the ox out of the mire."

"If you're calling me an ox, Ed Sparkleman, I'll—"

"You'll what?" he asked as he piloted the helicopter up into the air and headed it toward town, skimming just above the tops of the forest across from the meadow. "Jump?" came his final question.

Kayla saw his point. She realized she had just performed the most childish scene of her entire life. He made her so furious! Somehow he'd always had that power over her. She was reminded of days gone past when the "Dreadful Five" were on the prowl. How angry Ed could make her, even then! The memories brought so much happiness to her that she suddenly burst out laughing. She laughed so hard she would have fallen out of her chair if he hadn't fastened the safety belts so securely.

When Ed realized she was over her temper tantrum, he laughed with her. He could scarcely keep control of the helicopter because he laughed so hard. The more he laughed, the more she laughed and vice versa.

"Dang! Kayla Dawn!" he exclaimed. "Do you know how long it's been since I heard you laugh like that?"

She tried to suppress another giggle unsuccessfully. Then she couldn't answer him because she couldn't stop laughing all over again.

The helicopter did a dance over the tops of the forest as a new round of laughter broke out inside it. First it swerved to the left, then to the right, up and down, like a drunken sailor trying to maneuver a duck.

"Dang, if you don't stop laughing, we're gonna get ourselves arrested, Kayla Dawn!" Ed finally protested through gritted teeth. "If Sky Patrol catches us, we're gonna spend the night at the county jail!"

She finally stopped enough to say, "It would be your fault, Ed Sparkleman, throwing me over your shoulder like a heathen! You haven't been so bold since high school!"

"Maybe I should'a been brash and bold all along, I could'a saved us a world of hurt and misery," he suggested with a wink.

Kayla straightened the neckline on her dress and then gulped. "I forgot to wear my emerald necklace," she gasped as she realized how tacky her beautiful velvet dress appeared without it.

"We ain't going back, Kayla Dawn," he drawled. "Not for no necklace.

"I can't be seen at church like this," she complained. "This is all your fault! If you hadn't flustered me so."

"I flustered you?" he asked flippantly. "Hah! That'll be the day!"

"Well now what am I supposed to do?" she demanded.

"Here," he offered as he pulled his life jacket out from under the seat. "I got a whistle on this life vest here. Use it!"

"What? Are you crazy?"

"No, look. It's got a gold chain on it. Here," he fumbled with the catch while trying to hold onto the helicopter controls. Removing the whistle from the chain, he realized she was not going to make any effort to help him. He sighed in exasperation. "Kayla Dawn!" he scolded. "Can't you do anything for yourself?"

"I can't wear that!" she insisted. "It probably won't even fit around my neck." She refused to admit that the chain was one of the most beautiful gold pieces she'd ever seen.

"It'll fit," he assured her. "Trust me."

Kayla unfastened the catch and slipped it on, fastening it up at her nape. To her utter surprise the chain rested in perfect proportion around her neck. She rubbed it through her fingers, feeling the smooth edges.

"It fits me perfectly," she agreed. "But why are you using a piece of jewelry to keep your whistle attached to your life jacket?"

"It's a long story," he told her, refusing to answer. He would never confide that he'd bought the gold chain for her as a wedding gift, hoping to put miniature gold babies on it for each one they had through the years. He bit his lip and savored the pain because it took his mind off the dull aching in his heart. "There's the Church," he said, changing the subject.

"This will be embarrassing, arriving in a helicopter," she complained.

"We have a helipad next door to the Church grounds, on the other side. Look! Besides, the people are used to us arriving by helicopter in the winter, especially after a storm."

"You, maybe," she agreed. "But certainly not me!"

"Then why don't you jump out of the helicopter on this side of the building before I set it down on the helipad. That way no one will know," he suggested sarcastically.

"Funny man!" she quipped.

"You know, Kayla Dawn, you don't make life very easy on me," he drawled. "One of these days you're gonna push me too far and I won't be responsible for what happens afterward."

Ed piloted the helicopter down to a complete landing, turned off the controls and said, "We may as well wait here until she stops spinning. We've got fifteen minutes to spare anyway."

"At least my hair won't get wind blown," she agreed. Her heart had stopped racing since their hilarious bout in the sky on the way down. Now she felt at a definite disadvantage.

"You know, Kayla Dawn, you should laugh more often. It suits you," he said, his voice much softer, kinder than earlier.

"I do laugh," she responded. "Just not that hard." She rubbed her ribs where the laughing still hurt.

Ed became silent for a moment, and thoughtful. Finally he said, "So you're really crazy about Commander Clark, so much that you're going to marry him?"

The noise from the propellers softened considerably as she thought how to best answer his question. Carefully she removed the ear phones, as did Ed. "I wouldn't use that expression, exactly," she finally answered. "I would rather say that we fit together emotionally and intellectually like a fine pair of kid gloves."

"Does he make you laugh?" asked Ed. "I don't think you should spend your life 'fitting' into a glove without laughing to get there."

She thought seriously about Josh and her relationship with him. "Yes," she answered, "he does."

Ed opened the helicopter door and came around to help her out. Then he escorted her into the Church.

The chapel, still empty, was new and modern, unlike the one she'd known in her youth. Ed sat down beside Kayla on a back bench and waited with her until Sunday School let out and the congregation came in for Sacrament Meeting.

He reached out and touched her hand. Instinctively she turned it over, palm up. He traced tiny circles with his finger across her palm, as he had done many times before.

When he spoke to her, he whispered, but his voice still echoed in the acoustically enabled chapel. "Have you thought any more about our subject matter in the helicopter yesterday?"

"No," she whispered back. "But I haven't had much time for thinking."

"Doc Nillson goes to our meetings. Maybe you'd like to talk to him," he suggested.

"I'll keep it in mind."

"You sound just like your dad," he complained. "'I'll think on it a spell,'" he always says, "like he hasn't heard a word."

"He's a stubborn man," she offered.

"And you inherited a healthy dose of that," he insisted.

Kayla paused. "Well," she said, "at least we agree on one thing."

The chapel doors swung open and people started gathering inside. Kayla stood up to look for Mont and immediately realized that was a mistake. People she hadn't seen in years came up to her to shake her hand vigorously, as well as Ed's. "Welcome home, Kayla," came the warm and constant greeting.

She whispered to Ed between conversations, "I feel like I'm in a reception line."

"You mean we're not?" he asked, disappointment in his voice.

She couldn't think of a healthy retort before another woman shook her hand and welcomed her back home. Finally Mont and Sparky joined them.

"I see you had better success than I did at waking her," Mont said, nudging Ed in the ribs.

"She was already up when I got there," Ed responded.

"Aren't you a vision!" Sparky exclaimed, examining Kayla from head to toe. "Mighty pretty wrapping for our little girl, Mont."

"Yep, she looks like a real princess, doesn't she?" Mont agreed, giving Kayla a kiss on her cheek.

Sparky and Ed both nodded. Ed stepped aside so Sparky could sit beside her, as well as Mont. Kayla noticed and thought it a kind gesture from son to father. She smiled at Ed and nodded her thanks. He nodded back, sat down and looked straight ahead at the podium.

Kayla sat between the two men who raised her, grateful for both of them. Each one reached out and held her hand tenderly in theirs.

Since this was the last Sunday before Christmas the congregation was invited to sing a number of Christmas Carols while the young men and young women read the story of Christmas from the scriptures.

The advent of the Savior's birth was a story she hadn't heard in a long, long while. She closed her eyes so she could imagine it all happening: the angel coming to Mary; Joseph agreeing to keep Mary as his espoused wife; the long journey to Bethlehem on a little donkey; the miraculous birth of the Christ child; the Savior of all mankind.

Suddenly Kayla felt tears stinging her eyes. It seemed all so unfair, she thought. I want to believe the stories of the Savior, but it is impossible to conceive a child without . . . she hesitated and opened up a thought inside her heart. Something her father had told her repeatedly through her growing up years filled her mind and her heart with a warmth she'd not experienced since she was a child: "With God, all things are possible."

Somewhere deep within her Kayla found a prayer and repeated it silently in her mind: 'God, if you are there and you hear me, please don't be angry with me. I don't understand my feelings. Spiritual manifestations are not my forte. I'm a scientist, not a theologian. Help me find my way, somehow. I want to believe.'

A single tear slipped down her cheek. She felt something pressed into her hand and opened her eyes to see her father's handkerchief.

Mont smiled at her with all the love that a tender parent can. She dabbed at her face with the handkerchief and then gave it back to him, hoping with all her heart that he'd not read more into her tears than what was truly there.

Following the meeting they regrouped outside. It was impossible to break away and seek out Mike Nillson, M.D., without arousing suspicion so she let the matter slide. She hoped Ed wouldn't be too disappointed with her.

"Is Tom feeling any better?" Mont asked Sparky on the way to the helicopter.

"He's still hung over," Sparky admitted. "Will wanted to stay with him until we got back. He was going to try to get Tom to help him cook dinner today, but we may have to fend for ourselves."

"The boys cook?" Kayla asked in surprise.

"Heck, yes," Ed responded. "They figure they've got to if Melanie and Charlene are ever going to marry them. You know, Kayla, men play Mr. Mom almost as much as the women these days. We all need a few good skills we can fall back on." He laughed and held the helicopter door open for her.

Kayla sat in the back seat next to Mont. Ed climbed in front with his father. While they waited for the parking lot to clear out, Mont glanced at his lovely daughter.

"Pretty necklace, Princess," he grinned.

Kayla exchanged a glance with Ed. "Thank you," she whispered. She wanted to say it wasn't hers, but Ed placed a finger over his lips to silence her, so she remained silent. Though why he didn't want Mont to know it wasn't hers, she didn't know.

Finally all the cars had left and the parking lot was empty. Ed started the helicopter up. Within minutes they were headed back to the Bar M Ranch.

"You still want me to come on up Tuesday, Mont?" asked Ed from the pilot's seat.

"If you don't mind," Mont responded.

"If Sky Patrol doesn't have much on the docket, it should work. Unless there's some big emergency," Ed answered.

"Good. Crack of dawn all right with you?"

"Anxious to get started, hmm?" asked Ed.

Mont gave Ed a stern look from the back seat, one that said, 'watch what you say around Kayla.' "Something like that," Mont answered.

"Look," said Sparky, "A moose! Down by the river."

"Take her in for a closer look, Ed," Mont requested. "It's been a while since you've seen a moose, hasn't it Kayla?"

"Years," she agreed. "Oh, do take us down, Ed."

"I always was a sucker for a pretty face," he admitted as he adjusted controls in the cockpit. The helicopter swooped forward and circled back along the river until they had a good view of the moose, a fine female with cocoa brown hair tinged with ebony and a strong bone structure. The massive creature scarcely gave them a glance as they passed by overhead.

"She doesn't scare off too easily," noticed Ed. "Ain't that just like a woman, standing her ground in the face of danger."

"Aw," Sparky drawled, "she's probably heard this helicopter flying by overhead so many times she thinks its some noisy bird."

Kayla smiled at the analogy. "That could be," she agreed. "What have you got planned for Tuesday, Dad?"

He patted her hand affectionately. "You'll see, Princess."

"I hate it when you do that," she said.

"What did I do now?" Mont asked.

"You're patronizing me," she told him. "When are we going to open up and talk in this family, Dad? Or has my trip been nothing more than a ruse?"

"I can't say anything more yet, Kayla, but in time."

Kayla shook her head while Mont patted her hand. No wonder she felt so content and at peace in California. She didn't have to deal with her capricious father!

Chapter Nine

Arriving back at the Bar M Ranch, they were greeted by William and Tom Sparkleman, dressed in jeans, western shirts and boots, and white, bib aprons. The aroma from the kitchen filled the entire lodge with the savory scent of elk steak, potato casserole and spicy, minted beans.

William held a kitchen towel over his left arm and bowed before Kayla as she stepped into the living area. "This way, your highness," he said with an elaborate bow. He took her hand and escorted her to the dining room table.

"Why, thank you, Sir Knight," she answered as though she were truly royalty. "It smells delightful," she complimented Tom and Will.

They both bowed and took their places at the table. Mont, Sparky and Ed also sat down, Mont at the head of the table, Sparky at the other end.

The Bar M's everyday dishes were made of dark, blue enamel with small white splotches, and they'd seen their share of hard use over the past thirty years. These were set around the oval table in meticulous order, with blue and white checked napkins and tin cups for drinking. Mont's face turned red as he realized what dishes Tom and Will had used. "You could have used the good dishes," he complained.

"If you'd left the key where we could find it, we would have," Tom responded quickly.

"It's—" Then Mont stopped. "Oh, never mind. Let's eat, shall we?"

Tom pouted momentarily, but let the matter slide.

Kayla noticed his disappointment immediately. She thought it odd that her father had taken to locking things up and not letting Tom or Will know where the keys were. Did this have anything to do with what Ed had referred to earlier that day regarding Morning Sun? She didn't have any answers yet, she realized, but Mont was going to start answering questions soon, if she had anything to say about it.

Sparky pronounced a blessing on the meal, then the boys passed the food around and everyone began eating.

Timidly Tom looked over at Kayla. "I'm sorry," he apologized, "for spoiling your homecoming last night, Kayla." He looked down at the table in shame.

"Apology accepted," she nodded. "Are you feeling better today?"

"I've got a whopping big headache," he answered. "But other than that, I'll live."

"You'd better!" she grinned. "All of us care about you, Tom."

Sparky smiled and his afternoon whiskers sparkled in the dining room light. In years past, Kayla had wondered why he never shaved. She was surprised to learn that his facial hair, for unknown reasons, grew faster than it should. If he shaved in the morning, by noon he'd need to shave again. If he shaved at noon, by evening he'd need to again. He finally grew tired of shaving all the time so he decided that if he trimmed his whiskers with a sharp pair of scissors once a week, it'd be good enough. Fortunately none of his boys inherited Sparky's worst nightmare, as he affectionately called it.

The elk steak, Kayla decided, was delicious enough to die for. She hadn't enjoyed a meal as wholesome since her father had visited her in August and brought some elk meat with him. He knew, as did the Sparklemans, that elk was her favorite protein, though she rarely ever got to eat it anymore.

"Who got the elk?" she asked, savoring every bite full.

"William has become the family hunter," said Mont. "He's got the steadiest hand."

William blushed, "Well, next to Kayla that is." He forked another piece of meat into his mouth. "I got this one up Porcupine Ridge. It was so big I had to split it and make two trips down the mountain."

"Fortunately for Shepherd, it was downhill and not up," Ed commented.

"You're still riding old Shepherd?" Kayla questioned.

"No," said Will. "We named this one after him when Shepherd got mountain fever. We had to put him down."

"I'm sorry to hear that," said Kayla remembering the gray stallion with fondness. "But Daylight is still doing well, isn't she?"

"Yep," said Mont. "She's still as beautiful and frisky as the day you broke her in."

"She's getting old, then," said Kayla. "I'd like to ride her while I'm here. Or is the snow too deep?"

Sparky answered her question. "The boys and I are going to see if we can get us plowed out tomorrow, Kayla. If so, you could take her on the road."

Mont wiped his lips with a napkin and looked across at Kayla. "We thought you might like to pick out a Christmas tree tomorrow. We can spend the day sprucing up the place, making it like it used to be at Christmas time."

"I'd love to, Dad!" she exclaimed. "You know how much this old place sparkles when we put up all the holiday trimmings."

"Then it's agreed," smiled Mont.

Cleaning up after dinner was a family affair. Kayla washed the dishes because she was the fastest at it. Everyone else cleared the table, rinsed, dried and put away the dishes. Mont, Sparky, Tom and Will retired to the Gathering Room while Kayla rinsed out the sinks and Ed swept the floor.

"You men have become very domestic in Morning Sun's absence," she commented.

"Only when you're around," Ed confided. "Otherwise we just trash the place."

"Somehow I doubt that," she told him. She placed the dish cloth over the sink divider and dried her hands. Then she untied her apron. From the Gathering Room floated the soft, gentle music from Lawrence Welk's Champagne Waltz. Mont had evidently turned on the CD player.

Kayla tried to step around Ed, but he moved the broom in her way. She stepped to the other side, but he moved the broom again, blocking her way once more. She smiled. "Are you going to let me pass?"

"No," he drawled, "let's dance instead." He set the broom aside and began singing, "Dancing in the kitchen on a Saturday night," as he swept her into his arms and danced a fast polka totally out of tune with the tender waltz from the CD player.

Kayla laughed and matched him step for step. Every time he tried to trip her up she kept pace with him.

By this time Will and Tom wanted in on the game. They switched the CD to Mont's favorites from the fifties.

Ed maneuvered Kayla out into the Gathering Room where Tom and Will pushed the sofa back and took turns fighting to see who would dance with her next.

The moment Tequila came on Kayla knew they were in trouble. Mont and Sparky started dancing, as well. The entire group danced and laughed so hard that one couldn't tell where the dancing ended and the laughing began.

The telephone rang and Mont left the group momentarily to answer it. Sparky collapsed in a hysterical fit of laughter as Ed wiggled his slim body between Kayla and Will, taking his turn again at dancing with her. Will shrugged, turned and bowed to Tom and continued dancing to the ferocious beat. Kayla laughed so hard she could hardly stand up any longer.

When Mont tapped Ed on the shoulder as though ready to take his place with his daughter, Ed stepped back to let Mont have her. Instead of dancing, however, Mont handed Kayla the cordless phone. "It's Josh," he announced. "Something about you not calling him last night when you got in."

"You're in trouble now, Kayla Dawn," Ed whispered in her ear.

Kayla grabbed the phone and went up to the privacy of her bedroom. She wanted to hear the conversation without the sounds from downstairs where the boys were still strutting their stuff. Stretching out across her bed, she placed the receiver next to her ear and answered the call. "Josh?"

"Just me," he responded. "I was worried when you didn't call me last night."

"I'm sorry, Josh. By the time I got here I was so tired and hungry. Dad fed me and then put me on the sofa where he rubbed my feet."

"...and you fell deliciously asleep, I know," he finished for her. "I've seen that happen before."

Kayla remembered the incident he referred to when, fifteen months earlier, Josh had joined her at the ranch for the fall roundup. She smiled with the memory.

"What was all that noise I heard in the background?" he wanted to know.

"The Dreadful Five . . . only Abbot isn't here so it must be the Dreadful Four, dancing and singing in the Gathering Room," she answered.

"And no doubt driving your father insane," he suggested.

"No," she laughed. "He and Sparky couldn't dissuade us so they joined us. It was delightful!"

"Now I'm jealous," he teased. "You're up there dancing with five men and I'm stuck here all alone."

"Don't be," she told him. "They may have my dancing moves, but you've got my heart."

"That's what I needed to hear," he sighed. "I can't believe how much I miss you. How did you manage to survive without me last week when I was ship side?"

"I spent every waking moment at work," she reminded, "trying not to think about you."

"Did it work?" he asked.

"Ask my staff," she said ruefully, "they thought I was the evil Bavmorda reincarnated."

"I doubt that," he consoled her. "Has your father said anything yet? Do you know why he wanted you home?"

"He's pretty tight lipped, Josh," she answered. "But there are some strange things happening around here and I'm beginning to worry more all the time."

"Tell me."

"For one thing, Ed told me Dad collapsed last fall and the doctor thought he has a heart problem," she replied.

"Has Mont confirmed that?"

"We haven't had time to talk yet. Getting a moment alone with him around here is like trying to have a quiet picnic on the freeway."

"That bad?"

"Worse!" she exclaimed. "Now Ed claims he's worried about the ranch and he wants Dad to sell it so Dad can retire and move to California. But I don't think that's the answer."

"I doubt Mont would ever give up the ranch without a fight," Josh observed.

"I know, but Ed wants me to talk Dad into it or something. He says he's just concerned for Dad's welfare, but something bothers me about his interest in the ranch," she confessed. "Besides which, Tom has started drinking and when we arrived last night he made a big scene and passed out. The boys had to carry him home." Kayla sighed.

"Sounds like you've got enough to deal with," Josh confided.

"The worst thing, Josh, is that Dad has been keeping secrets from me," she confessed, "and that hurts the most." She pouted momentarily. Josh reminded her, "You said that Mont is a private person. Perhaps whatever he hasn't told you yet is the reason why he sent for you. If it's something serious and you were my daughter, I'd want to tell you in person."

"I keep telling myself that, but sometimes I get so angry with him," she confessed. "What harm would it have done to warn me ahead of time that Tom had taken to the bottle? I would have been much better prepared for last night," she mused aloud. "And why didn't he tell me last August that Morning Sun is pregnant?"

"She is?" he asked, unable to keep the surprise out of his voice.

"She's at least eight months along or more, so Dad had to have known about the baby when I took him sailing last summer, but he didn't say anything about it," she complained as she rolled over to a more comfortable position.

A knock came at her bedroom door. "Kayla Dawn," Ed said from the other side.

"Hold a minute, Josh." She placed her hand over the mouth piece and said, "Come in."

Ed opened the door and looked in, then froze right there, his tall frame taking up all the doorway's vertical space.

Kayla lifted her head and leaned upon one elbow, unaware of the feelings rumbling deep within Ed Sparkleman.

He gazed down upon her feminine features, from her slim legs to her full, inviting lips. Her honey gold hair was starting to unravel from the French twist and only made her seem more voluptuous than ever. The forest green velvet dress she wore gave her skin a delicate glow that beckoned him. It took every ounce of strength within him not to stretch out on the bed beside her and gather her in his arms. The gold chain he'd told her to wear still caressed the delicate lines on her neck and only added to her startling beauty. He had always known the necklace would suit her, regardless what she wore, and the memories connected to that gold chain nearly tore him apart.

Suddenly the entire time he'd spent with her that day made him feel exhausted and weary. What had he hoped to accomplish? She was marrying Lieutenant Commander Clark in May. He meant nothing to her except as a childhood chum who could make her laugh. "I've got to get back to town, Kayla Dawn," he said with a twinge of sadness. "Pa and the boys are heading home as well."

"I'm sorry," she said, "I didn't realize you were leaving so soon."

"It's okay, honey," he assured her, unaware that he had even used the endearing term. "We know you want to talk to Commander Clark for a spell. We just thought someone ought to say goodbye and we'll see you later."

"Oh!" she exclaimed, putting the phone on the bed momentarily. "Your gold chain!" She started fumbling with the clasp. "I forgot to give it back."

"I don't want it back!" he growled sharply. Then he softened, "It looks better on you than on my life preserver."

"Are you sure?" she asked, sensing something within him that made her want to take him in her arms and hold him until he felt better again. It was a feeling she'd not had for more than seven years.

He nodded.

"Thank you," she murmured. Then she remembered something else. "Tuesday?" she asked quickly.

He turned to leave, but her question troubled him. He turned back. "Come again?" he questioned.

"You told Dad you'd be back on Tuesday," she reminded. "I'll see you then, won't I?"

"Sure thing, Kayla Dawn," he assured her, finding himself powerless to tell her no. "Until Tuesday then."

"Bye, Ed, and thanks for making me laugh," she told him with a tender smile.

Ed gulped and turned quickly. He pulled the door closed behind him. She heard his heavy boots descend down the hall.

When she returned to her phone conversation, Josh was ready to tell her how he had survived the rest of Saturday without her. His parents had cornered him into going Christmas shopping with them and Sarah had "bought out the store" before they were finished.

They only talked a few more minutes and said goodbye. Kayla pressed the disconnect button and lay the phone on the bed beside her. She rubbed her flat abdomen and wondered for a moment what it would be like when she and Josh became first time parents. Somehow she couldn't imagine her belly being firm and rounded like Morning Sun's. The thought made her smile to herself.

Then she heard voices outside. It sounded like Mont and Ed were arguing about something. She remembered that she hadn't heard the helicopter leave, regardless that Ed had told her goodbye.

Quietly she got up and went to the outside door off her bedroom. It opened onto the second story deck. She opened it a moment and the voices became louder. Mont and Ed were downstairs on the front porch, arguing. She tiptoed out onto the deck in order to hear them more clearly.

"I'm not going there again, Mont," Ed argued crossly. "My heart couldn't stand it."

"I'm not asking you to do anything wrong," Mont persisted.

"Mont, I love you as though you were my own Pa. You're a good man and I'd do most anything for you, anything but this!"

"You'll do it," Mont told him. "Because deep down in your gut you know I'm right. You'll never be able to live with yourself if you don't."

"You think you have all the answers," Ed's voice grew in volume as his temper did to match it. "But this isn't just about Kayla Dawn, this is also about me and I'm not going there! Not again!"

Kayla heard Ed's boots stomp down the steps and out across the crunchy path to the helipad. She wondered what they were talking about that apparently had something to do with her. It seemed to her that Mont was trying to manipulate Ed into doing something for Kayla that he didn't want to do.

Fear formed a knot in the pit of her stomach until she felt it reaching up and grabbing at her heart.

Then the worst fear of all came as the helicopter lifted up. Expecting Ed to fly directly southeast, as had always been his pattern, she was dismayed to see him fly toward the front of the lodge where he hovered long enough for her to make eye contact with him. She could easily see from his expression that he was angry, terribly angry. The realization that he knew she had been eavesdropping unnerved her and she fled into the safety of her bedroom.

She listened several moments, waiting, expecting Ed to land the helicopter and rush upstairs to confront her. However, she only heard the helicopter hover a few more seconds before Ed piloted it around and flew southeast, back toward Vernal.

Sitting on the edge of her bed, Kayla wondered if Mont knew she'd been eavesdropping. She hoped the loud whipping of the helicopter propellers had muffled any sound of her running back into the bedroom. Nervously she fidgeted with the skirt of her velvet dress.

Finally she sighed, stripped the dress off her shoulders and unzipped it. She dressed in cream colored pants and a matching sweater with jade and sandstone navajo figurines embroidered on the front. One of the figures held a golden spear. She looked at herself in the mirror and realized the gold chain Ed had given her suited the outfit perfectly so she shrugged and left it on.

She felt vulnerable to attack if she went downstairs. She could hear that Mont had come indoors and was pacing nervously in the Gathering Room. If he'd heard her, it would mean a confrontation, at best. Why had she eavesdropped? It wasn't in her nature to do something so demeaning.

It was then that she realized Mont had set her up. He'd deliberately kept things from her so that she felt he didn't trust her. She'd eavesdropped to find out if her suspicions were correct. If he was angry with her for so doing, he had better be willing to put some of the blame on his own shoulders, she decided.

Her line of thinking gave her the courage she needed to face him. Ed had gone back to town. Sparky and the boys were across the meadow in the cabin. It was just Kayla and Mont. She stood up, determined to face her father and find out exactly what had been happening at the ranch in her absence.

Kayla took a deep breath and headed down the stairs. Her stocking feet muffled the sound of her entrance. When she reached the bottom she realized Mont did not know she had arrived.

Mont stood next to the fireplace, his hand outstretched as he leaned it against the mantle. With his back to her, he had neither seen her nor heard her come down the stairs.

He seemed vulnerable somehow and it made Kayla hesitate. She had respected his privacy her entire life. How could she demand that he tell her anything?

On the other hand, how could she not confront him? He'd deliberately kept things from her as though he couldn't trust her. What had she ever done that warranted his distrust? For herself, nothing had changed other than she was now engaged to be married.

In her classes at BYU and USC she had learned to ask questions if she wanted answers. And if she couldn't get the answers she wanted, she would seek out other sources of information until she found answers. If she had to go to Sparky or William or Abbot or Morning Sun and all those sources failed her, she would give Tom a bottle of whiskey and get answers that way. But first, she would go to the only man from whom she wanted to hear the truth.

She stepped across the floor and wrapped her arms around his waist, hugging him from behind. "Daddy," she said, "I love you with all my heart and I would never do anything to offend you. But right now I am so angry and so hurt that if we don't sit down and talk, and you give me some real answers to my questions, I'm liable to pack my things and go back to California."

He turned and stared at her in shocked surprise. "What?" he asked in almost a whisper.

"I mean it, Dad. Right now I feel like you don't trust me for some horrible reason and if that's the case, then this is no longer my home and I'm no longer welcome here."

Tears poured down her cheeks as a thousand drops of anger melted out of her.

Chapter Ten

Mont held Kayla in his arms long enough for her to spend her tears against him. Her body trembled until she controlled the crying. He'd never seen her so distraught and he wondered what on earth he'd done that would bring her to this emotional shambles. Finally the tears eased some and she wiped her eyes on his handkerchief.

"Now, what's this all about?" he asked, not knowing where to begin.

She sniffed and pulled away from him. "Come, sit and talk to me," she insisted.

"I'll tell you anything you want to know, Princess. What have I done?" He puzzled over the past and wondered how he had failed her.

She took his hands and pulled him over to the sofa where she made him sit down. Then she moved the rocking chair directly in front of him so they could have eye to eye contact. She sat in the rocking chair and placed one foot on either side of both his knees and studied his expression carefully.

"You've got me trapped now, Princess," he agreed. "I'm your captive, I guess. Tell me what I've done."

"It's not so much what you've done," she began, "but what you've omitted that I'm upset about."

She took the pins from her hair and let the French twist fall out in big ringlets on her shoulders. Shaking her head helped to loosen her hair even more and she seemed vulnerable and angelic to him. He remembered a scripture about fathers offending their tender children and he immediately felt duly chastened.

"Anything you want to know," he said, "that I've omitted, just ask me and I'll tell you."

"Why did you ask me to come home?" came her first question.

Stubbornly he bit his bottom lip and thought the question through. Finally he sighed. "I can't tell you!"

"That's it!" she snapped. "I'm going home." She stood up and started for the stairs. He grabbed her wrist, pulled her back, made her sit down in the rocking chair then placed one hand on each arm rest so that he had her captive.

"I want everything to be perfect," he explained, staring deep into her brown eyes so she would know he was stubbornly going to adhere to what he considered the perfect moment. "Your mother made me promise I would do something for you and I've never done it. And I'm not going to do it YOUR way when I know exactly how KayDawn would have wanted me to do it."

Kayla felt like he'd stolen the wind from her sails. "This whole trip is about KayDawn?" she asked. "About my mother?" She almost couldn't say the word 'mother' for the emotions the endearing term seemed to fuel within her.

"Now," said Mont, "that's all I'm going to say and you're going to have to exercise some patience until I tell you that the timing is perfect."

He studied her expression and hoped he caught a faint glimmer of compliance in her dark brown, flashing eyes. "All right, then," he continued. "Now, anything else you want to ask me, that you think I've omitted, I will tell you."

She pouted momentarily. "All right," she finally agreed.

"Now then. You think you have questions. Maybe I have answers. I'll try. What else would you like to know?"

Kayla sighed. "There are so many things spinning around in my head, Dad, that I hardly know where to begin, but let's start with my trip up here with Ed in the helicopter. He told me some things that upset me."

"Like?" he asked.

She didn't like the tone in his voice, but she didn't want any secrets kept from him when the conversation was over. "Ed is worried about you," she confessed. "He said you fainted a few months back and Doctor Nillson was concerned about your heart."

"The boy is daft! There ain't a dad gum thing wrong with my heart!" he complained.

"Ed is a man, Father. He is a grown adult capable of assessing whether or not the doctor has lied to him," she crossed her arms for emphasis. "Did you or did you not faint?" she insisted.

"I got dizzy," he explained. "It was a hot day. I'd been working with lumber all day long, making a new fence up in the northwest section of the ranch. We'd hiked three miles back to the meadow so the horses wouldn't get overheated. I hadn't had any water to drink for several hours. You'd have got dizzy, too."

"Did you or did you not faint?" she asked one more time, making her voice severe and demanding.

Mont sighed. "I don't know. The doctor said I did. I got dizzy and the next thing I knew I was laying on a stretcher heading for the hospital in an ambulance."

"What was the prognosis?" she asked.

"The prognosis was that if I didn't have a heart problem before I got the medical bills, I sure as thunder did afterward!" he snorted.

"Why are you being so stubborn about this?" she questioned. "If I had fainted in the meadow and I took the ambulance to town, you'd be just as stubborn the other way. You'd make sure they found out and fixed whatever was wrong with me, right?"

"It's not you," he complained. "It's me. You're young and you have your whole life ahead of you. I'm just a wasted down rancher who wouldn't mind if the Lord said, 'Come on home, Mont, it's your time now.'"

"What about your grandchildren, Dad?" she asked. "Don't you want to be here for your grandchildren?" She arched an eyebrow, but didn't notice any yielding. "You always said you wanted a handful of grandchildren. Now I'm going to marry Josh and he wants a large family. I don't want our children to grow up without their grandfather."

"Well," he acquiesced. "I don't want them to, either." He patted her knees. "Next question," he urged, ready to move on.

"Not until you explain about the prognosis."

"You are too stubborn for your own good!" he complained.

"The prognosis, Dad!"

"Who raised you, anyway?" he asked. Her expression did not soften so he conceded. "I have a slight arrhythmia. The doctor put me on some digitalis and it's been fine ever since. It's not life threatening. It's not serious. It's a nuisance," he added. "Next question?"

Kayla sighed, relieved that he had finally told her. She began with her next obstacle. "Ed was concerned about the ranch. He wondered if you ought to think about selling it. He thinks you should come live in California, near me."

He frowned. "Is that what you think I want?"

"No," she admitted. "This ranch is your whole life."

"You don't know me very well, Princess," he said, shaking his head. "You and KayDawn are my whole life. This ranch is just a piece of ground with some pretty trees on it. If I thought you needed me in California, that's where I'd be."

"Then you are thinking of selling?" she asked.

"No!" he exclaimed, his tone completely defiant. Seeing her startled expression he softened. "Not yet, Princess. What would I do about Sparky? He deserves better than a big old boot, don't you think?"

"So you're going to keep the ranch until you both die?" she asked.

"I hope so," he answered. "Unless the good Lord sees fit to make me an invalid. Then I'd have to just mosey my old wheelchair down to California where you'd have to take care of me, I reckon, but that's not what I want in my old age."

"And your grandchildren?" she asked patiently.

"Well, the way I figure, kids need to have a place to go where they can hike way up to the top of a mountain or catch trout in a clear mountain stream. The best thing I could do for them, besides traveling back and forth to see them often, is to keep the ranch for them."

"Like a summer home?" she asked.

"Exactly," agreed Mont. His eyes sparkled as he explained his plans to her. "Sparky and I were talking just last week about the ranch and our families and all. Abbot is getting his doctorate soon. He wants to be a surgeon and Heaven knows Vernal needs another good surgeon. William is sweet on that little gal whose father runs those river trips on the Green River out of Dutch John. I expect they're going to get married one of these first days and he's going to take over the business for his father in law. Tom . . . well, he's another story all together and we don't know yet what's going to become of him. Ed's starting to fit in nicely with the Sky Patrol. He enjoys that sheriff and police stuff.

Sparky and me, we figure that all the boys will be gone within the next few years. Then we plan to mosey on down the road, live in California in the winter, near you somewhere of course, and in the summer, we'll come back here and bring a couple of grandkids with us."

The gleam in his eyes made Kayla realize he was serious. "That's what you really want?" she asked, studying carefully his expression.

"Beats ten hours a day in the saddle," he answered.

"That's the only thing that you'd be happy doing?" she asked again.

"Other than being with your mother," he nodded, "I believe so." He had a firmness to his jaw that she had seen only a few times before, when he was doing something that gave him pure joy.

"Then let's move onto question number three," said Kayla.

"There's more?" he asked as his eyes widened with incredulity.

She nodded slowly and gave him a searching glare.

"All right, all right," he said, holding up his hand in protest. "Fire away."

"Why didn't you tell me last August that Morning Sun is pregnant?"

"You're treading on private ground, Princess. Are you sure you want to do that?" He arched an eyebrow and tried to stare her down to no avail.

"Dad!" she snapped. "Morning Sun is the closest thing to a mother I've ever known. Don't you think I would have enjoyed getting a present for the baby, or throwing her a baby shower while I was here, or crocheting a pair of booties or something?"

"You know how to crochet?" he asked, startled.

She hit him in the arm playfully. "No, but you know what I'm trying to say! Something so joyful should have been shared with me."

"Some things are better left unsaid," Mont insisted. "Some things aren't always as joyful as we may think."

"Morning Sun has wanted a baby since before I was five," Kayla was confused by his attitude. "She's prayed for a child of her own continually. Now that she's going to have one, what's not to be joyful about?"

He shook his head and addressed her like she was still the innocent child of long ago. "Kayla, remember when you were a young girl and you wanted a rattlesnake for a pet and I wouldn't let you have one?" he began carefully.

"Yes, Dad, but—"

He held up his hand. "Just let me finish this thought and then we'll see where you want to go with it, all right?"

Kayla nodded.

"You wanted a rattlesnake and I said no, it wouldn't be a good idea. You decided you would catch your own rattlesnake, even after I told you they were dangerous, they bite people, people get sick, sometimes they die when rattlesnakes bite them. You remember all this?" He asked.

"I remember," she agreed patiently.

"So you went out and you found a rattlesnake hole and you tried to get the snake out to keep for a pet and it bit you." He paused for emphasis.

It gave Kayla a moment to reflect on the memory. Her father had rushed her to the hospital where she spent the most miserable week of her life, hovering between headaches with nausea and headaches with blinding stomach pain.

Satisfied that she recalled the incident, Mont continued. "Sometimes we want something so bad we'll do anything to get it, but it really isn't good for us to have it," he explained. "Do you see where I'm going with this?"

"Yes, Dad," she agreed, "and I'm glad that you tried to protect me when I was a little girl and I didn't know any better, but I'm an adult now. I'm 29 years old, I have a good job, my own condominium, my own boat and a car and what's more, most of them are paid for. I think you should start treating me like I'm an adult and tell me everything that you're trying to protect me from." Her voice held just enough anger in it to be convincing.

Mont sighed. He stood up and started pacing back and forth across the hearth. "What a dilemma," he moaned. "You do everything you can to protect the innocence of your child only to find out she doesn't want you to protect her anymore."

"Dad!" she complained. "Give me some credit for maturity."

He studied her expression. Yes, she was definitely an adult now, but she was also his little princess and he just didn't want to trample on her sensitivity. He also knew that the time had come for him to realize she had grown up and would have to learn to face the stark reality of life. He drew in a deep breath and exhaled sharply.

"Last April," he began, trying to keep his voice steady without seeming too emotional about what had happened, "I went with Sparky down to Salt Lake City over Conference weekend. We had some car trouble on the way back and had to stay over in Heber Sunday night until someone opened up to get it fixed. You know how everything closes down over Conference. Will and Ed had gone with us. We had a great time, visited with Abbot and met Abbot's sweetheart.

"See, if I'd left Will or Ed back at the ranch, I could have phoned one of them, they could have driven out to Morning Sun's place and told her not to come in until the next day. I telephoned Tom because he was the only one we'd left behind. I guess he went out on a drunk and she didn't get the message.

"She came over to the house around nine in the morning, like she usually did. She didn't know that someone had broken into the lodge in our absence and was still there."

"Oh, no!" Kayla inhaled sharply, realizing where Mont was taking her.

"Are you all right?" he asked.

"Go on with the story, Dad. I'll be fine. It just caught me off guard," she assured him.

He stuffed his hands in his pockets to keep her from seeing the fists he was inclined to make automatically whenever he thought on the incident. "The intruder jumped her as she was coming up the stairs to put away some laundry," Mont continued. "She kept her cool and did-n't struggle, but the man beat her senseless, regardless." His voice choked as emotion made breathing difficult.

Kayla stood up and walked over to him, putting her arm around his back to comfort him. "It's all right, Dad. It wasn't your fault. I'm sure Morning Sun knows that."

"He raped her, Kayla," Mont confided. "Now she's carrying his child!"

Realization swept over her and she sank to her knees and wept for Morning Sun. Her father stooped beside her. "I'm sorry, Princess. What a terrible thing to have to tell you."

"I'm all right, Dad," she sniffed. After standing up she walked wearily over to the sofa.

Mont followed and sat beside her, taking her hands in his.

Kayla allowed Mont time to collect his thoughts. "You found her then?" she asked, when she hoped he'd regained his composure.

"No, Ed found her," he explained. "We got home late that night. Old Bessie was mooing like she was ready to burst so we hurried out to the barn to see what the problem was. Tom hadn't milked her at all that day. Sparky and I stayed with Bessie to relieve some of her discomfort while Will went to the cabin looking for Tom, and found him passed out on his bed, liquor bottles everywhere. In the meantime, Ed went on up to the lodge to look for Tom."

Kayla sighed, "What a terrible thing for Ed to see."

Mont gulped. "We heard Ed yelling so we left Bessie aching and bellowing and ran up to see what was going on. By the time we got there Ed had thrown a blanket over her naked body and was telephoning the sheriff."

A great sob came from deep within him and it was several minutes before he could continue. Finally he regained his composure and said, "Her whole face was swollen so bad we could hardly recognize her. The ambulance came and I went down with her to the hospital. She didn't regain consciousness until later the next day. The doctor wanted to do an abortion, to make sure she hadn't conceived from the rape, but she refused. She said she'd been through enough."

"Did they ever find the man who did this?" Kayla wanted to know.

"No," he admitted. "And maybe it's a good thing they didn't right away because Will or Ed, either one, would have probably killed him if they'd found him." He shuddered with the memory.

"How do you know Morning Sun's husband didn't father the baby?" she asked, not really certain she wanted to know.

"He's sterile, Princess. Always has been, according to Dr. Nillson."

"So Morning Sun is keeping the baby anyway?" Kayla asked.

"She says something good has to come from what happened," explained Mont. "She figures she had to suffer like that in order for God to bless her. I think it's part of her culture."

"How do you feel about the baby?" she asked.

"I reckon the baby's half hers and she's a mighty good woman. Maybe she's right," he admitted.

Kayla sighed in relief. "I can easily understand her wanting to keep the baby," she told him. "I would have kept it."

He patted her hand tenderly. "I know that," he whispered.

Kayla stood up. "I understand why you didn't tell me, Dad, but you need to stop treating me like I'm still a child. I've got to learn to face life's trials sometime and I think I'm old enough now, don't you?"

"I guess you are, Kayla," he agreed. "But sit down because there are a few things more I need to tell you. I don't want any more secrets between us. You need to know everything."

I don't either, Kayla thought to herself. "What is it, Dad?" she asked. "I'm here for you. Let me be your shoulder."

"This is between you and me and the sheriff and Doc Nillson, now," warned Mont. "Sparky and the boys, not even Ed, know about it and they won't until we know for sure. Is that agreed?"

"I would have to tell Josh, Dad. I don't keep secrets from him, except in the case of Christmas gifts," she shook her head and gave him a questioning glance.

Of course," he affirmed. "But no one else."

"Good," she admitted. "I don't want to start off on the wrong foot with my engagement to Josh."

"No, you shouldn't," agreed Mont, realizing full well that he had already talked the situation over with KayDawn a million times through the spirit. Mont began, "Sheriff Heartwell and I believe we know how to prove who raped and beat Morning Sun and he's got a plan. When the baby is born, they're going to do a DNA test on it and then they'll do a DNA on the suspects. When we get a match, we'll know."

"How many suspects are there?" she questioned.

"Just one as far as I'm concerned," Mont answered.

"Who is it? Or am I allowed to know?" she asked.

Mont explained, "Right now the sheriff has almost enough evidence to convict the guy, but it's such a tricky situation that, if we don't handle it just right, he could walk free."

"What do you mean, Dad?" Kayla inquired. "Do you know the person whom you believe did this to Morning Sun?"

Mont studied her for several long minutes. "Yes," he finally said, nodding his head. "And so do you. The man is Tom Sparkleman."

If he had hit her in the head with a frying pan, she wouldn't have been more stunned. She leaned back against the sofa cushion completely out of breath. All the color drained from her face.

"That's why I made you promise it wouldn't go beyond me and you, the sheriff and Doc Nillson," Mont explained, wringing his hands in despair.

"How do you know? What makes you suspect Tom?" she asked.

"The day after the robbery I went down to the barn to drag a salt lick out to the meadow for the horses. Next to the trash containers, which Tom had hauled to the county dump while we were gone, something he'd rarely done before, I found one of his gloves. Lucky for me the guys were in town that day, even Sparky. I phoned the sheriff and he came right up," Mont rolled his eyes, evidence of the pain calling the sheriff back again must have caused him. "I hadn't touched the glove. No one had. The sheriff told me not to say nothing to nobody, especially Ed on account of him working for Sky Patrol."

"Oh, Dad," Kayla sighed. "How terrible for you."

Mont nodded. "The sheriff told me later that the blood on the glove was Morning Sun's. It was a leather glove identical to a pair that Ed had given Tom the Christmas before April, smooth surfaced and highly polished. Evidently when Tom was taking the gloves off, he left one perfect finger print on the outside of the glove."

"I see," said Kayla. "So why haven't they arrested him yet?"

"Two reasons," explained Mont. "They think he might have been drunk when he attacked her. If so, they would approach the trial a little differently. The second reason is that the judge told Sheriff Heartwell that if the DNA matched up, it wouldn't have to go to trial. They'd have enough evidence to pressure Tom into confessing."

"That would be better for Morning Sun, not having to testify before a jury. I don't know how she could do that," agreed Kayla.

"She speaks broken English at best," Mont told her. "Any defense attorney could rip her to shreds, which would be worse for her. For the first few months after it happened, she would hardly speak at all. She's improved so much we hate to rock the boat."

"Does Tom know he's a suspect?" Kayla asked.

"Not that I'm aware," said Mont. "And I've done my best to keep my mouth shut. You'll have to do the same, Princess."

"I will," she vowed. "For Morning Sun I would do anything."

"So would I," he agreed.

Suddenly a thought occurred to her. "That's why you've locked up the den and the dishes and such in the house?"

"Yes," he nodded. "I don't know what Tom was looking for that day. I couldn't find anything missing. Whatever it was, he left a mess in the den. My files were strewn everywhere, things were tipped over and dumped out."

"At least I understand what Ed meant this morning," she told him. "He said he wasn't going to attack me, like I would really be worried about someone attacking me."

"That's why I sent Ed back for you," Mont explained. "I knew Will would keep an eye on Tom, especially after last night when he insulted you. But I didn't want you here when they came over to cook dinner. I don't know how drunk Tom has to be until he tries to hurt someone again."

"Do you think he will?" she asked.

"Princess, when Tom's drinking, he isn't someone you want to be around. You ever see him drunk and you're alone, shoot him first and ask him questions later, you hear?" He stared into her eyes with such a somber expression that Kayla knew he was serious.

"Did I tell you I've taken some self-defense classes for women down in San Diego?" she asked, hoping to brighten his mood.

Chapter Eleven

Mont popped corn at the stove while Kayla sat at the kitchen table stringing cranberries for tomorrow's decorating. "Do you remember the year those rascals put that frog in the dish pan the week Sparky and I took you and the boys up to Porcupine Ridge camping? It was your turn to do the dishes," he reminded as the corn popped boisterously inside the stainless steel pan.

"I recall that you laughed about it until I started crying," she responded.

He chuckled. "If you could have seen your face! I was sitting less than three feet from you by the fire ring when you screamed and turned around. There was that big old green frog setting pretty as a picture on your shirt, trying to lap up a piece of your hair with its tongue!" He recalled. "I wish we'd had the video camera running because your expression has never been duplicated."

His reference to videos stirred happy memories within her. "Oh, Dad!" she exclaimed. "We should watch home movies tonight!"

"You really want to, Princess?" he asked, hoping she would.

"I'd love to," she smiled. "Where are they?"

"Just let me get this popcorn in a bowl, Princess, and we can watch while we string. How does that sound?" Mont turned the stove off and poured the popped corn into a big metal bowl. Then he carried it to the Gathering Room and opened up the entertainment center.

Within minutes they were laughing over the antics of the Dreadful Five as the group tried to catch the bad guys, Mont and Sparky. By the time they had the popped corn and the cranberries strung and ready for tomorrow, they'd watched the Dreadful Five grow up from toddlers to teenagers. Then Mont put the last video into the machine and turned it on.

"This is the last one, Princess. I think it's your graduation from BYU, before you left here for USC," he said.

"Good," she exclaimed. "I want to see if I've changed much from seven years ago."

The pictures that came across the television screen showed Kayla stepping up in her graduation gown and cap to receive her degrees. After that, they viewed a shaky scene of the blue sky and Mont's nose as Mont tried to determine whether or not the camera was still working. The next part of the video caught her completely unprepared. Kayla was vividly reminded from the television screen that Ed had also attended her graduation. She watched in silent wonder as he took her into his arms and kissed her passionately.

"Oh, Princess," said Mont, stopping the film with the remote. "I'm sorry. I didn't realize . . ."

"It's all right, Dad," she tapped his arm. "Turn it back on. That's a part of my life I'm glad that I shared with Ed."

"If you say so, Princess," he responded as he pressed the play button.

The film began again with the same kiss. The graduation party came next. Kayla remembered it well. Mont had been too tired and went back to the motel. The Dreadful Five cut up the dance floor, with Abbot doing the filming and adding his own anecdotes. The last dance of the night aired and Kayla was once again in Ed's arms. He stared deep into her eyes and the love she saw within them radiated through her with sweet memories. He had a special look he always gave her right before he kissed her. It was an expression she would never forget, and a time she would always treasure.

Mont reached out and rubbed her shoulder. "You don't have to do this, Kayla. It must be painful," he comforted.

"I'm fine," she resisted. "It doesn't bother me."

But the truth of the matter pierced Kayla to the core. The reaction she felt watching Ed kiss her on the video bothered her more than she would ever be able to say.

She thought back to those days at USC when she arrived in California with her luggage and a broken heart in tow, knowing it was over between them. Over! It was such an impossible word for her back then. How could she have let it happen? Yet in her heart she knew the answer. She'd had an insatiable yearning for information. She felt like some huge sponge, soaking up data about an exciting and wonderful world that she had never known growing up in this serene, protected little valley. Without realizing, or weighing the consequences of her choices, she had let that thirst for knowledge overpower any other desire she may have had.

For seven years she had wondered what would have happened, had she asked Ed about the scholarship. Surely they could have worked something out so that she could continue her studies. If he loved her, he would have done anything to help her. Kayla also knew that his whole life had been the ranch. That's what he'd lived for and planned for every bit as much as Mont and Sparky. Would Ed have given up his hope of running the ranch so she could chase a dream somewhere else? The truth hurt her now like it had never hurt before. She hadn't given him the opportunity to tell her no. She'd told him goodbye without ever asking him if he loved her enough to sacrifice the ranch for her. A tear formed in her eye and she wiped it away before Mont would see it.

The rest of the film became a flurry of bitter sweet memories in front of her: images of Ed walking her across the meadow; Ed throwing her in the stream; Ed swinging her around on his shoulders so she could soar like an eagle; Ed arm wrestling Mont and winning him, his first win ever; Kayla dumping a pan of cold water on Ed as he lay sleeping under a pine tree; Ed wrestling her to the ground and kissing her into senselessness.

In every single image, she noticed her smile. She was laughing, genuinely laughing, just like twice earlier that same day.

Mont scooted off the sofa and sat on the floor when the video ended. He pressed the remote buttons and the television switched off. It was close to midnight and they had been watching videos for five hours. He pulled her stocking off and began his nightly ritual, rubbing her foot vigorously. It felt so good Kayla didn't want to resist. "Dad," she asked, "do you suppose Mother ever loved someone else before you?"

"I never thought about it," he answered. "All I cared about was that she loved me then."

"Did you ever love someone before Mom? You were twenty-six when you married her," Kayla persisted.

"I liked a little filly named Emily," he confided. "She was a pretty one, too."

"What happened between you?" she asked.

"I met your mother," he responded with a gentle smile. "So when the filly finally noticed me, I had to tell her no."

"Did you ever wonder what happened to her?"

"I heard she married some rancher over in Colorado and had nine children!" he exclaimed.

"Nine!" Her mouth dropped open.

"Mmm hmm, and you know what?"

"What?"

"Not one of the nine could ever hold a candle to you!"

"You're prejudiced," she complained.

"Nope," he disagreed. "I reckon the Lord said, 'Mont, you got one child coming and that's all you're going to get. I'll make her so special you won't need any more.' At least that's what I figure," he drawled with a wink.

"You've been a great father," she told him.

"I ain't going anywhere, Princess," he argued. "So don't put me in the past tense yet."

She kicked at him, but he dodged her foot and she missed. He took off her other stocking and started massaging that foot.

"You ARE a great father," she began again.

"That's better," he agreed. "I'm glad you think so, Princess."

"It must have been hard for you, being both mother and father to me," she mused.

"It was never hard," he disagreed. "Well, almost never!"

She kicked at him again. This time he grabbed her foot and started tickling. It was all she could do to get her foot away. Finally he held up his hands and said, "I just want to rub your feet, Kayla. Enough horsing around."

"Why did you ever say that?" she asked. "I always thought you meant I looked or acted like a horse."

"I guess because that's what your granddad used to say to me," was his fond reply.

"Well, if I say it to my children I hope someone shoots me!" she complained.

"You sound like you're about ready for parenthood," he observed.

She laughed. "What makes you say that?"

"You want to be a better parent than your own."

"I've thought a lot about being a mother ever since Josh proposed. I don't think I ever contemplated parenthood before these last two weeks. I want to be a good mother," she decided.

"How will you accomplish it?" he asked gently, studying her expression.

Kayla thought about his question before she answered, "I guess the best anyone can do is take the good that they learned from their own parents and use it wisely. The bad they learned should be thrown out of their parenting completely," she observed.

"What did I do that was so bad?" he laughed.

"Enough horsing around," she said in an imitating manner.

He smiled.

Kayla continued teasing him, "Or how about, 'If I've told you once I've told you a thousand times,' or worse," she accused as she held up her hand so he wouldn't protest. "I've called you a million times!" She laughed as she said it.

"You wouldn't answer, what was I supposed to say?" he complained.

"Do you remember when I was up sitting by the spring house eating watercress one evening and you called me to come to supper?" she asked.

"Of course. That happened at least once a day," he reminded.

"No, this one time you called me and I decided to put your statement to the test. I counted to discover if you really did call me a million times."

"You did?" he asked in surprise.

"Yes, and you only called my name fifty-seven times before you found me!" She grinned.

He nudged her playfully. Then he resumed rubbing her feet.

Kayla leaned back into the sofa remembering all the wonderful times they had together. Last summer when he'd come out to San Diego, they'd spent three weeks together sailing out to Catalina and northward as far as Santa Barbara, then back to her home port. It had been just Mont and Kayla for the first two weeks. Josh had joined them for the last week. It was an idyllic time and she had wanted it to last forever.

"Do you think I'm a fair sailor?" she mused as she stretched out completely on the sofa.

"What a question!" he remarked, climbing up into the rocking chair. "I'm still here and the Lady Dawn was floating when we got back. In my book that qualifies you."

"Do you think sailing suits me?"

"I don't know why not," he replied. "Lots of women sail. It's not an uncommon practice."

"Do you think I would have been better off marrying Ed and forgetting about the scholarship?" she studied his eyes in the lamplight as he answered.

He hesitated only for a moment. "I think you did what was best for you," he said, choosing his words carefully. Then, hoping to avoid anymore questions along those lines he said, "I also think if I don't go to bed, I won't be able to speak a civil word tomorrow."

"Oh, your gastritis. I didn't even think!" said Kayla. "Will you be all right?"

"I'll take a pill and be fine," he mused. "Little Mother!" And with that remark he went upstairs to bed.

Kayla didn't feel the least bit sleepy. She wandered out onto the porch, wrapping a heavy quilt about her as she did so. She sat down in the old rocking chair that her great-grandfather had made generations ago. The sky was clear, without a single cloud, and the moon was a mere sliver. The stars were startling, numerous and bright, and the milky way was clearly visible. She remembered sleeping out on the deck above and watching the sparkling sky on cool summer nights of her youth.

She thought about Ed and Josh and their differences. Josh was refined and scientific, a perfectionist in many ways. He loved sailing and water sports of all kinds, ballroom dancing, the theater, marine life and meteorology. Ed, on the other hand, though he'd graduated from ASU with a bachelor's degree in criminal law and animal husbandry, was anything but refined. He was a mountain man with every fibre of his being. His opinion of sailing and water sports was candid, if nothing else. To Ed, water was good for three things only, drinking, bathing and fishing. He hated the theater, and he thought ballroom dancing was for sissies. About the only things Ed and Josh had in common were fishing, and loving the same woman.

Kayla felt relieved to know that she didn't have to choose between the two loves of her life. Her choice had already been made. Loving Josh was the most natural feeling in the world. Besides, Ed would never want her in a romantic way again, she reasoned. She had hurt him terribly, and as punishment, she would feel guilty the rest of her life for so doing. However, she couldn't turn the clock back and start over. Still, she couldn't help feeling like she had lost an important part of herself when she'd said goodbye to Ed.

Strong, undeniable emotions regarding Ed stayed with her far into the morning hours as she sat snuggled up in a warm, cozy quilt on the front porch of her father's home.

Is it possible to love two men at the same time? She wondered. And if she did, what would it matter? Ed didn't want her, not anymore. And if he did, she could never break up with Josh when she loved him with all her heart! Was she getting loyalty mixed up with love again? She had too many questions and no easy answers.

Finally, unable to resolve any of the puzzles stirring around in her mind, she shrugged and went in to bed.

Daylight came too early as she heard her father calling from the bottom of the stairs. "Am I going to have to bring a glass of water and pour it on you, Kayla?"

She rolled over and moaned. "No, Dad," she called back. "I'm up."

"Then hurry!" he instructed. "We're all waiting on you." His voice had an uneasy edge to it and Kayla hoped he'd had a restful night.

Kayla jumped out of bed and stubbed her toe on the dresser. Hobbling around she managed to find a pair of leggings and a sweater, then her snow bibs and parka. Gloves, warm socks and boots were tossed by the stairs as she rushed down the hall to brush her teeth and hair. She pulled the long strands back in a pony tail at the nape of her neck and put a bright bow there to hide the hair wrap. A touch of makeup gave her face a healthy glow. Then she rushed down the hall where she grabbed her boots, stockings and gloves.

By the time she reached the front porch she was bent over, still trying to get one boot on, unsuccessfully. She heard a chorus of laughter and looked up to see Sparky, Tom, Will and Mont grinning at her.

"What?" she asked. "I always get dressed like this." She sat on the first step and finished putting her boot on, then laced it up quickly. She stood up and put her gloves on her hands as she walked down the steps to the horses.

Within moments they were trotting along the road that the boys had worked diligently to clear with the tractor since dawn that same morning. Now the sun shimmered through the tree branches heavily laden with snow. Across the white and frozen landscape a million brilliant diamonds glistened as the sun's rays were bent by each tiny ice crystal. The dazzling display of nature took her breath away far easier than the freezing temperature.

"When you see a pine tree you particularly like, Kayla, just let us know," said Sparky. "We'll cut it down and haul it back to the lodge."

Mont and Tom seemed unusually quiet this morning and Kayla hoped Tom hadn't discovered anything unusual from her own mannerisms.

When they'd gone a couple of miles, Mont grumbled, "Any time, Princess."

"Oh, Dad," she said, "It's your belly, isn't it?"

"Something like that," he moaned.

"Did you take your pill?" asked Kayla, concerned.

"Yes, I took my pill!" he snapped.

Sparky glanced at her, searching for an explanation.

"I kept him up too late," she told him. "I didn't even think about it," she apologized.

"He was in bed before 1:00 A.M.," offered Tom.

"How'd you know that?" Sparky asked.

"I saw Kayla sitting on the porch all by her lonesome when I came in from the barn," he grinned.

"That was around one," confirmed William.

The comment bothered Kayla. Had Tom been watching her all the time she'd sat on the porch last night? She looked over at Mont and realized he was thinking the exact same thing.

"I don't feel so good," said Mont, anxious apprehension etched upon his face.

"We can go back," said Kayla. "Sparky can pick out a tree."

"No," Sparky disagreed. "I'll take you back, Mont, and make you some sassafras tea. That'll help that gut of yours."

"No!" Mont protested, almost too vehemently. Kayla intuitively sensed that he didn't want Kayla around Tom without Mont by her side to protect her. When he said, "Tom, you come back with me," she knew her assumption was accurate.

When Mont issued an order like that there was no arguing with him.

"Sure thing, Mont," agreed Tom. He turned his horse back and took the reins from her father so he could lead Mont's horse back with him. Mont leaned over the horn of his saddle and groaned. "Git up!" Tom coaxed the two horses.

As she watched them head toward home, she worried. "Will he be all right?"

"He'll be fine," said Sparky. "But let's find that tree quickly now, Kayla. Your Dad will do better when I get back and make him some sassafras tea."

"Why did I keep him up so late?" Kayla moaned.

"He's a big boy, Kayla," reminded Sparky. "He knew what would happen to his gut if he misbehaved."

Kayla was not comforted. They traveled a short distance farther when Kayla decided to offer a little prayer in her mind so only God would hear her. 'It's me again, God. I still don't know if you're there, but watch over Dad if you are, please. And help me find the perfect tree for the lodge in an expeditious manner.' She lifted her head and hoped that William and Sparky hadn't noticed.

As she opened her eyes, a bright ray of sun burst through the trees, illuminating a small clearing where three tall pines hugged each other. The sight seemed so perfect that Kayla turned her horse toward it, forcing him to walk in the snow almost belly-deep to get there.

"Thank you, Lord," she whispered under her breath. Then, "Look!" she exclaimed. "I prayed for a tree and the Lord gave me three of them!"

"You want all three of these, Kayla?" asked William with sarcasm etched in his voice.

"All three," she agreed. "Let's get busy."

Both men grumbled about her choices, but they were obedient in helping fulfill her wishes.

Within a half hour they cut the three trees down and spread them out on a large, thick plastic tarp.

"They ain't going to stay on the tarp, Kayla," Sparky complained. "We didn't know you were going to want three trees or we'd have brought more tarps with us."

"They'll stay," she insisted. "And if they don't we'll come back for whichever fell off."

They tied two corners of the tarp to the saddle horns on Sparky and William's saddles. Afterward they tied more rope from the tree trunks to Kayla's saddle horn. Then they started back. By the time they reached the lodge the horses were sweating from their heavy workout.

"Take the horses in the barn and brush them down good," Sparky instructed William. "Kayla and I will check on Mont, then I'll hammer some braces on those tree trunks."

Kayla was well on her way up the steps to the lodge before Sparky was out of the saddle.

She brushed past Tom at the foot of the stairs and a terrible image of Morning Sun flashed through her mind. She shook the image away and smiled at Tom so as not to arouse his suspicion. "Is he all right?"

"He's resting. I think he'll be fine," Tom reassured her.

"Thanks, Tom. I appreciate you taking such good care of him."
Kayla turned to go up the stairs. Tom put his hand on her arm. She stopped and turned around to face him.

"He's a little grumpy," he warned her. "If he gets out of hand, call me."

"I will. Thank you, Tom." She turned once again, and although Tom released her this time, she could still feel the pressure of his hand upon her arm. The sensation of fear this caused left her stomach unsettled.

Mont lay under the blankets in his pajamas, sweating fiercely.
He smiled at her when she came into his room. "Did you get your tree?"

"Three of them," she announced with a bright smile.

"Three?" he moaned. "There's no room for three trees, Kayla, besides, we don't have enough decorations for three trees."

"Did you or did you not say I was to make the house as perfectly decorated as I could?" she questioned, putting her hands on her hips for emphasis.

Mont knew he was out gunned. He gave her a weak smile. "Do it your way, Princess," he told her. "Just let me rest."

"Sparky's making you some sassafras tea," she told him. "After you drink it, then we'll leave you alone."

"It tastes like soap, you know," he complained.

"Does it help?" she questioned.

"It helps, but it tastes like soap."

"You want a sick belly or a soapy taster?" she asked with a grin.

After Mont drank his tea, he fell asleep. While he slept, Kayla went downstairs and supervised decking the halls. She first sent Tom out to gather pine boughs for a huge wreath on the door, and to drape over the mantle.

Together the three men and Kayla worked all afternoon getting the house ready for Christmas. The Christmas tree grouping stood near the large picture window, one tall tree in the center, another tree two feet shorter to the left and the shortest tree to the right. After stringing all the lights, Kayla stood back to inspect their handiwork.

"There are not enough lights," she decided at once.

"I'll go to town and get some more," offered Tom.

She noticed Sparky raise an eyebrow over the suggestion. "Why don't we send both of you?" he suggested. "That way we know we'll get them back before supper."

Tom glared at his father momentarily, then snapped, "I don't need a baby sitter, Pa!"

"Then stop acting like you do," suggested William.

Tom's hands knotted into fists at his sides. "I'll get my coat!" he snapped as he stomped over to the closet at the foot of the stairs.

"I'll make a list," Kayla said, "because there are a few other things I could use here, as well."

William rolled his eyes wearily.

"Get used to it," Sparky suggested to his son. "When you and Melanie marry you'll discover a woman can find more things to put on a list than you can find paper to write it."

By the time Tom and William returned from town Sparky and Kayla had most of the decorations up. They finished stringing the lights on the three trees. Kayla spread cotton batting around the base of the trees. She felt it represented snow. Then she layered it with angel hair to represent Heaven's glow.

Chapter Twelve

Mont awakened to the smell of chicken noodle soup and pine boughs so he shuffled out of bed and stretched. His stomach felt much better after having rested and he was hungry.

Kneeling beside the bed, he bowed his head, a habit he had developed in his youth. His prayer was short, but to the point. He wanted tomorrow evening to be perfect for Kayla. He wanted to know whether or not KayDawn approved of what he had planned for their daughter, and he wanted to know if Kayla shared any of his spiritual inclination. One other thing he added, and certainly not the least important. Mont asked that the issues between Kayla and Ed be resolved, one way or the other. If she loved Ed, she should not marry Josh, and vice versa. When he finished, he stood up and nodded, feeling comfortable with the requests he'd made. For the first time in a long while, he felt that he was doing something right for his daughter, and for himself.

Putting on his robe and slippers, Mont went down the hall to the stairs. As he looked from the landing to the Gathering Room below, his heart leaped inside him. Although Kayla didn't know it, he realized, she was so much like her mother sometimes it seemed uncanny. The Christmas decorations were a perfect example. She certainly had KayDawn's flair where creativity came into play.

He thought back on their first Christmas together, when KayDawn had insisted they fill the whole house with pine boughs, on the mantle, over the doors and around the window arches. She'd wanted a tree grouping and Mont had tried to put his foot down about that. "One tree per house was good enough," he'd objected, but she wouldn't hear of it. She made him cut down three trees, placing two in the Gathering Room and one in their bedroom. She even dug up a sapling and decorated it in Kayla's bedroom on the dresser near the crib, even though it would be May before their baby would arrive.

He smiled to himself from the memories as he stepped down the stairs.

Kayla called to him from the kitchen. "Is that you, Dad?"

He wandered to the back of the house, to the big country kitchen. He told her with a smile, "You outdid yourself, Princess. Everything looks absolutely perfect."

Kayla finished up the few dishes she was washing. "I already fed Sparky and the boys. They've gone back to the cabin. I was just going to finish these dishes and then bring some soup up to you."

"I can eat down here, Princess," he said, sitting down at the kitchen table. "I'm not too keen on eating in bed."

"Are you feeling any better? You've slept most of the day away."

"Much," he agreed. "I guess I should stick to what the doc said twenty years ago, meals on time, adequate rest."

"I feel so guilty for keeping you up last night. It won't happen again," she promised. After drying her hands, she poured his soup into a stout mug and placed it beside him on the table. Crackers, milk and some vegetable sticks from the refrigerator rounded out his meal.

"Was Tom on his best behavior?" asked Mont.

"He was," she confirmed. "But I was just as worried as you were when he said he'd seen me sitting on the porch at one this morning."

"Don't do that again, Kayla," he warned. "And when you do go to bed, keep both bedroom doors locked."

"I doubt he could climb up onto the deck, Dad," she smiled.

"You didn't see Morning Sun," he answered. "If he can do that, he can do anything."

By seven-thirty that evening Kayla had Mont tucked back into bed, washed the rest of the dishes and tidied the main level of the Allen's family lodge. She curled up into the easy chair and watched as a log in the fireplace was whittled away by the flames.

She watched the clock until it was eight P.M. then she telephoned Joshua. He picked up the phone on the second ring. "Kayla?" he asked rather than his traditional hello.

"Yes," she answered.

"I hoped it was you," he admitted. "I miss you."

"And I miss you," she confessed.

"Do you know that without you at the lab, chaos reigns?" he questioned.

"Yes," she laughed, "I know that. I'm indispensable, aren't I?"

"You definitely have the rest of us spoiled," he admitted.

"So, other than chaos, how has your day been?" she asked.

Josh explained the problems he faced, placing a block of data on a graph, and she suggested a couple ways to improve the technique. Then he complained about the awful El Nino impact on San Diego weather. It had been raining buckets that day. The streets were flooded, three houses slipped off a cliff onto the beach. "And it's headed your way," he informed her.

"When you get in Thursday telephone Sky Patrol and ask for Ed Sparkleman," she told him. "The roads are open today, but they may not be by Thursday. Ed can bring you and your parents up by helicopter."

"Isn't he Sparky's oldest son?" Josh asked cautiously.

"Yes, Josh." She sensed the wariness in him. "Ed and I were engaged once, you remember?"

"I do," he said. "Has he simmered down much since you were up there fifteen months ago?"

"A lot," she admitted. "In fact, he's been pleasant and funny. He's made me laugh."

"That's good," he sighed. "I didn't want any altercations between you two while I'm not there to protect you."

"Don't worry," she soothed. "Ed is harmless."

The next hour she confided to Joshua all of the conversation between her father and herself the day prior. She wept when she made reference to Tom and his connection to Morning Sun's battering and rape. By the time she'd finished she was sobbing, the painful situation for sweet, gentle Morning Sun, almost too much for her to bear.

When they finally hung up, she replaced the receiver and walked to the dining room window where she looked out across the meadow to Sparky's cabin. Smoke puffed out of the chimney and headed east as a light breeze picked it up and carried it off until it dissipated. Kayla sighed heavily, worried how Sparky would react when the truth was finally known about Tom and his brutal attack on Morning Sun. It would kill him, she thought wearily. Those boys had been his whole life after Mary Sparkleman died. He had poured every ounce of his being into raising them well, teaching them to respect women.

Then Kayla remembered an incident she had forgotten completely, until that very moment. It happened the summer after she turned fifteen. The Dreadful five had been reduced to three while Ed and William were away on a fishing trip with the Priest's Quorum from her Church. She'd been bored to tears. Ed and Will were usually the life of the party. Abbot had taken to reading the summer away, and that left Kayla and Tom to occupy time in each other's company. She couldn't remember where Mont was that day, out on the range, she supposed.

She and Tom were sitting on the bridge in the meadow, fishing for fresh rainbow trout. It seemed innocent enough, she thought. Tom was two years younger and she felt responsible for him.

Tom started talking about things that only a man and his wife should have discussed, private things that he was feeling, dreams he'd been having. Then he put his arm around her and forced her to kiss him.

She hadn't wanted the kiss and it made her angry. Without thinking, she smacked him in the face.

To her surprise, Tom hit her right back. Then he pushed her down upon the ground where he climbed on top of her.

Shocked, she reached out and tried to push him off her, but he placed his mouth hard against hers and forced a searing kiss from her. "Stop it, Tom!" she hissed, struggling against him.

He raised his hand as though he intended to hit her again. His face was only a few inches from hers. "You want it! You know you want it!" he yelled.

The next thing she knew, Tom went flying over the bridge guard and through the air. He landed in the stream about ten feet away from her.

Then Sparky stood over her and lifted Kayla up to her feet. "Are you all right, honey?" Sparky asked tenderly.

She saw that Tom had cut his arm open on a rock in the stream where he'd landed. She nodded. "I'm okay," she said, brushing the dust from her clothes. "But look, Tom's hurt!"

"You broke my arm, Pa!" Tom accused, icy mountain water washing over him, cooling him off.

"I'll break more than that if you ever lay a hand on Kayla again!" Sparky snapped. She'd never seen Sparky angry before that day, or since. It wasn't a pleasant experience.

"My arm, Pa!" whimpered Tom.

Sparky softened enough to help Tom up and inspect his arm. It wasn't broken, but it needed a few stitches.

Kayla had dismissed the incident as a childish prank on Tom's part.

However, it seemed to her that the moment Ed and William arrived home they stopped coming over as much, and they didn't call themselves the Dreadful Five anymore. As Kayla looked back on the incident, she realized that was about the same time that Mont and Sparky started giving the boys extra duty out on the range while Kayla was given less to do ranching and more than her share of housework with Morning Sun. Now she could see where parental control and common sense worked hand in hand to protect her.

She sighed. An image of Sparky's face at hearing that his own flesh and blood had perpetrated such a horrible crime against someone as kind and innocent as Morning Sun, filled her imagination. If she thought he'd been angry about Tom forcing a kiss out of Kayla, how would Sparky react when he learned what Tom had apparently done to Morning Sun? Could Sparky survive such horrible news? How would he be able to endure it? She would have to voice this concern next time her father felt up to it.

The following morning Kayla was up at dawn, ready to do the chores for Mont if he should need her. She'd tossed and turned most of the night, worrying about Sparky and Tom and Mont's heart and gastritis. She tiptoed down the stairs and started some Pompanoosuc porridge, then she left it on a hot pad on the counter to let it thicken while she went out to the barn. Sparky was already milking Bessie so Kayla raked out the soiled straw from the stalls and scooped it into a wagon bed, then forked fresh straw onto the floor for the horses and gave them oats, hay and fresh water.

She'd forgotten how soiled her clothing would get and was glad she'd worn her oldest pair of jeans for the job.

"Looks like you've been the official pooper scooper today," Sparky grinned as he disconnected the milking tubes from Bessie.

"Someone has to," Kayla said. "Besides, I really don't mind." She soon gathered the eggs and returned to the lodge. Mont was up in his work clothes when she arrived.

"You won't need to go," she told him. "Sparky's bringing the milk in now and I brought the eggs."

"What about the horses?" he asked.

"I fed them and cleaned the manure out of their stalls."

"So that's what that lovely smell is," he sighed. "Guess this family doesn't need me anymore," he joked.

"Of course we do, silly," she said. "Who would drink sassafras tea if we didn't have you?"

"The porridge is ready," he said, ignoring her remark.

The kitchen door opened and Sparky came in with the milk. He poured it through a strainer into a stainless steel milk container, then put the milk in the refrigerator. Then he took out the container from yesterday morning's milk and carefully skimmed the cream off it. When he was satisfied that all the cream was separated, he poured the skim milk into two pitchers, capped them and put them back in the refrigerator.

"I'm going to send Ed with Kayla down to Morning Sun's place today," Mont announced. "I'm overstocked on milk, cream and eggs and she could use them."

Kayla was surprised at the announcement. "You're getting rid of me today?"

"Only for a few hours. You remember that I wanted everything perfect, and then I'd tell you why you're really here?" he asked.

"Yes," she admitted.

"Well, Ed's going to be your escort today. He's going to take you to visit with Morning Sun, do some Christmas Shopping in town, have lunch, pick up groceries, I've made a list for you," explained Mont. "He'll have you back here at 4:30 and then we'll begin to unravel the mystery." He winked and gave her a kiss on the forehead.

"I was hoping we'd do some cross country skiing before Josh and his parents arrive, Dad. I thought perhaps today, but it can wait until tomorrow," she agreed.

"That sounds fair," he nodded. "My plans today, your plans tomorrow."

She smiled. "How soon before Ed arrives?"

"He won't be here for another hour or two. You'll have plenty of time to shower and get that manure smell off you," said Mont.

Later that morning as Kayla sank into the deep, four-legged bathtub, a treasure out of history, she sighed. How she wished her father had chosen someone other than Ed as her companion for the day. The feelings she'd been having about him lately had left her emotions unsettled and she was concerned that it may not be in her best interest to spend a lot of time with him. Still, her father usually knew best. She would have to trust his good judgement.

When Ed arrived Kayla had dressed in chocolate brown velvet pants and cream turtle neck sweater with forest pine embroidered on the front. Her buffed suede ankle boots matched perfectly the suede jacket Josh had given her last Christmas. She still wore the gold chain Ed had told her to keep. For some unexplainable reason she felt it important to do so.

Kayla gave Ed a polite smile when he arrived.

He just nodded and looked past her to Mont. "I put your things by the kitchen door," Ed told him.

"Thanks," said Mont. "I appreciate your doing this for me, Ed. I really do." He reached out and shook Ed's hand respectfully.

"That's one of us," Ed replied, his voice a little more tense than normal. "You want her back by when?" he asked.

"By four-thirty," said Mont.

"All right, Mont. I hope you know what you're doing." Ed turned and said to Kayla. "Let's go then."

Sparky came through from the kitchen. "I put some things in the truck for Morning Sun."

"We'll deliver them right away," said Ed.

He opened the door for Kayla and they walked out to the Bar M Ranch truck, a rugged, white Ford F350 with four-wheel drive. Kayla boarded on the passenger side and buckled into the seat belt. Ed climbed in and did likewise, then turned on the ignition and they were on their way.

Uintah County maintained half of the ten mile dirt road that led down to Highway 121 between Lapoint and Maeser, a sleepy town meshed against the northwest edge of Vernal. From the halfway point up the mountain, where the road connected to the Bar M Ranch, all maintenance became Mont's responsibility.

Fortunately, Mont owned a dandy tractor with a snow blade that Sparky and the boys utilized to keep the gravel road open. Early yesterday morning, they'd run the tractor nonstop and plowed down the last few miles, making the road almost clear of snow. In the process, the amount of snow pushed to the sides made the road seem more like a white tunnel than a mountain lane.

For the first few miles Kayla and Ed were both silent. Kayla wondered what Ed was thinking and she supposed that Ed was doing the same.

Finally Ed broke the silence with, "The Christmas decorations make the lodge look nice, Kayla Dawn. Your mama would be real proud."

"Thanks," she mumbled, angry that he'd used her mother in the context of his praise. Kayla recognized her difficulty in accepting her mother as a part of any conversation. She didn't know why she felt so defensive, perhaps because she knew so little about the woman. She sighed and wondered if she would ever be able to come to terms with the anxiety she felt at the mere mention of her mother's name.

There was silence again until Kayla changed the subject with a confession, "Dad finally told me what happened to Morning Sun."

"It's about time," Ed nodded. "Dang fool should have told you right away, but he can't be reasoned with. He has to do everything his way."

"Guess his daughter is a lot like him," she observed.

He thought about her remark for only a second before he snorted, "Ain't that the truth!"

"You didn't have to agree so quickly," she complained, punching him playfully in the arm.

"I call it like I see it, Kayla Dawn. Even you should remember that about me," he defended.

"I wanted to talk to you about Thursday evening," she told him. "Josh is coming from San Diego, along with his parents, Admiral and Sarah Clark. They plan to arrive in Vernal sometime late in the afternoon. If the weather turns too bad, they'll need an airlift up to the ranch. Do you think that would be all right?"

"You'd better tell them to plan on a lot of snow," he answered. "Weather service says our sunshine and clear skies will be over tomorrow night. El Nino is sending another storm in, this time a bad one."

"I thought the last one was bad," she pointed out.

"It was," he replied, "just like the one that's coming."

"So you will fly them up for us?" she asked once again.

"Have mercy, Kayla Dawn!" he snapped. "How many pilots do you know in town with their own helicopter?"

"Just one," she replied. "You don't have to get testy!"

"Sorry," he said softly, unable to shake the feelings raging through him.

"I didn't mean to offend you, Ed," Kayla comforted. "I just didn't want to interfere with your Christmas Eve plans too much."

"My Christmas Eve plans," he said dryly, "include waiting around at the airport until Lieutenant Commander Clark and his folks arrive. Then I'm going to fly them up to the ranch where you and me, Pa and Mont, your Lieutenant Commander and his folks will all sit down for Christmas Eve dinner. I'll even open presents and be polite," he explained in total exasperation. "Pa already extracted my promise on that much."

"Oh," she sighed. "Mont hadn't said what the plans were for Christmas Eve. I just assumed you and the boys would be at the cabin."

"No, William and Tom left for Dutch John this morning where Melanie's folks are having a big Christmas celebration. Charlene is Melanie's best friend, which is why Tom went with him."

"When will they get home?" she asked.

"Sometime Christmas Day, probably late evening if I know William. He bought a ring and plans on giving it to Melanie Christmas Eve."

"Do you think she loves him?" Kayla asked.

"She acts like it," he answered. He couldn't resist adding, "Of course, that doesn't mean much, does it?"

"That was uncalled for," she complained. "Why are you so testy today when Sunday you were completely the opposite?"

"You know why," he answered. "You heard the conversation between me and Mont Sunday."

"No," she responded. "I heard the tail end and couldn't decide what it was all about."

"That was probably enough," he decided.

"Ed, I don't know what my father has asked you to do. Whatever it is, if you feel uncomfortable about it, don't do it," she suggested.

"Good advice," he admitted reluctantly, "but I have a lot of respect for Mont and for his advice. He's almost as much a father to me as Pa."

"Why don't you tell me what he wants from you? Maybe I can help," she suggested.

"That'd be a trick!" he growled sharply.

"Then don't tell me," she responded, "but don't yell at me either."

"I wasn't yelling," he grumbled.

"Maybe you should stop by Sky Patrol so you can go back to work," she suggested coldly. "I can run Dad's errands by myself." She had no intention of spending the day with him if he was going to maintain his current temperament.

He sighed, staring straight ahead. Kayla studied him carefully to discern any sign of softening, but she saw none. His jaw was set and determined. His eyebrows knit together in a frown. Both hands held the steering wheel so tightly his knuckles whitened almost to his fingertips.

His driving became erratic, as well. When they reached Highway 121, Ed squealed the truck onto the pavement. The truck spun off the snow-packed gravel and narrowly missed a car that was passing from the opposite direction.

"Stop the truck!" Kayla yelled. "Ed, you stop this truck this minute!"

He slammed on the brake and the truck came to a screeching halt.

"Pull over," she insisted.

Ed cursed under his breath and drove the truck off the pavement, onto the side of the road, where he braked to a screeching stop.

Kayla jumped out of the truck and started walking east, toward Maeser and Vernal.

Ed followed her in the truck. "I'm sorry, Kayla Dawn," he yelled. "You can get back in the truck now!" He tried to coax her to get back in, but he realized, with futility, that she wouldn't do it.

Kayla stared straight ahead and continued walking.

After several minutes of fruitless persuasion, Ed finally pulled the truck ahead of her, brought it to a stop and jumped out. He stomped back to her and stood in her way.

"I'm sorry, Kayla Dawn!" he insisted.

"Sorry doesn't cut it," she snapped. "If you cannot act mature enough to drive that truck safely, I won't ride with you."

"If you wouldn't make me so angry I could spit nails, maybe I could drive safely," he countered.

"What did I do?" she asked. "I offered to let you off the hook so you wouldn't feel obliged to spend the day with me, that's all."

"And how was I supposed to respond to that?" he demanded.

"It's obviously too much trouble for you to be around me and I don't want to inconvenience you any longer!" she snapped. She was more hurt than angry, she realized, as the tears started to well up in her eyes unbidden.

"Now there you go, crying just like a woman," he complained. He cradled her in his arms and pulled her tight against him in a protective gesture.

"I am a woman!" she sobbed against his shoulder, "And I never wanted you to hate me."

"Is that what you think?" he asked tenderly, the anger wrung out of him by her unexpected accusation. He felt as though his heart flipped over inside his chest and the emotional pain seemed excruciating. He hooked his hand beneath her chin and tilted her head up to face him. He looked deep into her brown eyes for several long moments, studying her sad expression. Her long hair whisked across her face from the wind. He pulled the blond strand aside and tucked it behind her ear. "Kayla Dawn," he whispered huskily. "I am so far away from hating you, it ain't right. I should hate you. I've wanted to hate you, but no matter how hard I try, I can't." He bent down and kissed her forehead tenderly, then pulled her close against him once again.

Kayla allowed his embrace willingly. She felt herself melt against him. He could be utterly gentle at times, or tenaciously stubborn and bull headed. It seemed he had always been this way, she decided.

He was like a big brother to her, she thought, in amazement. He was over protective, and like most big brothers, he always seemed to think he knew what was best for her.

# Chapter Thirteen

The drive to Morning Sun's mobile home south of Vernal took a little over half an hour due to the Christmas traffic. The roads were clear and people were rushing about trying to finish up the Christmas shopping. Even for a small town such as Vernal, the Holiday Season meant scurrying about and maneuvering your way through or around the crowds.

Ed turned into the trailer park and stopped the truck in front of a pleasant awning-covered deck that stood outside the front door of a double wide mobile home. Morning Sun opened the door and beamed when she saw Kayla.

"Dad sent us with some milk and eggs and Christmas groceries," she explained. "And a few Christmas presents."

Ed carried the milk and eggs in first, then went back for the remaining groceries.

Morning Sun was a superior homemaker. Her tidy home was "spit and polish" from top to bottom, as Josh would have observed, thought Kayla with a smile.

"Come," said Morning Sun. "You see."

While Ed busied himself with the groceries, Morning Sun took Kayla's hand and led her back to a bedroom that she had converted into a nursery. "For my baby," she explained simply.

Kayla grinned broadly. "It's lovely, Morning Sun. Yellows and greens would be my first choice for a baby's room, just like yours."

"Mr. Mont did not tell you," said Morning Sun, "about baby."

"No," confessed Kayla, "that's why I was so surprised the other day."

"Baby is not—" Morning Sun began.

Kayla interrupted. "I was angry that Dad had not shared this information," she confessed, "and when I told him so, he explained about what happened. I'm so sorry, Morning Sun."

The pleasant woman sighed. "It was very hard. I could not think. My head hurt bad. I fell asleep."

"I'm so glad you're all right now," Kayla hugged her. "And I AM happy about the baby. I would have kept the baby, too."

Morning Sun smiled from ear to ear. "It is right," she agreed. "Baby is innocent."

"That's right," said Kayla, placing her hand on Morning Sun's rounded belly. "And the baby is all yours!"

"It is good that has come from evil," said Morning Sun. "God has given this child as a sign."

"That may be true," smiled Kayla happily.

Kayla and Ed stayed with Morning Sun through lunch, snacking on cheese and crackers and telling stories about their childhood together. Morning Sun was glad to learn they had always considered her a wonderful mother to them.

Ed seemed to unwind from his anger earlier, and Kayla felt grateful that he was able to laugh with them.

Too soon it was time to go. They hugged and kissed farewell then boarded the truck and Ed drove them back to Vernal where they stopped for groceries. Mont had given them quite a list. Half of the things he wanted were at another store. By the time they'd found everything on the list it was almost four in the afternoon.

Ed headed the truck west on Highway 121 past Maeser.

"I am exhausted," said Kayla wearily. "I hardly slept last night."

"You, too, hmm?" he asked.

"Oh, I was worried about—" she hesitated. She could not tell him everything that had kept her awake. "I was worried about Tom's drinking and Morning Sun's baby and Josh flying out here Thursday, and whether or not his parents will get along well with Dad and Sparky."

"I was worried about today," he said somberly. "I thought it might be easier to drive the truck off Porcupine Ridge as do what Mont thought I should do."

"Why won't you tell me, Ed?" she questioned. "We used to be able to tell each other anything."

"That was a long time ago. Things change. You changed," he suggested.

"How?" she asked.

"Seven years ago you would have been content to be a rancher's wife," he reminded. "Now you're involved in science and sailing and you want to marry a Lieutenant Commander in the U.S. Navy."

"Seven years ago I was just beginning to learn who I was," she confessed. "And I didn't like that person."

"Why?" he questioned. "What happened?"

Kayla paused. She felt responsible for the past seven years of bitterness between them and hoped that, by sharing her feelings, she could help him get over her. "I don't know that I can explain it well enough, but I'll try. When I went to BYU, I felt like a caterpillar eating away at a huge leaf. There was so much to consume and so little time to do it in. As I began my studies, I felt my mind growing and expanding. There were new horizons everywhere that needed to be explored. I couldn't learn fast enough. I took more than 30 credit hours per quarter and I didn't come home those summers because I felt I had to learn more. My chance to learn would soon be over and I was still trying to digest all this fabulous information."

"So you graduated with your bachelors and your masters in the time it took me to get my bachelors," he said. "But after BYU?"

"You came to bring me home," she remembered, "you, your brothers, Sparky and Dad. On the way home I felt like I was still that caterpillar and I was suffocating. I felt like a cocoon was wrapping itself around me and I would never be free to be myself."

"But you told me you wanted to marry me," he reminded. "YOU told me!" The pain in his voice was unmistakable.

"Because that's what I thought you expected from me," she agreed. "I was so confused. I wanted to marry you, but I knew if I did, I would never be able to continue my studies. And I wanted to learn! I love learning!"

"I've realized that much over the years. You've got two doctorates," he elaborated. "And all those medals, honors and masters degrees. I don't know how you did it."

Ed turned the car back onto the unimproved, snow-packed road that led into the Ashley National Forest, toward the Bar M Ranch.

"I finally felt the cocoon fall off from around me, I spread my wings and I soared," she admitted. "It was the best thing I'd ever done for myself up to that point."

"So what about us, Kayla?" he asked. "Where did that leave us?"

Kayla looked across at him and he stopped the truck and turned off the ignition. On both sides of the truck, the pine trees stretched high overhead, putting them in shadow.

She sighed. "You are a mountain man, Ed," she managed. "All your life, up to that point, you had dreamed of running the ranch. That was all you'd ever talked about."

"And you thought that you couldn't have both, more college and me?" he guessed.

"Could I have?" she asked.

He didn't answer.

"Ed," she paused, wondering if she should even voice the words. However, she knew she had to ask, regardless what answer he may give. "If I had come to you then and said I've got this fantastic scholarship to get my doctorate's degree in one of the marine sciences. It'll take four more years. If you want to marry me, come with me while I go back to school. Would you have done it?"

"No," he admitted and she could hear the regret in his voice. "I would have told you that if you loved me, you would become my wife and stay at the ranch with me."

"Then I would have remained forever in that cocoon, Ed," she explained. "I would have suffocated and never found out who I really am."

He shook his head. He wanted to ask more. He needed to ask more. Mont had stated plainly that Kayla had some feelings for him still, and encouraged him that it would be in his best interest to find out exactly where he stood before she married Josh. Dare he even hope?

"And now?" she interrupted his thoughts. "If we were to go back seven years now, knowing what we know now, would you let me go to school, would you let me spread my wings?"

"Would you want to be a rancher's wife?" he answered her question with his own. "Or a helicopter pilot's wife?"

Kayla agonized for him. How could she answer? "I'd ask him to let me think about it for a while," she murmured.

"So would I," he responded as he turned the engine on and put the transmission in gear, then started back up the road toward the ranch. So that was it, he thought wearily. He would still have to wait. There were no easy answers from Kayla, no simple yes or no. It seemed he'd waited his whole life for Kayla to make up her mind what she really wanted, and he was still waiting.

Coming across Pine Bluff Ridge, they were able to look out upon the Bar M Ranch, with its lodge, meadow, barns and cabin. Ed parked the truck once again as though unwilling to go any farther.

"Have you talked with Mont about selling this place?" he asked.

"Yes," she smiled. "He has no interest in selling. He's worried what Sparky would do," she explained. "He also wants to keep the ranch for a summer home, when he does retire, for the grandchildren. I guess the only way it will ever be sold is when he dies, assuming I could bear to part with it."

Ed nodded and looked wistfully out over the small valley. "You know he's had an offer of several million dollars for it, don't you?"

"He said some investor woman was trying to buy it last Spring."

"She came to see me and my brothers," he confessed. "She told us that she would give us a million dollars to split amongst us if we could convince him to sell."

"So that's why you were so anxious the night I arrived!" she accused as swiftly as the anger building within her.

"Yes," he admitted, "but by Sunday I was fully repentant again, so simmer down."

"Why?" she asked, unwilling to believe him so easily.

"You gave me a taste of what it was like, back when we were kids, horsing around," he reminded. "You made me laugh. You got us dancing and acting like kids again. Ha! You even got Mont and Pa dancing!"

"And your point is?" She hoped the tension in her voice could not be discerned for she was still unconvinced.

"It was then that I realized the ranch should never be sold. This land is too beautiful to be ruined. It doesn't need bulldozers up here tearing the land up. It doesn't need builders putting in condominiums and cabins all over the place. It needs young boys and girls slinging mud across the stream at one another. It needs wiener roasts and marshmallows stuck between crackers and chocolate bars. It needs to stay the Bar M Ranch and it needs a good manager who would love it like we have."

Kayla sighed with deep pleasure. At last she knew where Ed's heart truly lay. "You're so right," she agreed. "And I know just the man who could do it." She gave him a wink.

"You can see our clearing from here," he said, changing the subject. "Look!"

Across the meadow and behind the lodge about 400 yards, there was a break in the pines and a small clearing big enough for a four-bedroom house. She and Ed had talked about that clearing when they'd planned to marry. He had wanted to build her a house there and raise no less than six children, three of each, he'd told her. She smiled with the memory.

"It's still a beautiful spot," she sighed dreamily.

"Dang right!" he exclaimed. He looked out across the valley while she looked across the space between them. She could still see the fever burn within him, the fever that he had for this land. His whole body tensed with his love for it. Unlike the other boys, Ed would take care of the land because he loved it. She wondered if Mont knew just how much. But Kayla was troubled by other matters as well as the ranch and she didn't quite know how to approach the subject without offending Ed. Finally she decided there was no easy way so she plunged in almost recklessly. "What can we do about Tom's drinking?" Kayla hoped her voice sounded more empathetic than critical.

"I've got no ideas," he told her. "Pa is beside himself with worry." He hung his head and looked at his knees, refusing to look up at her. "Pa thinks he's hung up over you, Kayla Dawn."

"What?" she asked, her voice betraying the feelings of fear this statement produced.

"Pa told me years ago about Tom and you on the bridge that day. I was angry enough that I wanted to pull his arm off and beat him to death with it," he confessed. "After that I made sure Tom and William were both out working, even though it meant I was out there with them."

"I thought Sparky had instigated that," she confided.

"No. He asked me what I thought should be done about it. I told him I'd see to it Tom would never have the energy to try anything with you again." He frowned with the memories.

"You kept your word," she responded. "Then Dad thought it was time I learned a few womanly skills, and he assigned me kitchen duty with Morning Sun."

"Yes," he remembered. "I knew Pa had told Mont about it. Mont came to me a few weeks later and praised me for keeping Tom under control." He smiled. "Guess he didn't know that kissing you was something I wanted to save for myself, not for my brothers."

She blushed. "You accomplished that," she agreed. "But now something has to be done about Tom's drinking. Dad is just as worried as Sparky. He considers you boys as though you were his very own sons."

"I know that, Kayla Dawn, but I sure don't know what to do about Tom. Until he's ready to admit he's got a problem, he won't change."

"Couldn't you send him through a detox program?"

"We tried," he admitted, cringing with the memory. The dang fool tried to kill himself."

"Then what's going to become of him?"

"He's going to get himself in real trouble one of these days and when he does, it'll either straighten him out or kill him, one or the other," he said as he stretched his arms and placed one across the back of the seat behind her. His hand rested just above her left shoulder.

"You don't think he's dangerous when he's drunk, do you?" she asked as innocently as she could force herself to sound.

"I'll tell you what I think," he turned and faced her. "I've seen him drunk enough that he could have killed me if I didn't have my wits about me."

"If you're that concerned, and if he's as hung up on me as Sparky thinks, should I worry? Do you think he could harm me if he were drunk enough?" she asked.

"To tell you the honest truth," he admitted, "none of us would let Tom be alone with you if he'd been drinking, not even Pa."

His words chilled her to the bone and she shivered. He massaged her shoulder and turned up the heater fan. "Cold?" he asked.

"Just worried," she admitted. "I've come home to two major situations in our families and it feels peculiar. I'm used to things running smoothly. It makes me wonder where it will end."

He returned to rubbing her shoulder and his fingers brushed against the gold chain she wore. He recognized it immediately. Until now he hadn't noticed because of the turtle neck sweater she'd worn.

"Still wearing my chain, I see," he observed, silently praying that the hope building up within him could not be heard in his voice.

"It suits me," she admitted with a soft smile. "Much more than it suits your life preserver."

"Ain't that the truth!" he smiled. Then he threw caution to the wind and said, "I bought it for you seven years and six months ago. I had planned to give it to you on our wedding night."

Kayla remained silent. She reached up and touched his hand still massaging her shoulder. "I wondered," she admitted. "I'm glad you finally gave it to me." Her eyes filled with tears and she tried to blink them back, but she knew he'd noticed. She hoped he hadn't read too much into them.

Ed reached out and caught a single tear with his index finger as it started to spill down her cheek. He brought the tear to his lips, savoring the taste of it. "Don't cry, Kayla," he said softly.

"I don't mean to," she answered. "I never meant to hurt you, Ed."

"I know, Honey," he said huskily. "I know."

He put his hands upon the steering wheel and stared out over the little valley where the Bar M Ranch awaited them. "I'd better get you back before Mont gets nervous," he said after a long hesitation between them. Then he started the truck up once again and drove her back to the lodge.

Chapter Fourteen

When Ed drove into the driveway, Sparky was there to meet him. "A good thing you got here," he said, "Mont's been pacing the floor."

Ed glanced at his watch. "We're only seven minutes late," he informed him.

"He's been in a dither all day. We'd better let him have his little girl back and head on home to the cabin."

Kayla smiled as she got out of the truck and Sparky got in. "This must be really important to him," she said.

"It is," he agreed. "We spent the better part of the day working on it together, but he's nervous as a pole cat."

Kayla stepped toward the lodge then turned back. "We're going cross country skiing tomorrow if anyone wants to come."

Ed shook his head. "I took today off to spend with you. I don't dare take another one. Sky Patrol may not like that."

"Count me in, Kayla," said Sparky. You know skiing is my favorite sport, next to riding in the saddle."

"Good," she smiled. Until tomorrow then?"

"Wild horses couldn't drag me away," Sparky grinned.

Ed put the truck in gear and headed it back down the driveway.

Kayla turned and walked into the house. Then she remembered the groceries. She turned back, but the truck was already too far for them to hear her. Oh, well, she thought. They'll have to bring them over later, when they remember.

The moment she opened the door Kayla smelled the halibut cooking in the kitchen. She took off her coat and hung it up, then went to find her father.

Mont had on a chef's apron as he stood near the stove, frying fresh halibut. A candlelight supper was set up on the dining room table, this time with the best dishes, real candles, and service for two.

"Hi, Dad. Sorry I'm late," said Kayla as she gave him a kiss on the cheek.

"Oh, that's okay, Princess," he lied.

"It couldn't be too okay with you," she scolded. "Sparky told us you were anxious."

"Hmm! Wait and see if I invite him to go cross country skiing with us tomorrow," he teased.

"I already did," she confessed. "Ooh, is that halibut I smell?"

"Yes, it's fresh halibut and it's nearly ready," he admitted.

"Fresh? How did you get fresh?" she asked in surprise.

"Josh told me about a place in Port Townsend that ships it out the same day. I ordered it special." He gave her a wink. "I know it's your favorite."

"You spoil me," she said. "But don't stop."

He smiled. "Go ahead and sit down. It's almost ready."

Kayla hugged him tightly. "First I'll dash up to the rest room."

"All right," he agreed. "I wasn't thinking."

"I'll be right back," she assured him.

While in the bath room, Kayla brushed her long hair until it sparkled like honey gold over her shoulders. She refreshed her makeup and studied her face in the mirror. The gold chain she wore was barely visible beneath the cream colored turtle neck. She rubbed it tenderly with her fingers and admired the way it matched her honey gold hair. What she had learned from Ed today had opened her eyes to a thought she had never before considered. She still loved Ed, loved him with all her heart. However, it was not the same kind of love that she felt for Josh. The way she felt about Ed was totally familial. She smiled as she realized it had always been this way. Seven years ago when she had planned to marry Ed, she truly loved him, but without any of the passion that she had for Josh. There had been no aching deep inside her for Ed to hold her, to touch or caress her. There had been lust, mainly because she'd never experienced any real romantic love before him. Perhaps his feelings for her had been more physical than what she had felt, she didn't know. But she did know, at last, that she had always loved Ed just as she would if her were her own dear, sweet brother. She always would, she realized happily as she studied her face in the mirror.

She brushed aside thoughts of Ed as easily as she brushed her long, blonde hair. Now she had another obstacle to face: whatever Mont had prepared for her regarding Kayla's mother. Was she ready for it? Her stomach tightened into a hard ball as she thought about what still lay ahead of her. Disregarding her uneasiness, she shook off the concern and hoped she could make the best of the situation.

Within moments Mont and Kayla were sitting at the dining room table. Mont gave a short blessing on the food then spooned up two bowls of fresh spinach salad. She slid a serving spatula under a slice of fresh fried halibut and placed it on her plate. It was perfectly cooked and split apart in tender, moist particles.

"This is divine!" she raved, savoring the flavor. "I'd forgotten how good," she confessed. "I haven't had any for months, since—"

"Since August," he interrupted. "We stopped at Oceanside on our way north, remember?"

"We ate at that little restaurant on the end of the pier, but it wasn't nearly this good!" she exclaimed.

"It's all the TLC," he told her.

Their meal couldn't have been more delicious. Soon they were too full to eat another bite and they retired to the Gathering Room.

In front of the Christmas tree grouping waited a large gift, wrapped in gold foil with a huge red velvet bow and ribbon. It's large enough to be a hope chest, thought Kayla to herself.

"Sit down," Mont instructed.

"Anywhere in particular?" she asked.

"I've got the video camera aimed at the sofa," he explained. I thought we should do this together and record it so you won't ever forget what it all means."

"Show me exactly where you want me, Dad," she smiled.

He placed her in the middle of the sofa then went over to the camera, mounted on a tripod. After looking in the lens he said, "Move to your left just about a foot." Kayla complied. He turned on the camera then slid the large package over to her.

"Sit beside me," she complained. "I want you on the video also."

"I'm coming," he laughed heartily and Kayla discerned that his anxiety was easing some. He sat down beside her and gave her a hug. Then he said, "Princess, when your mother died. Well, just before she died, she made me promise I would give this to you some day." He paused and his eyes misted slightly. "At first I didn't want to give it to you. I was selfish and you were too little. Then I didn't even want to look in it anymore; it made me sad. I finally put it in storage and left it there. Not too long ago I felt inspired that it was time. I want you to consider it as *one last gift* from your mother, something she would have given you fifteen years ago if she'd been here to do it."

Kayla felt a knot of apprehension within her. Mont rarely talked about her mother and she intuitively sensed that now she would learn more about KayDawn Allen than at any other time in her life. She didn't know whether she wanted to or not. Her mother had always been a mysterious nonentity, someone so unreal that she failed to exist, in Kayla's mind, on more than one occasion. Kayla gulped. Then she undid the bow and removed the gold wrapping paper.

Beneath the paper she found a beautiful hope chest, hand carved in cherry wood. The workmanship was exceedingly fine, with scrolls and roses hewn out of the wood in delicate patterns in the lid. She could tell Mont had been oiling and rubbing it recently. It smelled deliciously of lemon oil. A bronze clasp kept the lid secured with a small padlock.

Mont stretched forth his hand and gave Kayla the key. "Your great grandfather made it for KayDawn when she was twelve. It was his custom to present a fine trunk to each of his daughters and granddaughters on their twelfth birthday." He smiled with the memories the old chest evoked within him, surprised that he could finally do so. "We used to argue over whether it was a trunk or a chest," he admitted. "I always called it a trunk. Your mom insisted it's a hope chest."

"It IS a hope chest. Mother was right." Tenderly Kayla ran her fingers over the finely carved flowers. "Did she like roses?" she asked wistfully, thinking to herself how much she loved them.

"They were her favorite flowers," he replied. "Red ones, white ones, yellow, pink, it didn't matter. She always said that roses were God's most beautiful creation next to children."

"It's beautiful," she murmured. In her mind she could imagine her great-grandfather carving every intricate flower fastidiously.

Kayla slipped the key into the padlock and unlocked it, then gave the key and padlock to Mont. Carefully she opened the lid, wondering what she would find beneath it.

To her utter amazement she discovered a quilt inside the hope chest. However, this was not just any ordinary quilt in traditional floral or star shaped patterns. This quilt was covered with sailboats of every shape, size and color, embroidered on an aquamarine background with an ocean wave pattern. There were also seals and porpoises, sea shells of various sizes and varieties, and lighthouses. The quilt was entirely nautical from start to finish. Even the heavy flannel backing was made with a sailboat printed fabric.

Kayla gasped. Her face paled and her hands began to shake. She reached out and gently pulled the quilt up to her face and caressed her skin with it. "My mother liked the ocean?" she asked in a whisper, the words choking on her tears.

"She made that quilt when she was eighteen years old," Mont explained. "She was more like you than you've ever known, Princess."

"Why didn't you ever say anything?" she questioned softly. "I thought I was the odd one out in our family."

"I don't know why, exactly," he confessed. "I thought perhaps if you never knew, you'd never want to follow the same dreams. I guess I wanted you to marry Ed and be a rancher's wife forever, as though I could wrench from you something so intangible as a longing for the sea."

His eyes misted slightly and Kayla put her arms about him. "I've had sea fever ever since Sparky gave me that book about the little girl and the sea shore, remember?" she asked.

"How could I forget?" he wanted to know. "I was mad at him for weeks. Every time you wanted me to read it to you, I cringed," he confessed.

"Tell me about my mother," Kayla insisted. For the first time in her life she really wanted to know about this woman who loved the sea as much as Kayla herself.

"She grew up in Mission Beach. Her father was a marine biologist who worked for Sea World. KayDawn had dreams of going to college and becoming a marine biologist. Her father didn't want her to, he felt women should marry, have babies and stay at home." He smiled. "Before she met me, she had three loves: sailing, marine wildlife, and quilting."

"You never told me," Kayla wondered at his reasoning.

"For two reasons," he explained. "I didn't want you running off to the sea."

"Which I did anyway," she added for him.

"Second," he continued, "it was too painful. If I had not come into her life, she would have become a marine biologist. I stole from her two of those things she loved. Not only did I steal them from her, but I was also responsible for her death."

"She died of an embryo implanting in a fallopian tube," Kayla reminded.

"But who persuaded her to have another child?" he asked. "No, I accept full responsibility for what I did."

"Dad, that's hardly fair to blame yourself for something nature had a hand in," she complained. "Accidents happen, even those within the human body."

"I've made peace with it," he relented. "Besides, she hasn't held it against me," he winked.

"Did she sail before she met you?"

"She was born sailing, Princess. Her father owned a big ship with two masts."

"A ketch or a yawl?" she asked.

"You tell me," he suggested. He reached into the chest and pulled out a shoe box.

Inside the box, alphabetized by category, Kayla found dozens of photographs. She looked up a category called, Boats Daddy Owned, penned in neat block letters. The first photo in the section was a beautiful ketch with clean, distinct lines. Kayla recognized the design immediately. "It's a Dickerson 50," she told Mont. "They've been around since the early fifties," she informed him. Then she saw the ketch's name, Lady Dawn, etched across the stern. "He named it Lady Dawn," she said as tears filled her eyes. "Dad, that's impossible!"

"I've always told you your mother watches over you," he reminded. "When you named your sailboat Lady Dawn, I whimpered around here for a week like a love sick puppy. I was so happy to know your mother had influenced you in this regard."

Kayla studied his expression but she could not believe what he'd said to her. She hoped she could remain silent on the matter but an unsettling bitterness choked her. She almost gagged. It was just one of those weird coincidences of life that science hadn't yet deciphered. Probably a gene imprint from her mother, she decided. It certainly could not be some spiritual manifestation from a woman who'd been dead for twenty-seven years.

"Is it a ketch or yawl?" asked Mont tenderly changing the subject. He realized by her silence that she was digesting this information.

"A ketch. The aft mast is shorter than the front, see?" She held the photo up for his inspection.

As Kayla thumbed through the photographs, her father explained each one. There were photos of KayDawn when she was a toddler kissing an unidentified little boy. "Who is this?" she asked.

"I believe he was a neighbor," said Mont. "Did she write on the back?"

"Yes," said Kayla, turning the photo over to see. "It says, 'Mark Johnson kissing me at Mama's house. I was probably three in the photo.' My word, she kept photos that cover her entire life."

"Even our wedding reception," he told her, pulling an album out of the chest. It gave a detailed account of their wedding, from before Mont proposed until after Kayla was born, when she was pregnant with their second child.

Kayla placed it on the sofa beside her. "Good bedside reading material, I'll bet," she told him.

Next she pulled out a small, clasped diary. Every single page was filled out in neat, highly legible cursive.

"She was fourteen when her parents gave her that diary," said Mont. I believe she said it was for Christmas. She wrote in it every day. She said her father once offered her a hundred dollars for it but she wouldn't take it."

After the diary Kayla found a baby book that KayDawn had written in, all about Kayla's first smile, first tooth, first steps, as well as a pair of booties. "I didn't know she kept a baby book," said Kayla.

Kayla opened the book and saw her own hand and foot prints staring out at her from the front page. "Was I ever that small?" she asked in amazement. "Look at those tiny feet!"

Scanning over the writing on the next page, Kayla read aloud:

"Today is the second happiest of my whole life (the

first being the day I married the man of my dreams).
My darling daughter, Kayla Dawn Allen, was born
at 3:17 A.M. at the Ashley Valley Medical Center.
She is the most beautiful baby girl in the world.
I have never seen, before or since, such a perfect
little child. I will love her forever.

KD"

"Did she always sign her name KD?" asked Kayla.

"Always," he responded. "Her father called her that as a nickname and she seemed to like it. Her mother liked the more formal, KayDawn."

"I want to learn more about her, Dad," Kayla said, surprised at her request. She had never felt such a hunger for knowledge about anything so strongly in all her life, not even when she gave up marrying Ed for her scholarship at USC. "Will you tell me everything you remember about her?" she asked as tears dripped down her cheeks.

He wiped her tears away with his thumbs. "It's high time I did," whispered Mont. "She loves you very much, Kayla. She wants you to know that."

Kayla started laughing but tears came to her eyes as well. "Dad!" she complained. "You finally present me with something that makes my mother seem real to me, then you spoil it by talking about her in the present tense, as though she were still here!"

"She is!" he insisted. "She's often nearby, Kayla, watching over me and you."

Then why haven't I seen her?! She wanted to scream, but her voiceless expression remained totally impassive.

"I see," Mont said wearily, as though she had actually voiced her complaint. "You still don't believe in eternal life."

She sighed, realizing he had read her thoughts just as he had done so many years ago. She didn't want a confrontation, but with Mont being able to understand her thoughts as he did, perhaps it was time to discuss the issue. "Dad," she began tenderly. "I want to believe. I've even prayed to believe, but you are the one who raised me and you taught me that I should question everything."

"Not this," he explained tenderly. "This is something you must accept on faith."

"I'm sorry," she lamented. "But I'm a scientist first. It's not in my nature to pretend to have blind faith."

"Kayla Dawn Allen," he said sorrowfully, "how could I have failed you so completely? You attended Church and Seminary all through your youth. We read scriptures together. You even bore your testimony a time or two."

"I stopped attending when I went to BYU. Except when I'm here with you, Dad, I haven't been to Church for eleven years," she confessed.

"That long?" he questioned. "You never said."

"I didn't want to hurt your feelings," she responded.

"And now you do?" he asked quickly.

"No!" She shook her head. "No, Dad. I would never deliberately hurt you. Sunday evening, when we said we wouldn't keep any more secrets from one another, I felt that promise applied to this issue as well."

"I understand," he said. "But I also must bear fervent witness to you, Kayla, that the things I've taught you from the cradle up are all true. There is a God and he loves you very much. Your mother lives just as surely as I live. We just don't see her as clearly as we see each other. She is in spirit form. Her body is the only part of her missing right now. And she will receive that body back when she is resurrected."

"I want to believe that, Dad. Truly," she added. "But by all the laws of science it is impossible to bring a body back to life once it's completely died," Kayla said. "I respect you for having such strong religious convictions. I even envy your faith, but I have to be shown."

"If you would make an effort to know God, He would show you."

"You know," she advised, "you sound just like those angels on that t.v. show, what is it called? Something about angels," she shook her head sadly. "It's all so far fetched."

"That show does stretch the imagination a little," he agreed, "but only because the family relationship isn't clearly established. Our departed ancestors, your mother included, watch over us and help us from time to time as they see our need. I have sensed your mother's spirit on many occasions and have discussed important issues with her.

I know she lives across the veil from us and if we are truly faithful, we will see and know these things for ourselves."

"Oh, Dad," Kayla sighed. "I want to believe like you do, but right now I'm unconvinced. I can't believe something just because you say so. I have to take it apart and put it back together. I have to analyze it and consume it and digest it. When I can see that the science and logic match up in it, then, and only then, can I accept it as a fact. We live in a world where information is at our very fingertips. When I have substantiated proof that Mother is still alive and watches over me, then I will believe."

Mont shook his head. "I don't know what I ever did to send you away from the heart of the Gospel."

"You did nothing," she explained. "I did it all on my own." Hoping to change the subject, Kayla asked, "What is this?" as she picked up a small ivory vase made from genuine porcelain that she'd spotted inside the hope chest.

He sighed as he realized Kayla had just terminated the discussion. Mont doubted he would ever get another opportunity but he recognized the moment of religious confrontation had passed. He swallowed the lump that had risen in his throat and knew that he had failed her as a father. If she had shot him in the chest with buckshot, he wouldn't have felt more miserable. His body physically ached from the sadness and he sensed a deep and irregular beat to his heart that he ignored completely.

"It's a—" he hesitated, unable to continue for a moment. Finally, commanding his nerves to stillness he said, "It belonged to KayDawn's great-grandmother. Everyone in the family received some item from her personal collection and your mother received this vase. KayDawn was only seven years old when her great-grandmother died. She wrote about it in her diary. You'll read it later on."

Most of the next hour Mont told Kayla all the stories about her mother that she'd never heard before, from the moment he met her to the day Kayla was born; from their new experiences at parenthood to the moment KayDawn passed away at the hospital in Vernal. To Kayla, her mother finally became a real person, someone who loved Kayla more than she loved her own life. The thought made Kayla shiver as a new found love surged through her, love for her mother that she never knew existed. When the story ended as abruptly as KayDawn's life had, Kayla felt sad, reflecting the mood that Mont had reached by telling the painful account.

"What's this?" she asked, hoping to brighten his spirits. She picked up a manila envelope with paperwork stuffed into it.

"It's my Last Will And Testament, and the deed to the Bar M Ranch, Princess," he admitted. "Those are from me. I wanted you to know exactly where I stand concerning my financial affairs."

"Will you tell me?" she asked. "Or do I have to read it?"

He stretched and yawned. "It just explains that, in the event of my death, nothing is to happen to the ranch until after Sparky is gone, depending on which one of us goes first. Then when we're both gone, I'd like to see the ranch kept in the family for the grandchildren and future generations. So I've left it up to you... all of it. I hope you'll want to keep it. If you don't hire someone to work it, I'd like you to use the lodge for a summer home. Winters are hard and I don't know that any of Sparky's boys would want it now. Times have changed."

"Ed may want to run it, Dad," she suggested.

"What about Sky Patrol?" he asked. "He's all tied up with that now."

"You didn't see the look in his eyes today as he talked about the ranch and his love for it," she confessed. "If you and Sparky do retire, promise me you'll talk to Ed first before you turn the ranch over to anyone else."

"Are you sure, Princess?" he questioned. "It seems to me—"

"I'm positive," she interrupted. "He's always dreamed of taking over when you two are ready, and I don't think that dream has ever changed."

Mont gave her a broad smile. "Well, then that's what I'll do," he agreed heartily. "That would make me rest easy, knowing Ed was here to manage the ranch. I just assumed he wasn't all that interested in it anymore."

"Trust me," she encouraged. "He may not have told you all this, but I know what I saw in his eyes today as he talked about the ranch. That fire is still burning."

Pleased that Mont was so readily agreeable, Kayla changed the subject by digging deeper into the hope chest. She found a heavily framed photo of the musical play, <u>Li'l Abner</u>. Daisy Mae was posed next to Li'l Abner with the stage cabin in the background. Kayla couldn't remember doing Li'l Abner in school, yet the girl in the photo looked remarkably like herself at about age fifteen or sixteen. "Dad," she handed the photo to him. "I was never in Li'l Abner, was I?"

"That's your mother, Princess. She was wearing a blonde wig," he explained.

Kayla studied the photo carefully. The resemblance between KayDawn and her daughter was amazing. "I never realized we look so much alike," she said.

Mont smiled. "You got my hair coloring, Princess," he admitted. "But otherwise you are the image of your mother, almost entirely."

"I never recognized it before," she said. "What a wonderful gift, to know my mother and I are so much alike."

"I wasn't trying to hide the truth from you, KayDawn," he explained. "I guess I didn't realize how much you needed to know."

"Maybe it's a girl thing, Dad," she comforted. "Maybe men don't need all the emotional attachments that we do."

"That doesn't mean we're insensitive, Sweetheart," he defended.

"No," she agreed with a smile and a hug. "You're certainly not that. You are one of the kindest, most sensitive men I've ever met, next to Josh."

"Speaking of Josh," he said. "As a father, I have a couple of questions about him that I'd like to ask."

"Go ahead," she smiled.

"It's personal, Princess. I don't want to offend you."

"Dad, we can ask or tell each other anything, can't we?"

He nodded. She noticed the gulp of air he swallowed before asking, "Do you know for certain that you love Josh?"

She gave him an ear to ear smile in response. "Yes," she answered, and when she did the words sounded like sweet music. "I love Josh more than I've ever loved anyone."

"Hmm," he teased, "a father could get jealous over a statement like that."

"It's a different kind of love, Dad, you know that," she punched him playfully in the arm.

"If memory serves," he said, stroking his chin. "Tell me the difference between the way you love Ed and the way you love Josh," he requested. "Do you understand what I'm asking?"

"Yes," she answered. "I've always loved Ed. He is a great man in his own right. I want the very best in life for him."

"But—" he began.

"Let me finish," she said, "because it finally came to me today as we went on that outing together. By the way," she added, "I think your tactics are deplorable." She arched an eyebrow as he searched her expression. "And don't play dumb. You know what I'm talking about."

He raised his shoulders in a mock display. "Oops!" he squeaked.

"Enough said," she responded. "All right. I grew up loving Ed and William, Tom and Abbot. They have always been my buddies and my protectors. Well, nearly always," she added, remembering the incident with Tom on the bridge. "At around age seventeen when I finally started evolving from a child to an adult, my hormones went crazy, I suppose. And I had no mother to explain to me that my feelings were perfectly normal, remember?"

"And Morning Sun, she didn't—"

"No, she assumed you would and you assumed she would," she confessed. "So the feminine side of me fell for Ed in a big way. I think I was in lust... but certainly not in love. Think about it, Dad. The boys were practically the only men I knew. And they were still just boys long after I became a woman because men mature slower. I know, you disagree, but let me have my say in this, all right?"

He smiled. "I'm all ears, Princess."

"I thought I was in love with Ed, I truly did. But you wanted me to go to BYU, which I interpreted to mean that, because I had led such a sheltered life, you wanted to make sure I had a taste of the real world before I shackled myself to a rancher."

"That's close," he agreed. "And I felt a few years of separation would show both of you where your true feelings lay."

"You hadn't planned on the scholarship to USC," she continued, "or my insatiable thirst for knowledge. Neither had I but I will be forever grateful that it worked out to my benefit."

"And now?" he asked, hurrying her along. "How do you differentiate between the love you apparently feel for both men?"

"I know you think I still love Ed and I do, but it's different. I love Ed like I would love my dearest, closest confidante and brother," she announced. "I am protective of him. I want the best in life for him. I would do almost anything for him, but the physical attraction, the lusting, is completely gone," she confided. "I realized that this morning when Ed held me in his arms and kissed me on the forehead."

"He did?" came his swift response.

"Yes, and I think you put him up to it!" she accused.

Mont confessed, "I told him I knew that you loved him still, and that he should find out whether or not my instincts were on the mark. He said he wouldn't do it."

"I know," she admitted. "I overheard you and Ed arguing Sunday afternoon on the porch."

He bowed his head. "I've made a real mess of things, haven't I?"

"You have," she admitted, "because Ed almost proposed to me today and I didn't know what to tell him. It caught me completely off guard."

"What did you say?" he asked.

"I told him I would have to think about it," she answered somberly.

"I'm so sorry, Kayla. When I saw you laugh so hard Sunday after Church as you danced with Ed... I just knew I saw love in your eyes for him."

"I do love Ed. I love him with all my heart," she admitted. "But I love him as I would if he were my brother."

"And Josh?" he asked. "Explain the difference to me. Why is your love any different for Josh?"

"We complement each other," she explained. "We're totally compatible. He's understanding. He never yells at me. He tries to see the world from my perspective and I do the same for him. Yet there's also the passion," she confessed, feeling the longing for Josh grow painfully within her until it was all she could do to squash it. "I ache, Dad. I physically ache for Josh. When we're apart, I wander around like a lost puppy. If there is a God, if there is a Heaven like I want to believe, I think that Josh and I must have known and loved each other there because what we have transcends anything tangible on this earth."

Mont gathered her into his strong arms and held her as only a tender father can. "I'm so glad to hear it, Princess. I've been worried you were going to make a terrible mistake."

"Fathers have the right to protect their children," she conceded. "Even when they haven't the slightest idea what they're doing."

He smiled. "I'm glad you see it that way."

Kayla studied his face carefully. She still had one issue they hadn't discussed and it bothered her tremendously. Having no barriers now to interfere with the conversation, she began. "Dad, there's one more thing I'd like to talk about."

"What is it, Princess?" he asked patiently.

"I'm so worried about Sparky. What is he going to do when the truth comes out about Tom?"

"Now, that is a question," agreed Mont. "That day in the meadow when I passed out, I'd been stewing about Tom's involvement and how it would affect Sparky. And look what happened."

"Then what about Sparky?" she insisted. "What will this do to him?"

"I wish I knew," admitted Mont. "I hope his ticker is stronger than mine."

Chapter Fifteen

Kayla telephoned Josh shortly after Mont went to bed. It thrilled her to hear his voice and feel his love as he listened to her explain the events of the day. She confided every detail to him, including the discussions with Ed. She also explained about Mont sharing with her the events in her mother's life that now meant so much to her. She could hear his relief when she admitted that she loved Ed as though he was her own sweet brother. She was grateful that she could share everything with Josh, holding nothing back. Though how she would ever explain her feelings to Ed she didn't know, for she had sensed that he still cared about her in a more romantic way than as his sister.

After she had told Josh everything, he gave her a moment to moment account of life at the lab that day. He'd had a surprise visit from his father, who was worried about Grandmother's health. Then Josh expressed how utterly he loved Kayla.

He wanted to hear what her mother had written in the diary so Kayla read it entirely to him and they shared their feelings regarding it over the phone. As she read to him, her mother took on the dimensions of a real person, someone Kayla wanted to know, but hadn't been given the opportunity. Kayla's heart filled with love for KayDawn as quickly as her eyes did. She wept and wiped away her tears, then wept again. Through it all Joshua listened attentively, genuinely relieved for Kayla because of the bond she now felt with her mother.

At the end of the diary she read, "I wonder what tomorrow will bring. KD"

"That reminds me," said Josh. "I don't mean to interrupt, but are you still going skiing tomorrow?"

"Yes," Kayla informed him. "It'll just be Dad and Sparky going with me. Ed has to work while Tom and Will have gone to Dutch John to visit with Melanie."

"You be careful," he teased. "Don't let those two old codgers sway your affections from me."

"That'll never happen," she insisted.

"I'm glad," said Josh. "I'd better let you go so you can sleep. You've got a hard day ahead of you tomorrow."

"I know," she agreed. "But I've enjoyed hearing your voice so much!"

"And me back!" he exclaimed. "I probably won't bother calling you tomorrow night. With my luck, you'll come home exhausted, Mont will rub your feet, and you'll be gone to dreamland until morning."

"Probably," she admitted. "Don't know why that affects me like that."

"It's called environmental conditioning," he explained. "You must really get into a comfort zone on that sofa with your dad massaging your feet."

"I guess," she admitted with a smile.

"On Thursday we'll be leaving early, around ten in the morning, so I'll just wait and see you Christmas Eve. Will that work?"

"Sure," she agreed. "I usually sleep until noon the day after skiing, so does Dad."

"I love you, Kayla," he confessed.

"And I love you!"

When they finally hung up, Kayla was surprised to see that they had talked for four hours and it was almost one in the morning.

Snuggling up in her cozy bed, Kayla opened the baby book KayDawn had written in that first year of Kayla's existence. She read each page with renewed interest and laughed at some of the things "infant Kayla" did that brought joy to her mother's life. From KayDawn's writing, it became perfectly clear to Kayla that her mother loved her and had planned to spend a lifetime proving it.

One page in the book stood out in Kayla's mind as the most memorable of all. The page was titled, *Thoughts On Motherhood*. It had decorative roses and baby rattles etched around the perimeter. Within the frame KayDawn had written,

"Motherhood has given me a glimpse of the true meaning of eternal love. I have heard it said that Father in Heaven

loves us more than a mother loves her own child. If
this is true, and I believe that it is, then I must be the most
beloved of all His children. If my joy is this rewarding
with only one child, my Kayla Dawn, I want a meadow full
of children. Kayla is worth any and every sacrifice I've ever
made.   KD"

A blank space separated the next few lines on the same page. She
was surprised to find that her mother had written a message to Kayla
just below the blank space, a message that made her head spin with the
implications. She read it over and over again until she had committed
it to memory. As she did so, she wondered what had prompted her
mother to write her such a poignant message.

"Kayla, if I should ever be called home early I want you to
know that my love for you will never die. I will watch over
you through out all your life until we can be together again.
                          Love, Mama"

Had her mother known she would die young? "Called home early,"
was a phrase she had heard Mont use on more than one occasion. He
had likened it to dying, saying something about the spirit going home
to God, while the body remained to be buried in the earth. KayDawn
evidently believed that she and Kayla would be together again at some
future point in time. Her mother's faith seemed stronger than Mont's,
Kayla thought wistfully. What must it be like to have such faith?
    Kayla thought on her mother's words until the wee hours of morn-
ing forced her eyelids to close. Then she slept soundly.
    The sun rose Wednesday morning in a glorious display of reds and
crimsons across the eastern sky and Kayla was ready for it. Fully
dressed and ready for a new day, Kayla stood on the deck outside her
bedroom door and looked across the snow-covered meadow.
Tomorrow is Christmas Eve, she thought joyfully. And this will be the
best Christmas I've ever had. I know who my mother was and I love
her with all my heart. Perhaps more importantly, she loved me.
Thinking ahead, she thrilled to realize that tomorrow night Josh would

arrive and they would be able to hold one another again. Mont, Sarah and the Admiral would help them make wedding plans for May.

She felt her heart softening a little more toward spiritual matters as well. It seemed that her mother's faith had somehow touched Kayla's heart. She wished she had known her mother all those years, growing up. Admitting it only to herself, Kayla realized that her youth had been spent almost hating her mother, hating her for not being there while pretending her mother really didn't exist at all. Had KayDawn lived to raise her, Kayla now believed that she would have far greater spiritual inclinations than she did. For the first time in her life, Kayla felt a ray of hope that there truly was a God in Heaven, and that He was mindful of her needs.

Across the meadow at the cabin, Kayla saw Sparky coming out the door with his skis and backpack. He tossed them into the back of the truck, then drove the short distance over to the lodge.

The radio report came across the airwaves from Mont's weather radio below her. Kayla looked down from the deck. "Are you down there, Dad?" she called.

Mont stepped to the end of the porch and looked up. Kayla waved to him from the deck overhead. "Just checking the weather report, Princess," he said.

"What's the forecast?" she asked.

"Clear and sunny today, but heavy snow is expected later tonight," he answered.

"And Christmas Eve?" She was worried whether Josh and his parents would be able to arrive by helicopter.

"It's supposed to be overcast and cloudy, but the snow is supposed to ease up Christmas Eve morning."

"Good," she said cheerily. "We'll have a wonderful day today, and a great holiday, too!"

Kayla pulled her hair back to the nape of her neck with a ribbon. Then she went downstairs for breakfast. After a hot bowl of oatmeal she heated a large can of soup and poured it into a thermos, made fresh sandwiches and stuffed them all into a small back pack along with some dehydrated apple and banana slices. She used the pack Mont had set on the table for her, noticing he'd already put into it a few emergency items they may need: a whistle to use if they became separated;

a headlamp in case they couldn't get back by dark; a lighter to start a fire, if necessary, etc. By the time she finished, Mont and Sparky were waiting for her on the front porch.

"I have the food pack," Kayla told them, putting her arms through the straps.

"Sparky has the emergency kit and I have hot water and hot chocolate," said Mont. "I guess we're ready."

Kayla fastened the latches on her skis and grabbed her poles. She started out across the meadow ahead of them, west toward the open meadows high in the Uintah mountains that she loved so well.

The snow sparkled like a million diamonds scattered across the white terrain, catching the sun and reflecting it back in myriad bursts of light. The swishing of her skis on the surface caused momentary bursts of powder to spray out around her and Kayla relished the swishing sound of it, remembering an almost countless number of times she'd taken to these mountain meadows on snow skis. Mont and Sparky followed closely, never far from her but allowing her plenty of room to zigzag across the valley floor.

Porcupine Ridge, in the distance, stood ruggedly before them, with its sheer cliff face and gentler slopes east and west. On the opposite side, the north face, was one of the finest snow runs anywhere, Kayla knew from experience.

Sparky suggested they climb over Porcupine Ridge with its rugged terrain and ski down the opposite side. It would be an arduous journey, but each agreed they felt capable.

Porcupine Ridge was one of the tallest peaks in Ashley National Forest. It stood above the valley floor a good three thousand feet. Steep on the north, the east and west slopes graduated into other ranges such as pine bluff and devil's fork. With ten to twelve feet of snow on the slopes, the climbing would not be easy.

Their work began in earnest as they climbed in switch back patterns, one ski at a time, higher and higher. It took the better part of three hours to reach the top. By the time they did, all three were winded, Kayla probably more than Mont and Sparky.

"Whoa," she groaned. "I'm out of shape."

"I may not be out of shape," Sparky added, "but I'm out of air."

They rested and ate lunch on top of Porcupine Ridge, looking back at the distance they had traveled. "When you're hiking to Porcupine," Kayla observed, "it seems to take forever. On skis, it's not too bad."

"Do you still have your whistles and headlamps?" asked Mont.

Always one to plan ahead, Mont set a pattern of safety Kayla followed all her life. "Yes," she answered, knowing that Mont had hand-selected these items before they left the ranch. Each pack always had small emergency gear ready for nearly any event.

"Good," said Mont. "We'll want to see our way back if it gets dark before we get there."

"I'm a little concerned about avalanche danger," observed Sparky. "We've had two heavy snowfalls with a melting spell between them."

"There haven't been any avalanche signs yet," said Mont.

Sparky nodded. "That was one thing I checked out with Ed this morning before we left. Sky Patrol says they haven't seen any evidence of sliding snow."

"Just in case," Mont continued, "do you remember what to do in an avalanche, Kayla?"

"Yes," she nodded. "The objective is to allow the slide to carry you forward on your skis, using the snow's momentum to 'surf' the slide like you would if you were riding a big wave."

"I've been in an avalanche," Mont told her. "Keep your skis together as much as possible and your knees slightly bent. Then ride like your life depends on it," he added, "because it does. That's the only reason why I'm still alive."

Sparky nodded. "Try to stay diagonal to an avalanche, Kayla, approximately 45 degrees from the coming snow. And no matter what happens, remember that the only person you might be able to save in an avalanche is yourself. Don't worry about us until after you're safe. Is that clear?"

"It may be clear," she admitted, "but it's also impossible. My first concern would be for you and Dad. Besides, has there ever been a slide down Porcupine Ridge?"

"Not that I know about," admitted Sparky.

"You both ski these mountains at least weekly in the winter," Kayla reasoned. "In all your years of skiing, Dad's only seen one avalanche and you've seen none. I think you're both worrying unduly."

Mont smiled. "You told me last night that a father has a right to protect his child," he reminded.

"I give!" Kayla laughed and it broke the moment of tension.

Soon they were ready to start the treacherous, yet exciting, descent. The three long hours they'd taken to climb Porcupine Ridge seemed worth it as they began their journey down the other side. With very few trees on the top two-thirds of it, Porcupine Ridge was steep and somewhat unpredictable. The mountain side swiftly passed beneath them as they almost flew down it on their skis.

The wind whisked Kayla's hair free from the ribbon as her parka hood came loose part way down. She stopped momentarily and tied the hood's strap with a better knot. Mont and Sparky passed her only after determining that she was not in need of any assistance. Soon she started back down. Snow sprayed all around her in a trail that she left behind as her speed increased. Quickly she caught up with Mont and Sparky and passed them up without any problem, realizing as she did that they had deliberately slowed their pace for her benefit.

Kayla enjoyed the thrill of the slope and laughed so hard her cheeks ached, as did Mont and Sparky. "I'll bet it's been twelve years since I've done that run," she called to them. "I'm usually not brave enough to tackle it."

"It's a killer slope," Mont called back in agreement.

They traveled down the steep mountain side more than a mile before they finally reached the forest edge. They slowed their pace until the trees became so dense that traveling through them became a danger rather than a thrill.

They finally rested in a small clearing where they could enjoy the sunshine. Kayla folded back her parka hood and shook her hair loose. The golden strands fell like spun gold against her shoulders.

Mont pulled off his ski mask and let the sun bake against his face. She could easily see the similarities in their hair color. His hair was long and curly, grown just below his ears in winter. Usually he got a good haircut in the spring and let it grow thereafter until the following spring. He considered comfort most important, and this way he would be cooler during the summer and warmer in the winter months. The only difference Kayla could tell was that his hair had silver streaks throughout it as he'd aged.

Mont and Sparky started talking about the good old days, before there were wives and children to worry about. Kayla delighted in listening to them as they spread out an emergency blanket from Sparky's pack and rested on it. The metallic fibre reflected the sun's heat back to them, while keeping the cold snow from penetrating to chill them. The afternoon had warmed up considerably, so much that tiny rivulets of water trickled down crevices in the deep layers of snow.

They only rested fifteen minutes before Mont said, "It's two o'clock. We need to start back."

Kayla folded up the emergency blanket and stowed it away in Sparky's back pack. "I see you brought plenty of Jell-O," she grinned as she moved two large boxes aside to make room for the blanket.

"It always pays to go prepared," Sparky shot back. "I've never used it yet, but I'm never going to not have it," he winked.

"Always good boy scouts," she teased.

The started their ascent, heading a good distance farther east, before doing switch backs up to the ridge again. By the time they were almost back on top the sun began to sink in the western sky.

"We should just be able to clear the ridge and down the other side before it gets dark," said Mont. "Check your head lamps while we rest a minute, just to make sure they're still working."

Kayla removed hers from her pack. She flipped the switch on and the light responded. Mont and Sparky's head lamps worked equally as well.

Within minutes they were back on the climb. Another two hundred yards and they would clear the top, thought Kayla, having learned distances by sight in a special class at USC. Just as that thought formed in her mind she heard the rumbling. It was a sound she couldn't recognize, one she'd never heard before.

Mont knew what would cause such a muffled, almost stifled roar. He stiffened. His eyes searched the valley below them and the ridges surrounding the valley but he didn't see anything suspicious.

"Probably a small slide down in the forest," he suggested. "Let's go."

Suddenly there was a horrifying crack, like a huge crevasse opening up in a ten-mile glacier.

Mont, realizing their situation immediately, yelled, "Avalanche! Follow me down!"

It happened so fast Kayla didn't get a chance to catch her breath. The snow beneath her seemed to come alive and push its way down the mountainside. The roar it made deafened her.

Mont turned his skis down the steep slope and fairly flew down the mountain side. Glancing back, he saw that Kayla was just a few feet behind him with Sparky about the same distance behind her.

Kayla's heart raced faster than her skis as she followed after Mont at break neck speed. The snow beneath her was no longer solid but shifted like some white quick sand wanting to swallow her completely. Vaguely she remembered what she had been warned about keeping her skis together and her knees slightly bent. She tried not to think about the avalanche. Instead she placed all her concentration on watching and imitating every movement Mont made in front of her.

She could hardly keep up with Mont as she felt the snow toss her around like a limp doll. It seemed like some white monster was using her for a toy. She felt a huge hand of snow toss her about, tumble her around, tip her over and upright her once again. It seemed as though she was flying higher and higher into the crisp winter sky.

Sparky was also tossed around by the snow, but he seemed oblivious to it. He stretched out his hands with all his strength, releasing his hold on his poles as he pushed the bottom of Kayla's skis heavenward, as though trying to toss her even higher.

For a few brief moments it seemed to Kayla that time actually stood still. She felt herself flying through the air and realized that the snow structure beneath her had become a viable, raging monster. The roaring around her had completely deafened her and she could no longer hear herself think. She looked down and watched in amazement as the tops of the trees went sailing by below her, some of them breaking like match sticks. She wondered if she'd already died and her spirit was flying above the avalanche. Her body turned head over heels at least twice that she counted. In one of these somersaults she saw Sparky reaching out for her. He was holding her skis, pushing her up toward the sky.

Suddenly she felt something hard strike both her legs causing the most excruciating pain she had ever felt in her entire life. Her shins felt like they were on fire. The agonizing pain within them soon became unbearable. Her mouth opened in an effort to scream out, but nothing could be heard above the awful, terrible roaring of the white monster.

Then the oddest thing of all occurred. Kayla saw a beautiful woman dressed in clothing far whiter than the snow around her. The woman reached out in front of her and took Kayla's hands in hers, then crossed Kayla's arms over her face, forming a small tunnel for Kayla's face to rest. The angelic woman seemed exquisitely divine beyond all belief, with sparkling auburn hair and tender brown eyes, much like Kayla's.

Maybe I'm dead, thought Kayla. It was her last conscious thought for quite a while.

Chapter Sixteen

Josh glanced at his watch when the strange sensation settled upon him. His spine tensed and he felt a prickling feeling all the way from his neck to his toes. He hadn't had a similar feeling since the day his grandfather, Johannes Joshua Hansen, passed away. It was 3:27 P.M. He went to the phone and dialed his parents' number.

JonPaul answered immediately. "Clark Residence."

"Is Mother all right?" asked Josh.

"Yes, sir," replied JonPaul. "She and your grandmother are working on the biography."

"Would you please go check on them?" asked Josh. "Make sure they're both well."

"Straight away, sir," he responded.

Josh waited a few moments until JonPaul returned. "They are both in good spirits, sir. Your mother suggests you take two aspirin and go home to rest," said JonPaul.

Josh sighed. "Very well, thank you," he said. He hung up the phone and dialed his father's number at work.

A secretary answered, "Bridger Clark's office."

"Is my father available?" asked Josh.

"One moment, Commander Clark," replied the secretary.

Soon the Admiral came on the line. "Josh?"

"Dad, I apologize for bothering you at the office," said Josh.

"No problem, son. How may I help you?"

"Actually, I—" he paused. Would his father understand? Finally he admitted, "I wanted to hear your voice. I thought something might be wrong."

"Say no more, son," said the Admiral. "You're the one who inherited your grandfather's gift of intuition."

"Thanks," said Josh. "But I don't feel like it's much of a gift right now."

"Have you phoned your mother?"

"Yes, JonPaul said everything's fine at home."

"Then you must consider the others in your life, son," the Admiral advised.

"I don't even want to think about that," Josh admitted.

"For once, I hope your feelings are wrong," the Admiral confessed.

"Me, too. Thanks, Dad. I'll see you this evening."

"Good bye, son." The Admiral replaced the receiver and looked thoughtfully out upon San Diego bay from his office window. "Odd," he whispered under his breath. "The last time he telephoned to hear my voice, his grandfather had passed away." Bridger decided to check on his wife and her mother, regardless that Josh had indicated they were both fine. He pressed the intercom button at his elbow. "Will you telephone my wife?" he asked his secretary. "Let me know the moment she gets on the line."

Josh fumbled with the receiver for a moment. It couldn't possibly be Kayla, he thought as a lump of fear grew in his throat. He gulped, trying to swallow it, to no avail.

He knew Kayla was going cross country skiing with Mont and Sparky today. He doubted she would be back much before five. He dialed the number, and as he expected, there was no answer. He glanced at his watch again. He would have to wait at least an hour or two before he could expect her to return.

Still, the foreboding feeling that something terrible had happened to someone he loved made him edgy. He could imagine every sort of disaster conceivable. Perhaps she'd fallen off a cliff, or run into a tree, or maybe they were lost. He shrugged that thought away. Mont? Lost in the Uintah mountains? Never.

Josh hated this feeling. It was different from Saturday night when Kayla forgot to call him and had fallen asleep on the sofa instead. That night it was just one of those fleeting things: 'Oh, well, she was probably too tired by the time she arrived. I'll touch bases with her tomorrow.' The Saturday night in question, it was the sort of feelings one really doesn't worry about.

But now . . . he rubbed his face with both hands as if trying to rub away the emotions churning inside him. Now it was different. He didn't know how he knew. He just did. He intuitively knew that something was terribly wrong. And he had a fairly creative imagination, which made the feeling worse.

Impatiently, he paced around the lab, making a nuisance of himself. Finally he clocked out early and drove back home to the Marina Bay Club, where he headed for Bridger's Child on the run. Once on board Josh stripped and showered, scrubbing fitfully, but he couldn't shake the feeling within him. He dried off and dressed in his jogging pants and a light jacket.

Within minutes he was jogging along Shelter Island through the parking lots, from one end of the island to the other. After six trips around the island he did not feel any less restless so he stopped and sat down on the grass. Sweat poured from him and he wiped it off his face with his jacket sleeve.

From his viewpoint he could see across the bay to the Navy base. The Navy helicopters were beginning to patrol.

He glanced at his watch. Now five-thirty, it was already dark, and the time he would ordinarily be getting home from work. He pulled his cell phone out of his jacket pocket and dialed Mont's number. After nine rings he disconnected the call. "Surely she would be home by now," he said aloud.

He stood up and walked home to Bridger's Child. Once inside he dialed the operator from the boat phone.

"Directory Services," a pleasant voice answered.

"I need the phone number for Ed Sparkleman in Vernal, Utah," he requested.

"I have two listings for that name," said the operator.

"Give me both of them."

Joshua wrote down both telephone numbers on a piece of paper. He dialed the first number but received no answer. The second number forwarded the call to voice mail. He heard a man say, "This is Ed. I'm unable to take your call. Please leave a message at the tone."

Josh pressed the disconnect button in frustration.

The feeling of dread that had begun two hours earlier had not diminished in the least. If anything, he felt more apprehensive than ever.

He took another shower, dressed meticulously in military whites, then rushed out to the parking lot where he drove away in his white Toyota. En route to the Clark Estate, he dialed the three Utah numbers once again: The Bar M Ranch, and both Ed Sparkleman residences. Still, he received no answer. His watch indicated it was now 6:20 P.M. That would make it 7:20 at the Bar M Ranch.

It would be dark in Utah, probably black in the mountains, he worried. They should have been home from skiing at least two hours ago. Since he'd called steadily every fifteen minutes for the past several hours, he knew he hadn't missed them arriving home.

He'd listened to the weather reports, a snow storm had started to blanket eastern Utah, as promised by forecasters previously. If Kayla, Mont and Sparky were still on the mountain at this time of night, they would be caught in a blizzard.

WHERE ARE THEY??!!! he wanted to yell.

Realizing a serious panic had begun to control him, Josh shook his head and forced himself to focus on this evening and the party his mother had planned. He couldn't show up there in a dither. Especially after the phone call to his father. The Admiral would be particularly attentive tonight.

Finally he started analyzing reasons why Kayla, Mont and Sparky would not be at the ranch. He discarded all the excuses he could think of but one: Perhaps they had all gone into town to take in a movie or dinner. Surely by the time the party was over at his parent's estate, Kayla would be back at the lodge getting her feet rubbed by her father.

He held onto that hope. It was the only thought that could get him through the rest of the evening. Josh then did his utmost to drive away all thoughts to the contrary. He had to hold onto something, anything but what he could imagine might have happened on a lonely, snow packed slope in the Uintah Mountains.

# Chapter Seventeen

When Kayla awakened from a deep and comfortable sleep she tried to move but she couldn't. It's dark tonight, she thought sleepily, blinking her eyes, but she was still unable to see anything. Her body felt oddly contorted, almost compressed. For several seconds she had to think about her body before she began to understand her predicament.

She wiggled the fingers on her right hand and then her left. They seemed to move but they were icy stiff. "Why are my hands so cold?" she asked aloud.

Then she remembered the avalanche. "Dear God!" she gasped in a shocked plea to Heaven, "Do you know I've been buried alive??!"

Panic, her first instinct, was only overcome with desperate persuasion. She firmly and patiently talked her way out of a deep and terrible panic. "All right, Kayla, assess the situation and see what your options are," she told herself.

She moved her fingers once again and could not feel any pressure around them. "Hopefully, that means I'm vertical and my hands are above the snow's surface," she reasoned, knowing full well that, with the snow pressing in against her everywhere except her face, she could be standing on her head and not realize it. And in the darkness, there was no light source for which to seek.

She tried to move her toes but she couldn't even feel them. In fact, she couldn't feel much of anything below her shoulders except the sensation that she had become an insignificant object sandwiched by so much white snow there was no space left in which to feel anything.

"Dear God," she prayed in earnest. "Am I paralyzed? I can't feel anything below my shoulders!"

Another wave of panic hit her and she redoubled her efforts to remain calm. With some experimentation she could finally discern some feeling in her abdomen and middle back.

"I'm obviously still breathing," she said in an effort to assuage the second panic attack. She tried to expand her lungs but there was not enough space. "Shallow, but enough to stay alive," she whispered to herself.

Next she assessed her head and neck position. Fortunately her arms were crossed over her face, giving her a pocket of air. Her right elbow could move more than her left, and as she nudged it a little, she found she could almost stretch her right arm out straight and bring it back into a slight bend at the elbow again. She heard a far off whistling sound and thought it must be the wind howling down a canyon wall. At least she hoped it was the wind and not some creature of the night prowling around up there.

Moving her left arm was impossible. "Let's start with what you have," she told herself. "You have movement in your right arm and your right hand. What can you do with it?"

Immediately she moved her fingers enough, inside her gloved hand, to push the snow away from it. Slowly Kayla moved the snow away, inch by precious inch. She felt time pass as though it was crawling and it seemed to her that it took at least an hour before she could feel her left arm with her right hand. "Well, hello," she said to herself, as though making contact with a long lost friend. "Now we're getting somewhere."

Many more minutes of intense, concentrated digging in the hard, compressed snow, enabled her to uncover both arms above the elbows. She moved both forearms freely, bending them at the elbows, striving to discern whether or not either was injured. To her great relief, she felt no pain in either arm. She was now able to dig a little easier.

The next half hour went by slowly as Kayla dug the packed snow off her head. Every time she felt she was making progress, a mound of snow would fall in on top of her and she'd have to start over again. Another thirty minutes and she had her face completely unburied.

It wouldn't stay snow free for very long, Kayla decided as she felt big snow flakes settle across her cheeks and forehead. "That's reassuring," she sighed with a trace of sarcasm. "One hurdle down and another to go."

The new falling snow did not impede her vision, however, because it was pitch black outside and the top of her head was a good sixteen inches below the snow's surface. She had no more advantage in seeing the terrain than a gopher, hidden away in an underground tunnel, waiting for winter to pass. She couldn't even see the stars for all the dark clouds obscuring the sky above her.

Her greatest fear, now that her face was free and she felt relatively safe for the moment, was her concern for Mont and Sparky. "Dad!" She tried to call out, but she couldn't get enough air in her lungs to make it more than a feeble effort.

She would have to reach her back pack, she decided at once, if it was still on her back. She knew that Mont and Sparky, as well as herself, had carried an emergency whistle in their packs, just as readily as Ed had kept a whistle attached to his life preserver. For the first time in her life she was truly grateful her father, an Eagle Scout in his youth, had lived by the motto: Be Prepared! She began digging behind her, stretching her arms diligently to dig at the hard, almost brittle snow. Somehow she would have to get her whistle.

"It wouldn't hurt to have some light, either," she added aloud.

Kayla spent the next half hour trying to dig enough snow from the back of her head and shoulders until she could reach what she thought was a zipper. She couldn't undo it with her glove, however, so she removed the glove from her right hand and began to feel behind her head to where the zipper was. Unfortunately, it was the zipper to her parka hood. She sighed in exasperation.

Maybe if I remove the snow from my chest, an idea formed in her mind, I could bend forward and free my back pack. Courageously she started digging snow away from her neck and chest. Soon she ran out of places to put the snow. The piles around her were beginning to slide back down on her. Fresh, increasingly heavy snow flakes that the black sky kept dumping on her only impeded her progress. Every time she pushed the snow out of the way an equal amount seemed to return from another area.

After a while she finally felt some expansion in her lungs and she tried to call out again. "Dad! Sparky!" She listened for a response only to hear the faint echo of her own voice.

Kayla watched the hours pass by as she continued trying to move the snow around until she could finally bend forward, reach behind her and pull on her back pack. After some serious tugging, she was able to get it off her back and into the hole in front of her chest. Just those few inches along her spine gave her lungs a lot more breathing room.

Encouraged for the first time, she felt that if she continued digging, she could possibly free herself.

Inside the backpack Kayla found her head lamp and an even greater miracle, it still worked. She turned it on and held it in the air above her head, hoping the new snow would not bury it before someone could find her. She unbuckled the strap and slid the light to the end of it, letting it dangle freely. Then she took the strap in one hand and the light in the other. She tossed the light out of the hole, still hanging onto the strap. The headlamp came to rest at the edge of the hole she had dug.

By this time the new falling snow had almost buried the back pack so she brushed the snow off and removed the whistle from the pack. With all her might she blew into the mouthpiece. The whistle made a screeching, echoing sound. Kayla made it a point to blow on the whistle every three minutes as she continued trying to dig her way out.

Her fingers felt numb inside the gloves but she disregarded the sensation and continued digging relentlessly.

By the time Kayla had removed the snow in a circle around her, just past her waist, she discovered something terrible. It happened so quickly it took her by surprise and she was not the least prepared for it. As she lifted a handful of snow away from her right hip, she encountered an excruciatingly painful discovery. She was not paralyzed as she feared earlier that evening. An agonizing, hot flame of pain shot through her legs with horrendous impact. The realization of her true predicament was nothing short of a slow motion, bone-sawing nightmare. She heard an ear-piercing scream and realized, just before her body slumped limply into a complete faint, that the woman screaming was herself.

Mont continued his struggle up the steep mountain slope, searching for Kayla and Sparky. He'd been fortunate once again, having ridden the avalanche almost to its conclusion before his legs were buried to his waist. As soon as the slide stabilized, he worked his way free. The hot chocolate thermos had shattered on impact and he realized that the avalanche could have easily broken his back. His skis were useless, broken like twigs by the force of the snow. It would make travel difficult but his daughter and his lifelong friend were depending on him. How far back up the mountain they were, he had no idea. He started blowing on his whistle, three rapid successions, in 15 minute increments as he began the climb.

By nightfall he'd barely made a hundred yards, the heavy snow impeding his progress. Every time he took a step forward he'd sink back again. He finally worked his way over to the tops of some trees that were sticking out and used the branches as hand grips, both pulling his way up and pushing his way, whichever seemed best in the position of the moment. His head lamp was busted and he couldn't see a thing.

He could, however, feel the snowflakes hitting his face. Mont also felt the heavy weight as new snow collected on his shoulders. If he didn't find Kayla and Sparky soon, any sign they may have left regarding their whereabouts might well be buried until Spring. He shook that thought off immediately and continued on.

His eyes filled with tears and dripped down to his chin as he looked for signs of his loved ones. About halfway through the night he thought he heard a whistle some distance away.

At the same time he heard a familiar voice, one he'd heard many times before. His beloved wife, KayDawn, whispered to him anxiously. "To your left, Mont. Up and to your left." Mont immediately veered left, heeding the voice, knowing that KayDawn was still watching out for their Princess.

Within moments he saw a light that seemed to play for a moment on the forest wall. Encouraged, Mont headed for the light, brushing another load of snow off his shoulders as he did so. His lungs felt so frozen with the cold he could barely breathe, yet alone blow on the whistle.

That was when he heard his daughter scream. He'd heard it once before, in a less mature voice, the day she was bit by a rattlesnake that she'd tried to pull out of a hole in the ground. It was the most horrible sound he'd ever heard, even more frightening now because his little girl was no longer a child. She would not scream in such a manner without a good reason.

Mont rushed toward the source with all his might, putting forth more effort than he knew he had within him. It amazed him to realize that he had so much more energy waiting in reserve. He almost smiled as a new revelation settled upon him. The strength he felt did not come from within, it came from God.

"Look for the light," his spirit wife whispered, her voice sounded distinctly, not only in his ears but in his heart as well. "You'll find Kayla near the light."

Lamont looked, squinting his eyes to make his vision clearer. Then, off in the distance he saw a faint, motionless light. He rushed toward it and saw that it was a headlamp laying on a mound of snow. He rushed over to it, grabbed it up and pointed it toward the ground in a sweeping motion. His heart nearly failed him as he saw his unconscious daughter, half buried in a snow packed tunnel from which she had obviously been trying to free herself.

"Kayla!" Fresh tears stung at his eyes as he kneeled beside her.

Was he too late? Fear consumed him. Mont brushed fresh snow off her face and neck. He removed a glove and placed his hand against her carotid artery, feeling for a pulse. He sobbed all the more when he found one. It was a little thready but she was breathing steadily.

Opening the hot water thermos from his back pack, he poured a small amount into the cup. Then he held it to Kayla's lips and forced some of the warm liquid between her teeth. She swallowed and choked a moment before her eyes opened.

"Kayla!" he exclaimed. "Are you all right?" The fear in his voice was plainly obvious but he was so distraught he could not control it.

"My legs," she complained. "I think they're broken, Dad."

"What about your neck? Your back?" he asked anxiously.

"I can move my neck and shoulders and bend at the waist. It's just my legs. I think my shins are broken."

"I'll get you free, Princess," he comforted. I'll get you home."

"Where's Sparky?" she asked, tears filling her eyes.

"I haven't found him," said Mont. "But let's not worry about that right now. Let's take care of you and then I'm sure we'll find Sparky."

"No, Dad!" she gasped. "I think he's near me somewhere. The last thing I remember is..." she paused for a moment, remembering it all: the race for life down the mountain side; flying over the tree tops;

doing somersaults inside the moving snow; Sparky, beneath her, pushing her upward, ever upward; and last, but certainly not least, the angelic woman who crossed Kayla's arms in front of her face. She shuddered as she realized the woman's identity. "My mother," Kayla sighed. "She made me a breathing space. She followed the laws of nature, knowing I'd need that space so I could breathe."

Mont sighed aloud, "Your mother led me to you, Kayla. She's always watching out for us."

"And Sparky..." Kayla persisted. "He was pushing me up to the surface so I wouldn't be completely buried. Sparky was right there, Dad. He was right there, trying to save me."

Mont shined Kayla's light around the area and looked for signs that Sparky was nearby, but saw nothing obvious. "If Sparky's around here," he said, "I don't see any evidence of it. Let's get you free and stable. Then I'll look for him."

Fighting not only freshly falling snow, but snow impacted by the force of the avalanche, Mont could only dig away a small amount at a time.

Kayla's legs were wedged so tightly it took Mont several hours of digging to work her free without damaging her legs any worse than they were. He found one of her skis during the process and set it aside to use as a brace. Then he resumed the digging.

Every fraction of movement or pressure on her legs was excruciating and several times she fainted. Each time Mont would revive her with a little water. He soon realized they were getting nowhere fast as fresh new snow fell upon them steadily.

When he felt he had cleared enough snow away to finally lift her out of the deep hole, she couldn't tolerate the pain. She fainted once again. Mont lifted her out of the hole while she was still unconscious and stretched her body out flat on the snow, noticing her other ski, which had evidently been beneath her all the time.

Mont unzipped the left leg of her snow bibs to examine her injuries. The left leg was definitely broken, he decided, but it would mend. He zipped the left snow bib leg back up, then unzipped the right leg covering. Unprepared for what he saw there, he gasped. Small shards of bone were sticking through Kayla's legging and there was blood everywhere. He knew it would have to be made immobile while she was unconscious or they would never make it back to the ranch. He tied her right leg flat against the first ski, lashing her whole body up to her armpit to the ski. He would use the other ski against her left side, then lash both legs together. He would have to make the braces snug enough that her knees, ankles and hips could not be bent.

He slid down into the hole from which he'd dug her and tried to retrieve the ski that had been partially buried beneath her. He grabbed the ski and tugged on it but it wouldn't budge. He began to dig away at the snow until he'd enlarged the hole considerably. The ski was deeply imbedded in a horizontal position about two thirds the depth of the hole. When he had finally unburied most of the ski, he felt something strangely familiar frozen to the end of it. A lump of agony arose from deep within him as he dug more furiously than ever. The first thing Mont found was a glove. He tugged on it, removed it completely, and found Sparky's frozen hand still clutching the ski in a peculiar gesture, as though trying to push Kayla up with it, up to the surface and out of the snow, where she would have a chance to live.

Mont dug like a mad man to get Sparky free, but he knew, long before he even reached Sparky's face, that he was far too late. Great sobs consumed him as he cradled his friend's head in his big hands. Rocking back and forth on his knees, Mont wept softly, incessantly.

Kayla awakened to hear Mont crying. He was down in the hole from which he'd dug her free, sobbing as though his world had ended. She forced herself to turn her head and look back down into the hole. Mont was huddled over something. Then she realized it was not a thing. Rather, it was a special man, a hero. She heard his agonized voice as Mont stroked the lifeless hand.

"You did it, Partner," said Mont. "You saved her life. I'll get her home. Then I'll come back for you," he promised.

"Sparky?" Kayla fearfully questioned.

"He's gone, Princess," Mont whispered, the ragged words choking in his throat.

"No-o-o-o!" she screamed. "No-o-o-o!" Kayla felt her body shake with terror as she realized what Sparky had done for her. She remembered how she had seen Sparky pushing on her skis, pushing her up toward the surface of the moving snow. Tears coursed down the sides of her face as she wept for the loss of her dear, beloved Sparky.

Life, in all it's brutal reality, came rushing in upon her. Sparky had died trying to save her life. Yet he was the one who had insisted that in an avalanche the skier was to concentrate on staying alive first and seeking to help the others only after it was over. Sparky had gone against everything he'd ever taught her to do in such a situation.

Sparky and the angelic woman, her mother, had saved Kayla's life. Then the rational, scientific side of her tried to discard the memory of KayDawn appearing to her during the avalanche. A battle waged within Kayla, a war between her heart and her mind, when something deep inside her screamed rationality into an abrupt halt. It was a feeling she could neither analyze nor explain and it clamored to win Kayla's focus.

"She was my mother," Kayla whispered faintly. "My mother."

"What, Princess?" asked Mont as he stood up and turned to her. Tenderly he cradled her hand in his. "What about your mother?"

Kayla opened her moist eyes momentarily and tried to focus on Mont. She must tell him about her mother, but her voice seemed stuck in the back of her throat. Her lips trembled and she choked on the words she wanted to use. Then a deep and unexplainable feeling of peace and content settled upon her, more readily than the snow planting kisses all over her face. She closed her eyes and fell into a deep and blissful sleep.

The event completely unraveled Mont's emotions. He dropped to his knees in that awful white hole, bowed his head and began one of the most fervent prayers of his life. "Dear Father in Heaven, I am so thankful to thee for the life of my daughter, Kayla. Please don't take her home yet. If you need someone on the other side to help you out, I hope you'll consider taking me instead of her. She's young and has a lot of hope and promise now that she's engaged to marry Josh. I'm old and cantankerous, I know, but my spirit is strong and I would be a much better choice if you're thinking on calling anyone else from my family home tonight. I know you've got to do what you think is best, Father, but I've not asked for too much from you over the years. So if you'd grant this one request, I'd appreciate it. And thank you, Father, for giving me all these years with Sparky. He's been the best ranch hand and partner a fellow could ever have. He's helped me raise my little Princess and he's shared his four sons with me unselfishly. Next to

KayDawn and Kayla, he's the best thing that ever happened to me. One last thing, Father. I need the strength to get Kayla back, to get her the medical attention she needs. I know I can't do it alone, I'm going to need help. So if you'd care to send Sparky and KayDawn along to help me, I'd appreciate it."

Mont remained on his knees a few more minutes, feasting upon the sensations of the spirit. He felt Sparky's presence nearer to him than he'd ever felt before. From years of practice, he knew that KayDawn had been present long before he found Kayla. Satisfied that his prayer had not only been heard, but immediately answered, Mont allowed fresh tears to flow down his cheeks. Then he wiped his face with his gloved hands and began the tasks that lay ahead of him.

Chapter Eighteen

Ed kicked off his boots and stretched out upon the bed at his apartment. He'd just come from the airport where he'd pulled a double shift. It had been unexpected. At the last minute he'd filled in for a co-worker whose wife had a burst appendix. He'd expected to finish up his Christmas shopping after work last night, but not now. Everything was closed up tighter than a cinch on a saddle. He sighed as he glanced at the clock. It was already 1:30 A.M. Fortunately he wouldn't have to get back to work for another seven hours. And with the current winter storm bearing down on them, he doubted sky patrol would have anything to do tomorrow but monitor radio traffic.

He closed his eyes and fell into a deep sleep, not bothering to undress or crawl under the blankets on his bed.

The telephone jarred Ed into wakefulness. He grabbed it and rolled over on the bed, glancing at the clock. It read 2:00 A.M. "Yes," he grumbled.

"Is this Ed Sparkleman?" came a male voice on the other end.

"Yes."

"This is Josh Clark," said the voice. "I'm worried about Kayla and her father."

The mention of Kayla's name forced Ed into complete wakefulness, "Why?" he asked, tensing painfully. "What's happened?"

"I don't know that anything's happened," explained Josh. "It's just that I've been calling the ranch all night long and there's no response."

"Did you try Dad's place?" Ed asked, rubbing his belly.

"I couldn't reach anyone there, either," said Josh.

Ed sat up and rubbed his face vigorously, trying to rid the sleepiness from him., "Hold on a minute," he drawled. He stood and walked over to the bedroom window. Snow was still coming down, perhaps twice as hard as earlier. It looked like a white out storm if he'd ever seen one. "Hmm!" he said to himself. He went back to the phone. "There's a blizzard out, Commander Clark. The lines are probably down."

"Does that happen often?" asked Josh. He hadn't thought about the storm knocking the phone lines out, and as he heard the words, he searched his soul for a hint of softening. Still, the relentless fear that something was terribly wrong consumed him. From past experience, he had learned to trust his instincts.

"About every bad storm, I'd say," Ed replied. "As soon as it clears I'll try to reach them. If I do, I'll call you back."

Josh hesitated only for a moment. "I'll be flying into Hill Air Force Base soon. You'll have to use my cellular number."

Ed wrote down the number on a note pad by his bed. "I thought you weren't due in until tonight," observed Ed.

"I was able to catch an earlier flight through military channels," said Josh. "I'll try to rent a four-wheel drive truck or jeep in Layton and drive the rest of the way from there. Will the ranch road be open?"

"Nope," said Ed. "I'll have to take you up in my Li'l Posse."

"If it won't be too much of an inconvenience," said Joshua. "I would appreciate it."

"What time you expect to get here?" Ed asked.

"Around 0900 hours, if that will suit you."

"If you can get here by four wheeling," Ed warned. "The roads are liable to be treacherous."

"Oh, I'll get there," promised Joshua. "Will you be able to fly in a blizzard?"

"Nope," drawled Ed. "But a lot can change in five hours."

"I'll see you then," said Josh.

"Yeah," Ed responded. "Just check in at the airport. I'll be there on duty anyway." Ed hung up the phone. "Dang fool," he muttered.

He thought seriously about going back to bed, especially since he'd only been asleep half an hour, but a nagging thought persisted. There might be something wrong, he worried, regardless of the fact that he knew the Bar M Ranch phones went down regularly during a storm.

First Ed telephoned Sparky's number, then the Bar M. He could hear the lines ring in, but no one answered. Then he dialed a local telephone number and waited a moment. Before long he heard a sleepy voice say, "Sky Patrol, Keyser here."

"You out there sleeping on the job?" Ed teased.

"Almost," said Joe Keyser sheepishly, recognizing Ed's voice. "Things aren't any more lively than when you left here, Ed."

"Get on the radio and see if you can reach the Bar M, would you, Joe?"

"Sure, Ed. What's up?" Joe asked.

"Probably nothing," said Ed. "Will you keep trying to reach Mont until I get back to you? If you reach him, you call me back."

"Deal," said Keyser. "Talk to you soon."

Ed replaced the receiver, then went into the bathroom where he turned on the shower, stripped naked and climbed inside. He let the steam open his lungs and scrubbed his lean body from head to foot.

By the time he stepped out of the shower, Joe Keyser had not telephoned back and Ed began to get edgy. If Mont was at the ranch, he would have answered the radio signal by now. No one could have slept through the noise that new system made.

After toweling off, Ed slipped into fresh clothing and pulled on his boots. Then he put on his heaviest over coat and headed out to the truck.

The winter storm was in full swing, he realized as he headed west of town toward the airport. Although the plows had already been through the center of town, he knew they'd find just as much snow piled up on the return trip.

Within fifteen minutes Ed reached the Sky Patrol office at the airport. Joe Keyser frowned when he saw Ed open the door. "I thought you were going to call me back," Keyser complained.

"Sorry," grumbled Ed. "I thought I'd better come out here and help. I won't be able to sleep now."

"What's the scoop?" Joe asked.

"Don't know," said Ed. "Kayla's fiancé phoned and said he'd been trying to reach the Bar M all evening. No one answers and he's worried."

Ed walked over to the space heater and rubbed his cold hands together to warm them. He spent the next hour trying to raise Sparky or Mont on the telephone while Joe tried to reach them on the radio, both to no avail. What concerned him was that it sounded like the phone was ringing in. Usually when the lines went dead they'd get a busy signal, as if someone were using the telephone.

Ed knew he could always get through to the ranch via the airport radio with its high output tower antennae. Although Keyser consistently radioed out to the Bar M, he received nothing back in response.

Hill Air Force Base sits on top of a massive hill between the Wasatch Mountain Range and the Great Salt Lake. Military planes arrive irregularly throughout the day and night. Josh arrived at Hill Air Force Base by six in the morning.

It's Christmas Eve Day, thought Josh wearily as he stepped off the plane. He hadn't slept or eaten since noon the previous day and his body was beginning to show the first signs of exhaustion. He knew, however, that he could physically endure far more sleepless nights and days and very little food, if he had to. What he could not endure was the ache within his heart as he worried about his beloved Kayla. Certainly his thoughts fleetingly dwelled on Mont and Sparky periodically, as well, but his main focus was the woman who had stolen his heart away more than two years previous.

Having no formal background in religion, he'd been taught at his mother's knee to believe in God, and he did with all his might. Since the feeling of dread had come over him yesterday, he had carried a prayer in his heart, one that he'd uttered both silently and aloud, when he could do so with some privacy. He asked God repeatedly to protect Kayla and her family, to spare her and allow them to marry and raise a family together, had been his constant plea.

Arriving at the military base, he went directly to the Procurer's Office where he was identified immediately. Josh realized the Admiral must have had a hand in expediting his affairs on base.

A crisply attired Air Force Private met him with a proper salute. Josh returned the salute, then offered a brief, "At ease, Private."

"Yes, sir," came the response. "We have a four wheel drive Ford Bronco standing by for you, sir. Will you need a driver?"

"No," said Josh. "I'll drive."

"Very well, sir," said the Private. "Your keys and map, sir."

"Thank you. I suppose Admiral Clark vouched for the Bronco?"

"Yes, sir."

"Will you relay the message back to the Admiral that I arrived on base safely and that I appreciate his intervention in my behalf?" asked Josh.

"Straight away, sir. And good luck." The Private saluted him once again.

Josh responded in kind. Within minutes he was headed toward Ogden in the Bronco, where he would pick up Interstate 84. He knew the drive would take at least three hours under good conditions and he prayed that would be the case.

Unfortunately, the weather had other plans. By the time he reached the turnoff to Interstate 80 and headed toward the Heber cut off, large snowflakes were playing havoc with his visibility.

Near Heber he telephoned Sky Patrol, hoping Ed would be there. To his relief, Ed answered the call.

"It's Josh," came the worried response. "Any word?"

"No," Ed drawled. "The Bar M doesn't respond to radio or telephone, Josh."

"Is it snowing there?"

"In buckets," Ed replied. "Weather reports say it won't clear up until noon or later. Where are you?"

"I'm at Heber, about to head out of town."

"Well, fill up with gas before you go any further," Ed told him. "If you end up in a spin out, it could take hours for an emergency crew to reach you."

"Will do," said Josh.

"And don't hurry," warned Ed. "We won't be able to get in the air until the storm lifts. Sky Patrol won't let us go up until then."

"I'll be careful," sighed Josh, frustrated at the stormy weather.

Ed heard the uneasiness in Josh's voice and added, "I'll bet the lines are just down. That's happened before, you know."

"I know," said Josh. "I'm praying for that."

"So are we," comforted Ed. "So are we."

Josh turned the Bronco around and headed back toward Heber. He stopped at a small filling station and topped off the gas tank, grabbed a bottle of spring water and headed out again. He didn't feel hungry but he knew he would need to keep up his liquid intake so that he didn't become a risk himself.

How he hated the waiting. Even though he was driving the Bronco toward Vernal and had been involved in travel coordinating, he still felt like he'd been in limbo ever since yesterday afternoon. He couldn't explain why he'd felt so certain something was wrong. He only knew that he did, and now he would have to find out why he still felt so anxious. If something had happened to Kayla, he doubted he would be able to forgive himself for not coming with her. He'd had a feeling that he should have gone with her, but had pushed it aside, considering her feelings and Mont's before his own. That was Josh. He seemed always to place other people's needs and wants ahead of his own.

Now he made a promise to himself. When he finally reached Kayla he was going to persuade her to marry him much earlier than May. Tomorrow wouldn't be soon enough, he decided. He couldn't live the lonely existence he'd been living any longer. He wanted to protect her, comfort, cheer, encourage her, and love her forever. He wanted to come home and find her living in the same place he did. He didn't think, after enduring all this worry about where she was and what may have befallen her, that he could endure another day without her by his side. She had become a part of him, and without that part he was just an empty shell with no purpose, and no reason for being.

His mind was so wrapped up in Kayla that he couldn't take proper note of the beautiful scenery surrounding him. Passing through a portion of Uintah National Forest, he didn't notice the frozen condition of Strawberry or Starvation Reservoirs. He just kept his eyes on the road as the windshield wipers swished a clear line of vision past the snowflakes. Traveling was slow, the roads slippery and snow packed, regardless of the road crews efforts to keep it cleared.

It took Josh almost three hours to reach Roosevelt from Heber. Another thirty miles or so and he would reach his destination. He stopped long enough to fill up the Bronco once again. Then he was back on Highway 40 headed toward Vernal.

Half of the journey he'd spent offering vocal prayer to his Father in Heaven, pleading for the safety of Kayla and her family. The other half he'd worried how he would ever live without her, if something terrible had happened to her.

# Chapter Nineteen

The next time Kayla gained consciousness, she was bundled up under some tree branches with a silver emergency blanket. It was already dawn. A small, smoky fire gave off a glorious amount of heat but she could easily see that the storm had dumped at least an extra two or three feet of snow. It was still snowing, she noticed, but not nearly as hard as last night.

She didn't know where she was, but she knew that Mont was nearby because she could hear the sound of a hatchet hacking away at some wood. She tried to lift her head to see where Mont was exactly, but she couldn't because her head felt heavy, as though she were sedated. She noticed that Mont had completely immobilized her from the waist down by using her two skis and half of another, probably Sparky's.

"Dad," she whispered hoarsely.

Almost immediately Mont was by her side. "I'm right here," he comforted. "How are you feeling?"

"Rough," she admitted. "I'm having trouble breathing, Dad."

"I know," he said. "I listened to your lungs. You've probably got pneumonia from exposure."

"I'm not running a fever," she told him, lifting her hand to feel her forehead with her wrist.

"Not yet," he agreed.

"Dad, what did you do with Sparky?" she asked. "We can't just leave him here. The wolves will get him."

"I took from him what we would need to keep you alive," he confessed. "Then I buried him right there in that pitiful hole. I left his broken ski standing upright with my red neckerchief attached to it. Right before we leave, I'll sprinkle those Jell-O packets all over the area so we can find him easier from the air."

"Shouldn't we stay with him?" she asked. "Isn't that what the survival manual says?"

"Stay in one place is the normal rule," he answered. "But no one will even know we're missing until Ed brings Josh and his folks up to the ranch tonight. By then it'll be too dark to start a search party. Even with Sky Patrol covering the normal grid formations, it's going to be at least noon or later, tomorrow, before they find the Jell-O tracings, and that's if the snow stops and the storm lifts."

"I can't walk," she pressed her hand against his arm, knowing what he was planning to do.

"I can." He turned away from her and finished cutting off the branches of a young aspen tree. "I figure if I use those snow shoes I've made for me and the stretcher you'll be on, and taking into account the snow drifts once the wind picks up, we ought to be able to make the lodge by midnight or a little after. That's at least twelve hours earlier than the first possible moment that they even stand a chance of finding us."

"That's only twelve hours, Dad. Maybe we should wait it out."

"Kayla, your right leg looks bad," he admitted, refusing to look at her, unable to endure the pain he would see when she heard the news. "I'm not going to sugar coat it for you, Princess. With your lungs developing something dangerous, it's going to take oxygen away from your extremities, the perfect situation for gangrene to set in. The sooner we get you on antibiotics, the best chance you're going to have of keeping your leg."

"Let me look at it," she said bravely.

"It ain't pretty," he warned.

She gave him her most determined look.

"All right." He helped her sit up. Then he unzipped her blood soaked right legging. He had not removed the legging liner. Rather, he had split it open in order to dress her wounds, but had pinned it back together, Kayla realized, so he could keep pressure on the leg as it swelled. And it was swollen, she realized as he removed the elastic wrap, if only for a moment.

Kayla studied the leg carefully. It was definitely broken. She could see bone fragments poking out through the skin in several places along the shin. Mont was right, she decided ruefully. Her right leg didn't look good at all.

Mont lowered her head back down and redressed her leg, pulling the inner legging liner tight, then pinning it to keep it secure. Then he zipped her bib leg closed.

"The left one," she said, "hurts almost worse than the right."

He frowned and Kayla knew what he was thinking. "That ain't so good," he told her. "The left one's busted in one place but it's not poking through the skin anywhere. I was able to set it nicely while you were unconscious."

Kayla assessed the situation. With both legs broken and the possibility of gangrene festering, she knew it was imperative to get medical care as quickly as possible, but there was also Mont's heart condition to consider. They were miles from the ranch in fresh snow. The strain may be too much for him. Yet she saw the look of anxiety on his rugged face. She was his only child, his Princess. He would never stay put and disregard her needs over his own. She sighed heavily.

If anything happened to Mont en route to the ranch she didn't know how she could endure it. So Kayla offered a silent prayer, this time believing it would reach its destination. 'Dear God, it's me again. I know that you sent my mother to protect me during the avalanche. Will you send her again to protect Dad as he tries to drag me home. Please.'

For the first time in more than a dozen years Kayla felt complete and content. Intuitively she sensed that a greater power than her own was working for her good. She would now have to place her trust in God to get her and Mont through the trials that lay ahead of them.

"Let's go," she said finally. "I guess we've got no choice."

"I'm going to offer a word of prayer first," he told her. "I gave you a Father's Blessing but an extra prayer isn't going to hurt."

Kayla nodded. Mont bent and offered a prayer as sweet as any she'd ever heard. She felt warm inside and hopeful they would make it to the lodge before it was too late.

Josh arrived in Vernal around 10:30 that Christmas Eve morning. Ed was waiting for him at the airport. Josh brushed the snow off his parka before he entered the Sky Patrol building.

"Commander Clark," Ed nodded.

"Call me Josh," came the quick response.

"I understand your concern," Ed told him immediately. "I haven't been able to raise Pa on the radio or the phone. It's unusual. Mont wired the place eight months ago so that any emergency can be reported, from or to the ranch. They installed a whole new system right after Morning Sun—" Ed paused.

"It's all right," said Josh. "Kayla told me about it. She was devastated."

"Yeah. Well, they ought to be answering."

"When do you expect the storm to clear?" asked Josh.

"Another hour or two. Sky Patrol has us grounded until it lets up but the second they clear us to go, we're out of here."

"In the meantime?" asked Josh.

"We wait," Ed answered. "And keep trying to get through on the radio."

Josh sighed. The feeling that something was terribly wrong had nearly driven him to the edge of insanity ever since it first began eighteen hours ago. And now, to have to wait for a storm to pass before he could even get up to the lodge was almost more than he could tolerate. He stuffed his hands in his coat pockets and walked outside.

Ed watched him through the window.

When Josh reached the truck he kicked the tire and cursed.

"I know just how he feels," whispered Ed. "But it ain't only Kayla I'm worried about." He debated whether or not to telephone William up at Dutch John, then he decided against it. He didn't want to give Tom another reason to open up a bottle, not until he knew for sure there was a problem.

By the time the snow finally stopped falling, Mont had pulled Kayla on the makeshift stretcher nearly halfway up the far side of

Porcupine Ridge, forming a neat switch back trail behind them. The higher up they traveled, the easier it was to see the devastation caused by the avalanche. A huge path of tall douglas firs had been knocked down like bowling pins. The stark cliff area just beyond where they had skied yesterday appeared more brittle and rugged from the uprooted trees now buried in a mountain of snow at the edge of the valley below it.

Kayla could easily see the Jell-O marker Mont had made to locate Sparky's body. The red dye had spread and gave a bright pattern, easily recognizable to any plane overhead. She knew as soon as the weather cleared and Sky Patrol was notified, they would be able to find Sparky's body. She sighed with relief. Sparky would be able to have a decent burial. She couldn't imagine how the boys would endure losing Sparky, nor how she and Mont were going to live with the memories of what had happened.

She thought that, as bad as her legs had hurt before Mont brought her up out of that hole, they should be agonizingly painful now. However, Kayla's lungs hurt worse than her legs. She coughed and could hear a deep rattling sound in her chest that frightened her. Pneumonia was something she'd never experienced before and she didn't know what to expect.

Mont didn't say much. He kept his eyes focused on the next ten yards and when that distance was covered he looked to the next ten. That was the only way he would ever be able to get Kayla home. He refused to think about the cold, wet snow or the rigorous climb, the threatening weather or the gnawing hunger deep within his raw and burning stomach.

As long as Kayla could look at the foot of the stretcher and see a little bit of progress every few minutes, she felt confident they would make it. In her anxiety over her father's health, she insisted he stop to rest periodically, regardless of his protests. If he could strive to protect her, she should be able to reciprocate.

Truth be known, thought Mont, he probably wouldn't have made it this far without those little rest stops.

The heavy propeller blades whipped the air about them as Ed ascended up above the airport. It was well after one in the afternoon and they had just received clearance to take Li'l Posse up to the Bar M ranch. Josh was strapped in beside him and Ed glanced over at him for a moment on the way up. To his point of view, Ed thought, Josh looked terrible. He tried to draw an analogy in his mind but Josh's expression was worse than death, he decided. The man must be so crazy mad in love with Kayla that he's become a part of her. Even Ed, in his worst and darkest hour over losing Kayla, had still been able to function. In direct contrast, Josh seemed totally devastated. It relieved Ed, somewhat, to see the condition Josh was in, for he knew he would never have to worry about her as long as she had Josh by her side. The thought unsettled Ed for a moment and he pondered on it long and hard.

Soon they were skimming over the tops of the trees on their way to the Bar M ranch. "You really love Kayla Dawn," Ed observed quietly, though why he'd chosen this line of questioning he didn't know.

"More than my own life," Josh answered, wringing his hands through his thick hair.

"I'm glad to see it," said Ed. He wondered where these feelings were coming from. Hadn't Kayla been the woman he'd almost proposed to, again, just two days ago? Yet he found himself genuinely pleased that Kayla had found someone who loved her so much. He began to question his own feelings for Kayla as he watched Josh suffer for her.

"Coming from you, Ed," Josh responded, "that means a lot to me. I know you wanted Kayla to reconsider, we talked about it on the telephone two nights ago."

"You did?" Ed wondered aloud, surprised that Kayla had confided in him.

"Yes," answered Josh. "We tell each other everything."

Ed nodded. "Hmm," came his subtle response. "Then tell me, Josh. You love Kayla and you're planning to marry her. What if she came to you today and said, 'Josh, I want to go back to school. I want another two doctorates and it'll take at least another four to six years. Will you wait for me?' What would you do?"

Josh smiled faintly and it made Ed feel good that he'd been the cause of it. "I see where you're going with this," Josh admitted. "But the answer is simple. If she wasn't ready to marry now, I'd wait until Heaven fell from the sky in order to marry Kayla. First, however, I'd try to persuade her to marry me AND go back to school at the same time. With my background, I could help her with her studies, be her mentor as well as her husband."

Ed's voice softened. "Then you DO love her."

"I didn't realize there was any doubt of that," Josh said soberly.

"No, I don't mean to throw you off," Ed hurried on. "It's just, I've always thought I was the only one who could love her enough and protect her enough. Now I find out that, not only would you wait until she's ready for you, it's possible you may love her more than I do. Believe me, Josh, that's a sobering thought." He nodded his head thoughtfully as the idea struck him and bounced around inside him for a moment.

"Maybe it's not the amount of love that you feel for Kayla," Josh suggested carefully, "but rather why you love her that's most important."

"Now that's another thought all together," drawled Ed. "You may be onto something there."

Josh wanted to say more but thought to himself that he'd probably pressed Ed as far as he dared for the moment. Sometimes silence is a better friend than conversation.

Ed watched carefully around him at the storm clouds. The snow had nearly stopped and they were only a few moments away from the ranch now. Hopefully they would arrive and find that everyone was well and healthy, but as he studied Josh's demeanor over the last couple of hours, he knew that the man was intuitive. And that thought scared him most of all.

He also knew that Josh had been trying to say something important to him about the way Ed loved Kayla. If it's not how much he loved her, then maybe he should consider why he loved her. What kind of love did Ed have for her?

Lust came to mind immediately, a topic he'd learned a lot about over the past seven years. However lust came in a fleeting moment of passion. Astonishingly enough, Ed had learned that some of the most important considerations in relationships, in addition to the physical bonding that couples share together, had to do with selflessness, compatibility, similar interests and faithfulness.

Love, too, was an elusive element because there are so many kinds: A child has a special bond for his parents, and the flip side of that coin occurs when parents love their child. Siblings shared a different kind of love, altogether, as well as grandparents for grandchildren.

Then there was true, romantic love, heart wrenching, gut wringing, night sweating love that consumed a person so much they could never be the same. Ed was not fool enough to think that romantic love was fueled only by sex. Hopefully, real love made a person better. It forced them to look beyond themselves to someone else, making them selfless and empathetic, joyful, powerful and, during a crises, miserable at the same time. This is the kind of love he had seen from Josh.

He suddenly realized that the love he'd felt for Kayla all these years was strong and powerful, but not like he'd seen from Josh. However, one thing Ed knew with all his heart and soul was that he loved Kayla. He had always loved her, and even after she married Josh, he would still love her. He reasoned that this knowledge left him with only one question. What kind of love was it? Unfortunately, that was a question for which he had no easy answers.

"There it is!" Josh said anxiously as he pointed out the rooftop of the lodge.

"Yep," said Ed as he lowered the helicopter toward the helipad. It was buried in several more feet of snow since he'd been there Tuesday. He hesitated for a moment, letting the wind from the blades blow the snow away from the helipad before he touched down. Ed shut the helicopter down, and with the propeller blades still spinning, both Josh and Ed left the helicopter and headed toward the lodge, wading through snow up to their thighs to get there.

While Josh was brushing some of the snow off his pants, Ed used his key to unlock the front door, a painful reminder of the attack on Morning Sun. Before then, the ranch had never known a lock. "They're not home," he announced before they went inside. "Otherwise the door would have been unlocked."

"How are we to know whether they've been here at all since yesterday?" asked Josh, concern etched deeply in the lines on his forehead.

"Bessie will be able to tell us," said Ed.

Josh remembered the milking schedule from when he'd been there fifteen months earlier.

Ed ran up the stairs to the bedrooms, calling Mont and Kayla to no avail while Josh searched the main floor. Then the two men plowed through snow almost to their waists, through the snow drifts the helicopter blades had created, in order to get to the barn. Ed pulled open the door and went inside, Josh following close behind him.

Bessie was lying on her side, her teats engorged worse than he'd ever seen. "Do you remember how to milk her?" asked Ed.

"I can try," Josh answered. "Is that important just now?"

"She could die if you don't get some of the pressure off," instructed Ed. "I'll get the tractor out and plow a path to the cabin, see if I can find anyone there. If not, I'll call Sky Patrol and get a grid started."

"Is there a bucket?" Josh asked.

Ed nodded toward the wall where a large plastic bucket hung. "Don't drink it," he said, going out the door. "By now it's liable to be full of bacteria."

Josh turned to ask another question but Ed had slipped out the door and down to the next set of doors. Josh grabbed the bucket and started hand expressing milk from Bessie's teats. She bellowed and cried and kicked until Josh got her on her feet. Then he maneuvered her head into the stanchion so she couldn't get away. He coaxed and soothed her with his voice as he worked diligently to drain as much milk from her as possible. He heard the tractor start up and knew that Ed was on his way.

When Ed reached the cabin he braked the tractor hard, right at the door, jumped off and let himself inside with a key. "Pa!" he yelled, searching each room. The cabin was empty, as he had expected.

He went into the kitchen where a little desk stood in one corner. A modern radio stood waiting for him. He flipped a few switches and barked into the microphone. "This is the Bar M Ranch calling Sky Patrol. Come back."

A second of static and then the voice of Sheriff Heartwell came clearly over the speaker. "This is Sky Patrol, Bar M Ranch, is that you Ed?"

"Yes," replied Ed. "We've got a situation up here. Kayla, Pa and Mont went cross country skiing yesterday morning and they haven't been seen or heard from since. Over."

"I'll lay out a grid and get back to you. Over."

"I got Li'l Posse up here along with Kayla's fiancé. We're going to start on the western grid right away. Over."

"Roger that, we're on our way. Sky Patrol out."

Ed turned swiftly and hurried back to the tractor. He spun it around and headed back to the barns. By the time he got there, Josh had a bucket full of milk and Bessie was mooing like a satisfied customer. "Looks like you got the hang of it," observed Ed.

Josh continued expressing milk while Ed talked. "I've got to phone Will and let him know what's going on. He can notify the others. Then I'll grab some gear and meet you back at the helicopter. I guess you're familiar with rescue procedures?"

"Yes," Josh answered. "I am."

Within minutes they were airborne once again. "We're taking the western grid," Ed explained. "We've only got four planes so we'll cover west, southwest, west, northwest, and repeat the rotation every tenth of a mile."

"I'll man the binoculars," nodded Josh.

Before long, the radio was alive with air traffic. Sky Patrol, true to its promise, had planes starting from the Bar M Ranch and working outward on north, south and east grids.

The worst problem they faced was the dense, puffy clouds that wanted to lay right along the ground. Cumulus had a way of sleeping over the mountain tops and along the valley floors at this altitude. With the obscured vision, they would be lucky to find anything of importance.

Chapter Twenty

By four in the afternoon, Mont reached the summit of Porcupine Ridge. Although it had not snowed much since noon, the clouds were still thick and heavy. They had been trying to reach the top when a cloud had rolled over them, completely obscuring them from view. He thought he heard a plane about the same time, which surprised him, but he couldn't see anything. If a search party had been called out, he was sure they would never see them under the current conditions.

At least Kayla is sleeping, he thought, looking back at his daughter. Her face is so pale, though. She lost a lot of blood from the cuts in her right leg while she lay buried in the avalanche. Mont found evidence of it, but he did not tell her. She was distraught enough.

If he could only rest a little while, he thought, and laid down in the snow next to Kayla's stretcher. He tenderly touched her forehead to see whether or not she was feverish. A frown knitted across his brow.

"I'm burning up," she whispered, unwilling or unable to open her eyes. He couldn't decide which.

"You're a little warm," he agreed.

"We're at the top now, aren't we?" she asked.

"Yes, we've reached the summit."

"Why don't you go on without me?" she asked. "I'm too heavy. I'm wearing you down."

"I'll be fine," he assured her.

But Kayla persisted stubbornly. "There aren't any trees up here. I'll be easily seen from the air. You could make it back to the ranch in three hours if you hurried."

"What about the wolves?" he asked her. "I wasn't satisfied leaving Sparky until I'd dug the hole deeper. How am I supposed to bury you?" He rubbed her hand. "You're tough, Kayla, you're going to make it through this."

"I'm tired," she whispered. "I just want to sleep."

"Look at me," he insisted with growing concern.

Kayla opened her eyes. They no longer seemed brown to him. More like a gray brown. Her sleepiness worried him.

"It's hypothermia," he told her. "You must fight it, Kayla. You must try to stay awake."

"I'm trying, Dad," she whispered hoarsely.

"Then sing!" he demanded. "Come on, I'll help you."

He started singing nursery rhyme songs that she'd learned back when she was a toddler. "Sing, Kayla. Isn't Commander Joshua Bridger Clark worth fighting for? You want him to be a widower before he ever marries you?"

The thought of Josh spurred Kayla on. He would be devastated if she died. "I'm not going to die," she told Mont stubbornly. "I'm going to live and marry Josh and have a meadow full of children."

Mont smiled. "You read your baby book. That's good. Now you must sing with me. Come on." He lifted the top portion of the stretcher and started down the other side.

As they traveled down the south slope, Kayla sang with him. They sang every song she could ever think of, and by the time they reached the bottom of Porcupine Ridge, it was dark.

Mont's energy was spent. He knew he could not hold out much longer. His chest felt like a thousand-pound vice was wringing the life out of him. How could he possibly go on? He gently placed the head of the stretcher against a boulder near a thicket of dense pine trees so that Kayla could see a little better. Then he gathered her into his arms and held her to keep them both warm.

"Dad, you're sweating and pale," she complained.

"I'll be fine," he insisted. "I just need to rest a little while. Here, I'll set the alarm on my watch for twenty minutes. As soon as it goes off, we'll begin again."

She readily agreed. She'd been singing so long her voice was hoarse and her throat hurt. They drank the last of the warm water and let the thermos slide off the stretcher and into the snow. Then they both fell blissfully asleep.

Josh and Ed maintained a tight-lipped vigil in the helicopter as they completed their grid. They'd been in the air almost seven hours, with exception of refueling and checking back at the ranch at half hour intervals, in case Kayla, Mont or Sparky showed up there. Christmas Eve had fallen upon them unbidden, for they didn't want the pitch black night to impede their progress even more. Visibility had been poor to terrible all day. Regardless of the obstacles, several members of Sky Patrol were still anxiously engaged in the search for Kayla, Mont and Sparky.

Josh glanced at his watch, it was almost 9:00 P.M. He nervously kept his night scope binoculars focused on the surrounding terrain, but the only thing they had seen all day were clouds, fog, and the tops of a few pine trees when the cumulus would thin a little. Wearily he hoped the search would not be called off for the night. He couldn't imagine going back to the lodge and waiting there until dawn, empty handed. He marveled at the dedication of the Sky Patrol members, their families waiting at home for the Christmas festivities while they continued flying in grid patterns through heavy skies.

William and Tom, unable to help in the air search, talked with the county commissioner and got permission to clear the road to the ranch with county equipment. They could have asked Ed to bring them up and use the Bar M tractor, but they didn't want to deter Ed from his search with Sky Patrol. As Tom and Will manned the county's tractor, they scooped huge buckets of snow off the Bar M road on their way up the mountain side. The snowfall had been particularly wet and heavy, making progress difficult. They were only three miles up the gravel road and would not reach the ranch until dawn at their current rate of progress, but they were both stubborn and would not give up digging any more than their brother, Ed, would give up searching from the skies. Tenacity was a trait ingrained in all of them.

Bridger and Sarah Clark had arrived in Vernal shortly after dark. Bridger suggested they rent a motel room in Vernal until in the morning. By then the roads would be cleared and they could drive up in

Josh's rented Bronco. Besides, they had no way to get up to the Bar M Ranch until Ed came after them in his helicopter. And he was working with Sky Patrol in the search.

When Sky Patrol called the search off at 9:30 P.M., Ed sighed wearily. "We have to comply," he told Josh. "I could be grounded if I don't."

"I know," said Josh. "I just wish we knew which direction they went. There must be a dozen ways from the ranch to go cross country skiing."

"That is a problem," said Ed. "But even if we knew, without the clouds lifting some, it's still the proverbial needle in the haystack."

Suddenly Josh remembered, "Say, Kayla mentioned the other night that she and Mont had taped their whole evening together when she unwrapped her mom's hope chest. Maybe they talked about the ski trip."

"It's worth a try," said Ed as he maneuvered the helicopter back toward the lodge.

"Sky Patrol," he said, pressing the radio button, "This is Li'l Posse, over."

"This is Sky Patrol," came a voice.

"We're going back to the ranch, should you hear anything, over." Ed's voice sounded encouraged.

"Copy that, Li'l Posse. We'll keep in touch," came the response.

Within moments Ed landed the helicopter on the helipad at the ranch and shut it down. Together Ed and Josh pushed their way through the deep snow back to the lodge. Once inside, they located the video in question and started rewinding it.

"You go ahead and start it without me," said Ed. I've got to milk Bessie, feed the horses and work a few miracles with the tractor so that we can get around a little easier out there. If they say anything of importance, come on out and flag me down."

"Will do," said Josh, impatiently waiting for the video to rewind.

Finally he heard the click and the video stopped. He pressed the play button on the remote and sat down in Mont's big, stuffed leather chair. Watching the special evening between Kayla and her father made Josh feel, at first, like an intruder, even though he knew Kayla would show it to him eventually. He knew he had to listen to every word carefully in case they mentioned anything, however casual it may seem, about where they were going to ski.

He knew he'd been assigned the wrong job within five minutes of viewing the video. Just seeing Kayla again, knowing the predicament she must be in at that very moment, was almost more than he could take. He felt mesmerized by her grace and beauty, even on film. She was such a tender, gentle person. And she loved her mother dearly, he realized, watching her shed tears as she learned that KayDawn had hand-stitched a quilt covered with sailboats and sea life. He heard the door close about two-thirds through the tape and realized Ed had joined him, but he was so wrapped up in the video that he couldn't take his eyes off it, nor acknowledge Ed's presence.

Kayla had just picked up a manila envelope and asked Mont, "What's this?"

Ed sat down on the sofa opposite Josh. "Anything?" he asked, wondering whether or not to hope.

"No," said Josh holding up a finger as though asking Ed to be quiet for just a few more minutes.

Ed soon found himself just as wrapped up in the video as was Josh, learning quickly that Mont had no intention of selling the ranch, he would leave it all to Kayla when he died. Then Ed was surprised to learn that Kayla had gone to bat for him, telling Mont, "You didn't see the look in his eyes today as he talked about the ranch and his love for it. If you and Sparky do retire, promise me you'll talk to Ed first before you turn the ranch over to anyone else."

"Are you sure, Princess?" Mont questioned. "It seems to me—"

"I'm positive. He's always dreamed of taking over when you two are ready, and I don't think that dream has ever changed."

Mont gave her a broad smile. "Well, then that's what I'll do. That would make me rest easy, knowing Ed was here to manage the ranch. I just assumed he wasn't all that interested in it anymore."

"Trust me," Kayla encouraged.

Ed sighed as he realized she had protected his interest in the ranch for him, and he hadn't even asked her, nor would he have. Pride still carried him a long ways, he admitted.

Soon Mont was asking her, "Do you know for certain that you love Josh?"

Josh pressed the pause button. "Hmm," he observed. "This could put one of us in the hot seat."

"I'm ready," replied Ed, still pleased at the way Kayla had almost insisted Ed be the first consideration for ranch manager.

Josh shrugged. "So am I." He pressed the play button again and delighted in the ear to ear smile Kayla gave Mont in response to his question.

"Yes," she answered, and when she did the words sounded like sweet music. "I love Josh more than I've ever loved anyone."

"Hmm," Mont teased, "a father could get jealous over a statement like that."

"It's a different kind of love, Dad, you know that," she punched him playfully in the arm.

"If memory serves," said Mont. "Tell me the difference between the way you love Ed and the way you love Josh. Do you understand what I'm asking?"

It took a while before Kayla had explained her feelings between Ed and Josh. Finally she finished the conversation with, "I do love Ed. I love him with all my heart, but I love him as I would if he were my brother."

"And Josh?" Mont asked. "You really do love him, don't you Princess?"

"Josh and I complement each other," said Kayla. "We're totally compatible. He's understanding. He never yells at me. He tries to see the world from my perspective and I do the same for him. Yet there's also the passion," she confessed.

Suddenly Josh sensed the great longing for him that she really had and the feeling quite unsettled him.

Kayla continued, "I ache, Dad. I physically ache for Josh. When we're apart, I wander around like a lost puppy. If there is a God, if there is a Heaven like I want to believe, I think that Josh and I must have known and loved each other there because what we have transcends anything tangible on this earth."

Josh pressed the pause button. "Are you all right," he asked Ed, concerned for the man Kayla considered her brother.

"This is what you were trying to tell me," Ed realized aloud. "Kayla and me, we love one another as siblings."

"On her part, anyway," said Josh, hopeful that Ed would consider carefully his position.

Ed nodded but said only, "Please, continue with the video."

Josh pressed the button, disappointed that he could see nothing evident in Ed's manner or voice that would indicate whether or not he could reciprocate the kind of love Kayla had offered him.

That was when Josh realized that playing this video for Ed was a total mistake. He had forgotten all about Kayla's concern for Sparky when the day arrived that Sparky would learn about Tom's involvement in Morning Sun's assault. In horror Josh watched as Kayla said, "I'm so worried about Sparky. What is he going to do when the truth comes out about Tom?"

"Now, that is a question," said Mont. "That day in the meadow when I passed out... I'd been stewing about Tom's involvement and how it would affect Sparky... and look what happened."

"Then you've sensed my concern," said Kayla. "What about Sparky? What will this do to him?"

"I wish I knew," admitted Mont. "I hope his ticker is stronger than mine. Here, let's turn the video off now so we can discuss this without taping it, shall we?"

"Oh!" said Kayla. "I'd quite forgotten the camera, Dad. Sorry."

On the screen they watched Mont stand and walk toward the camera. Then the television went blank.

Josh pressed the off button and stood up stretching, pretending he hadn't paid any attention to the last few comments.

"What was that all about?" asked Ed, fear tightening in his throat.

Josh hardly knew how to respond. He'd been so distraught over Kayla that he hadn't thought ahead about Tom, he hadn't considered the ramifications if Ed had the slightest inkling that Tom may have been involved in the assault against Morning Sun.

"Hmm?" Josh mumbled, walking toward the kitchen. "Are you hungry?"

"You heard me, Josh," Ed drawled. "I've been straight with you all day, about Kayla, about my feelings. Now you'd better be straight with me!"

Josh sighed and turned to face him. "If you'd promised Kayla not to discuss this with anyone, what would you do?"

Ed paused. He knew he was treading in deep water and he felt like he was drowning. He paced back and forth for a moment, much like a caged tiger anxious for freedom. "What would Tom do that was so terrible Mont nearly had a heart attack over it?" He asked, more to himself than to Josh.

Which didn't help the agony Josh felt for the man. Ed's father was missing and now Ed was about to discover something horrible about his own brother. Would it never end for Ed, this bitter torment?

Ed continued the pacing. "What did Tom do, Josh? What was so terrible that Mont would keep it from Pa?"

"Concentrate on the current situation," Josh said calmly, stepping cautiously toward the door. "You're not going to help your father if you go off on some tangent, Ed."

Suddenly Ed bristled. "It was Morning Sun!" he whispered hoarsely, his voice hollow as he realized what had happened. "That day I found her, she was delirious, she said something about the fire water. I thought she wanted me to put out some fire that she'd seen in hallucination. She was really talking about liquor, wasn't she?"

Josh kept his voice steady, authoritative. "Think about your father and what we need to do to help him," he said. "Focus on what's important right now."

"No!" Ed cursed vehemently. "You tell me! Was it Tom that beat Morning Sun to a pulp that day?"

Josh arched an eyebrow. "Your father doesn't expect you to chase after any more nightmares tonight but the one they're living," he said calmly, trying to gain control of a terrible situation.

"Tell me straight, Josh!" demanded Ed. "I've got a lot of respect for you, seeing what you've gone through with Kayla missing. Don't you know that Morning Sun is like my own mother? You tell me it straight or I'll go wring it out of Tom."

"I'll tell you," Josh affirmed. "But only on the condition that you give me the keys to Li'l Posse."

"It wouldn't do much good," Ed admitted. "I know how to start her without the key, but I'm a man of my word, Josh. You know that much about me. You tell me what you know, and I won't do anything about it until after we find Pa, Kayla and Mont."

"Your word of honor?" questioned Josh, praying that Ed would have the integrity to keep the promise.

"Yes," clipped Ed. "You have my word of honor."

Josh sighed and shook his head. "Sit down," he instructed quietly. "I'll tell you everything I know."

Chapter
Twenty-One

"Dang! Would you sit down! You're driving me nuts!" Ed complained as the clock on the mantle struck midnight. The loud chimes reminded them that Christmas Day had arrived.

Josh nodded. Then he wandered out to the front porch and looked out over the little valley where the snow lay eight or nine feet deep. He had the sensation of being in a mountain meadow in the Swiss Alps.

Ed followed him out. "I owe you one," he admitted ruefully. "You need to know that our odds have gone down quite a bit with the second night passing."

"The sky is clearing," said Josh. "It's Christmas! We're going to find them today, I just know it. God works His finest miracles on Christmas Day."

"If we get a break in the weather, if we get lucky, and if they're still alive," replied Ed. "I don't mean to startle you, Josh. I know this country like the back of my hand. We're dealing with rugged mountain terrain that can snatch a body away and keep it for years before it gives up its secrets."

"You believe we may never find them?" asked Josh.

"If we don't find them by tomorrow night, the search will probably be called off completely," Ed confessed. "Believe me, I know how it works. Unless they've dug themselves into a snow cave somewhere, they're likely already gone."

Josh didn't know how to respond. The information had unsettled him, but had not been unexpected. "Why did you wait until now to tell me this?"

"Because you have so much hope for Kayla," confessed Ed. "Truthfully, Josh, they may not have lasted through the snow storm."

Josh nodded, his mind in a daze. "I expected as much. So I'll tell you something that I know for a fact. Kayla is alive. I can feel her. Don't ask me to explain. I don't know about Mont or your father, but right now, Kayla is alive."

"Maybe you're intuitive enough with spiritual matters that you would know," Ed conceded, realizing an argument with the Commander would be fruitless. He placed his hat on his head and walked toward the steps.

Josh gave him a questioning glance.

"Don't worry," said Ed. "I'm only going over to the cabin to get a shower and a change of clothes. Besides, I do my praying in private."

Josh almost smiled. "I understand," he offered.

Ed stomped down the front steps and out across the meadow along the plowed path. When he arrived at the cabin he entered and slammed the door shut. He had so many mixed emotions coursing through him he didn't know what to do with himself.

Anger seemed to be the worst emotion for the moment. He'd learned to deal with anger long ago, when Kayla broke off their engagement. The first thing he did was climb in a hot shower and let it pour over him until it ran cold. He finally scrubbed down after the water chilled him so bad he felt numb. Afterward, he put on clean clothing and stretched out on Sparky's bed.

The odds of finding Sparky, Mont or Kayla alive when daylight arrived were slim to none. He knew it, and he knew Josh knew it. A deep sadness seemed to start in his toes and work it's way up his body. When it finally reached his throat he thought he would choke on it. The three people whom he loved more than anything else in the world may never be found. The sadness stretched painfully within him, not only in regards to the possibility of not finding the trio, but also to the information Josh had given him about Tom. Perhaps it was for the best, where Sparky was concerned. If they made it back and Pa learned about Tom, well, he just didn't know what it would do to his father.

"Oh, Pa!" he moaned. "Mont was right. If you knew about Tom, it'd kill you." He pulled the pillow over his face and wept bitterly.

With Ed at the cabin, Josh was left to his own thoughts. He paced back and forth across the front porch. He wandered through the lodge and felt like whimpering, like a lost puppy, just as Kayla had said to her father. In the kitchen he opened the refrigerator and looked inside. But nothing struck his interest. He closed the door softly and went back out on the front porch to watch, and wait.

Then he offered up another brief prayer, almost exactly like the thousands he'd offered in the last thirty-two hours. "Is she alive, Lord? Will you help her?"

When he raised his eyes he had tears in them. However, they were tears of joy, mingled with fear. Yes, he thought to himself, Kayla is alive, but where? Where?

Kayla smiled as she listened to her mother sing a little melody. It was a lullaby she hadn't heard her sing since she was a toddler. The dulcet tones seemed almost angelic and Kayla breathed peacefully as she heard it.

> "Sleep my Kayla, close your eyes
> When you wake, you'll be surprised.
> Daddy loves you, Mama, too.
> Heaven sent us just for you."

Kayla yawned and looked out over the valley that lay ahead. The snow sparkled in the faint moonlight. Heavenward the skies had cleared. Stars shone brightly and the moon, little more than a sliver, cast a dim light across the valley floor. Yet it seemed much brighter to her and she reasoned it was due to illumination from the snow.

Listening carefully beyond her mother's song, Kayla could hear the tender prayer of her father, from somewhere in the forest. Smiling to herself, Kayla offered a soft-spoken prayer of her own. "Dear God, it's me, Kayla. I don't know what more I could ask from you right now. You've given me everything: a mother who sings to me, a father who prays for me, a man who loves me and wants to marry me. I'm sorry I didn't recognize you before now. I don't know what was wrong with me, but that was a lifetime ago. So here I am, knowing how much you've blessed me and loving you for it. Anyway, I just wanted you to know."

She waited a long time for God to answer her, but she didn't hear Him this time. She listened intently but no, she couldn't even hear her mother's beautiful song anymore. Anxiously she realized that Mont had finished his prayer and was no longer talking to the Lord as he'd been just moments before. The uneasiness grew within her until, all of a sudden, she jerked into full consciousness.

Mont had stepped into the forest some time ago and had not returned. She panicked. Where was he?

"Dad," Kayla mumbled. "Dad, where are you?"

When Mont did not answer, Kayla trembled. "Dad!" she said sharply, "Where are you?"

"Right here," he whispered softly. "I'm right here beside you." Mont bent down and gave her a gentle kiss. "I think your fever's gone," he announced. "And your breathing sounds better."

Kayla realized that he was right but she ignored any reference to herself for the moment. She was more concerned about Mont. "You were gone so long," she whispered. "I was afraid."

"You have no reason to be afraid now," said Mont. "I'm feeling much better."

"I heard you praying," confessed Kayla. "I've been praying, too."

"I know," he assured her. "I know." He picked up the head of the stretcher and headed east across the valley that stretched ahead of them. "Let's go. It won't take long now."

"What time is it?" she asked.

"Around two in the morning," he answered.

"We slept too long, didn't we?"

"It helped," he confessed. "I can make it the rest of the way now."

Kayla settled back against the stretcher. Mont was right, she decided, listening carefully to her lungs within her. She couldn't hear the rattling sound that had disturbed her earlier. A strange and peaceful calm settled over her. She also noticed that her teeth were not chattering any longer and she actually felt warm. She wondered for a moment if it was hypothermia setting in, but realized immediately that a greater power than nature was at work for her benefit. She closed her eyes and slept while Mont pulled her forward, ever forward.

Josh looked out over the meadow as he paced up and down the porch. His heart filled with prayer as he waited and worried.

He sighed wearily and sat down in the old rocking chair that had spent almost eight decades on the big, wide porch. The clouds had fled eastward and stars appeared in a brilliant display across the night sky. He looked across the meadow to the cabin where a soft light came from the windows and he knew that Ed was still awake, waiting, just like him.

The night had turned bitter cold and Josh was keenly aware of terms like hypothermia and dehydration. He sat on the porch until he felt so chilled he had to seek warmth from the fireplace inside.

After stirring the hot coals and adding more wood, Josh removed his shoes and put them on the hearth to warm up. Then he leaned back in the recliner, resting, waiting. Before long the warmth from the fire spread through him. He closed his eyes for the first time in almost 45 hours. Unable to control the slumber that permeated his whole body, Josh fell into a deep and restful sleep.

"There it is," Kayla, sighed Mont, disturbing her rest. "I see lights ahead."

Kayla opened her eyes and tried to turn enough to see the lodge but she was too weary. "Thank you, Lord," she whispered. "Thank you." Kayla looked back from whence they came. The snow lay crisp and sparkly as far back as she could see. She closed her eyes to stop the tears from streaming down her cheeks. They were almost home. Almost home.

When they finally reached the path in front of the porch, Mont laid the stretcher down and leaned over her. "Princess," he whispered softly, taking her hand. "You're going to be all right now," he comforted. "You have a whole world of joy waiting for you. You'll be able to marry and raise a big family. You'll have lots of children and live to a ripe old age."

"I know," she sniffed through her tears.

"Don't spend your life worrying about what's happened these past two days, Princess. I'll never be far from you, I promise."

"I know, Dad," she reassured him.

"And Kayla, he said, giving her the best smile she'd ever seen, "Remember, with God, all things are possible."

Mont gave her a tender kiss on the forehead, then stood and walked up the steps to the porch.

She heard the front door open and close. She wondered why Josh wasn't here yet. Was it still Christmas Eve or Christmas Day? She'd lost track of time and couldn't remember. It must be Christmas, she thought happily. Josh once said God works His finest miracles on Christmas Day. And this Christmas day, she knew it was true.

Josh heard the door close and it startled him. He sat upright and saw Mont standing in the Gathering Room. "She needs your help," Mont nodded toward the door. "I'll call Ed to fire up the chopper."

Josh brushed past him in an instant as he fled outside and down the porch steps.

On the ground, strapped to a makeshift stretcher, he found his beloved Kayla. Both her legs were bound tightly to a pair of skis. "Kayla!" he cried. "Kayla!" He knelt beside her.

"There you are," she whispered. "I've been looking for you."

He laughed and cried, all at the same time. Then he kissed her face, her eyes, her hair. His tears mingled with hers. "You're hurt," he offered lamely. "What happened?"

But Kayla couldn't answer immediately. All she could do was cry as she savored the sweet, husky smell of him, and the taste of his tears against her lips.

Across the meadow, at the cabin, Ed was jolted awake by the telephone ringing. "Yes!" he snapped as he grabbed the phone.

From the other end of the receiver he heard Mont's familiar voice. "Better fire up the Li'l Posse, Ed."

"Mont?" came Ed's startled response. "You're back?"

"Kayla needs a quick transport to the hospital, son."

"I'm on my way!" Ed shouted as he hung down the receiver and reached for his coat.

Kayla sobbed uncontrollably into Josh's strong shoulder as he cradled her tenderly upon the plowed down snow in front of the porch. "It's all right, Kayla. Take your time."

She heard the cabin door slam shut across the meadow and footsteps crunching rapidly on the snow down the lane as Ed raced toward them.

Josh took a handkerchief from his pocket and wiped her face. She had a bruise across the right side of her forehead. "What happened?" asked Josh tenderly.

Ed arrived and slid onto his knees beside her.

"Avalanche," she whispered. She wanted Mont to tell Ed about Sparky, knowing she didn't have the courage to tell him herself.

"Are you all right, Kayla Dawn?" asked Ed tearfully. His sister was home, he thought wildly. His sister was safe! The realization that Kayla was, indeed, his beloved sister, freed him forever from all the anger and aching of the past seven years. The lump in his throat melted as tears slipped carelessly from his eyes. He hugged her and kissed her cheek tenderly.

Kayla gulped. "There was an avalanche on the far side of Porcupine Ridge," she whispered.

She saw the look in Ed's eyes and knew he was wondering about his father.

She looked at Josh. "Where's Dad?" she asked.

"Mont went in the kitchen," answered Josh. "Go check on him, will you, Ed?"

Kayla nodded. It would be easier on her if Ed would go inside where Mont could tell him about Sparky.

"Where's Pa?" asked Ed. "Did he go in the house with Mont?"

"I didn't see him," answered Josh. "Kayla?"

Kayla pulled Josh's head closer to her. "Get Dad," Kayla whispered in his ear.

Ed stood up and jumped over Kayla in one swift motion. He raced up the front steps and across the porch where he flung the door open and called out, "Mont! Pa!"

Kayla sobbed for what seemed an eternity as Josh cradled her against him. While she was crying, Ed returned, unnoticed by her. He was pale and tight-lipped.

"Sparky's gone, isn't he?" Josh asked softly.

Kayla nodded. "How am I ever going to face my brothers?" she asked Josh. "Sparky died in the avalanche while trying to save me."

"Where did you say the avalanche was?" Ed asked, his face ashen, almost white in the pale light.

Kayla looked up at him, surprised to find him standing there. She gulped. "On the far side of Porcupine Ridge," she answered. "Is Dad all right?"

"As well as can be expected," said Ed. "He brought you in from the west?"

"Yes," she said, clearing her throat. "We had to come up over the ridge and back down into Mountain Meadow, then up through the valley."

Ed removed his hat and studied the snow-covered valley, faintly illuminated by the stars overhead and a slim, silver moon.

Josh stood momentarily and listened carefully as Ed spoke in a hushed whisper to him, but Kayla couldn't hear them. Kayla thought she heard Josh say something like, "That's impossible." Then Josh looked out across the valley and followed the smooth, even contours of the snow for some distance before his vision blurred.

Kayla began to feel uneasy about their whispering. "What's wrong?" she questioned. "Where's Dad?"

Ed knelt beside her and took her hand. "We need to get you to the hospital right away," he comforted. "Mont doesn't want you to worry about him right now. He wants you to see Doc Nillson, and afterward, we'll talk about what happened up on Porcupine Ridge. All right?"

"No!" she snapped, angry at Ed for patronizing her. "Will you stop treating me like I'm a child?!! Where is my father?"

Josh, stunned and silent until now, bent down beside her and cradled her in his strong arms. "Kayla, we don't know what happened after the avalanche, perhaps God is the only one who does."

"Before you begin," she said, holding back her tears as a peaceful calm settled upon her, "while I was in the avalanche I learned about

God. He's real, Josh. He's real and He loves us. What ever has happened to my father, I'm ready."

Josh sighed in relief. "Good," he said, "then you need to know that Ed searched everywhere in the lodge for Mont, but he's not in there."

"What?" asked Kayla, uncertain she had heard correctly.

"Mont's not in the lodge, darling," Josh reiterated. "And there are no tracks in the snow."

"But he carried me here," Kayla said. "Josh, you saw him, didn't you?"

Josh nodded. "I did. He told me you were outside and he was going to telephone Ed to get the helicopter ready for you."

"Ed," she asked quickly. "Did he call you?"

"Yes," Ed answered, tears stinging the back of his eyes as he kept them in reserve. "He said that I'd better fire up the Li'l Posse because you need a quick transport to the hospital. He called me 'son,'" Ed realized aloud.

"Are you sure he's not in the lodge?" Kayla asked. "Maybe he went upstairs to lay down."

"I searched every room," Ed sighed wearily. "He's not in there. I don't know where he is."

"We can't see any tracks in the snow, Kayla," Josh persuaded. "Ed, where are my night binoculars?"

"In Li'l Posse," said Ed, standing. "I'll fire her up and bring the binoculars back with me."

"I have to see this, Josh," pleaded Kayla. "I have to see the meadow with my own eyes."

Soon the helicopter roared to life and Ed returned, giving Kayla the binoculars. She made the men position her so she could scope out the entire meadow. To her utter amazement, they were absolutely right. There was not a single track across the snow anywhere.

Yet here she was, she thought, as though it were all some crazy, unexplainable dream. She hadn't walked back to the lodge. Both her legs were broken. She was strapped to a makeshift stretcher that Mont had hewn with his own hands. The skis had been strapped to her body by Mont. He had carried her up to the top of Porcupine Ridge and down again to the other side. And he had fallen asleep next to her at the bottom of the slope, near the stand of pine trees and a large boulder. He had kissed her cheek right before he went into the house to wake Josh.

"When we arrived," she said calmly, "he spoke to me. I can still hear his words. He said, 'Don't spend your life worrying about what's happened these past two days, Princess. I'll never be far from you, I promise.' I reassured him that I knew this. Then he gave me the most wonderful smile I'd ever seen him give and he said, 'Remember, with God, all things are possible.' Then he went inside."

"He called me son," remembered Ed quietly as tears slipped from his eyes. "But he's gone just as surely as Pa is gone, isn't he?"

"I remember tracks coming down the south slope," Kayla recalled. "But at the bottom we both fell asleep. I don't remember seeing the tracks after that. We have to find the tracks, Ed. Otherwise, the wolves will get him."

"We need to get you to the hospital," Josh reminded her sternly.

"No!" she protested. "I'm not going to the hospital until I know where my father is. Ed, you've got to take us up. The weather has cleared. With the night binoculars I can show you where we were tonight."

"Kayla Dawn," Ed began. "Josh is right. You need to—"

"I need to find my father!" she snapped angrily. "And if you don't take me there, I may find it difficult to forgive either one of you!"

The two men exchanged glances. Josh shrugged. "She's right, you know. She's too stubborn for her own good."

"Dang right," drawled Ed. "Let's go then."

Moments later Kayla was in the helicopter and Ed was flying over the meadow. With the night vision binoculars she surveyed the meadows carefully. Yet there were no tracks in the snow anywhere until they reached the stand of trees. Then the tracks were clearly visible, coming from the south slope and going up over the top of Porcupine Ridge.

A peaceful calm settled upon Kayla as she looked through the binoculars and saw with her own eyes that the snow had been completely disturbed where Mont and she had slept that night. "Let me go, Kayla," came Mont's voice in her heart and in her mind. "I'm content now to be with your mom, and with Sparky."

"Goodbye, Daddy," she whispered as tears of peace spilled from her dark brown eyes. "I love you so."

Then she wiped the tears away and said to Josh, "Dad's in those trees." She intuitively sensed where her father's body would be found. "He went in there to pray for us." She looked at Ed. "When it's daylight, you follow our tracks from here, Ed, up over the Ridge and down again. You'll find Sparky where Dad left Jell-O traces."

"Thank God," Ed whispered hoarsely, unable to keep the tears at bay any longer.

Chapter Twenty-Two

"The surgery went very well," Doctor Nillson spoke to the group at the hospital. "The right leg will take longer to heal and she will need some physical therapy, but I expect a complete recovery."

Josh sighed heavily. "When can I see her?"

"She'll be in recovery for at least another half hour. You could go down to 207 and wait. That's where they'll bring her once she awakens." The doctor smiled and gave Josh a handshake. "She comes from strong stock, Josh. You may be surprised at her resilience."

Josh nodded. "Thanks." he said.

Sarah rubbed Josh's back while the Admiral sat on the other side of Josh. "I think we should go down to the cafeteria," suggested Sarah.

"I'm really not hungry and I promised I would let Ed know the minute she's out of surgery," protested Josh.

"As you wish, Son," Admiral Bridger Clark smiled and nodded at Sarah. "Come along, Mother. Let's give him some space."

Sarah took Bridger's offered hand. "We'll be back shortly," she said.

"I'll wait in her room," Josh told them.

They nodded and left him sitting there as they walked down the hall to the elevator.

Josh stood up and stretched. He located room 207 and stepped inside. The room smelled sterile, like a mixture of ammonia and alcohol and deodorizer all mixed together.

Josh picked up the telephone and dialed the airport number. A man's voice answered, "Ashley Valley Airport."

"This is Joshua Clark."

"How's Kayla?" asked the voice.

Joshua didn't even know this man but he seemed to know Kayla.

"She's out of surgery and the doctor expects her to make a full recovery," said Josh.

"You give her our love," said the man. "I'll radio Ed and let him know."

"Did they get—?" Josh hesitated.

"They brought their Pa's body down about a half hour ago," said the voice. "Now they've gone after Mont."

"Thank you," said Josh. "I'll let them know if there's any change."

Goodbyes were said and Josh hung up the phone. He walked over to the window and looked out onto the street. It was nearly one in the afternoon, he noticed, glancing at his watch. The skies were clear and blue.

He was relieved Ed, Tom and Will had found the location of Sparky's body. He hoped they were equally successful in their search for Mont. His mind had wandered back through the scene in front of the lodge so many times that day he felt dizzy with it. Yet he knew that Mont had awakened him. He could still hear Mont's exact words: "She needs your help. I'll call Ed to fire up the chopper." Josh had actually seen Mont. He was there!

Ed, the third witness to support Mont's presence, had listened to Mont's voice on the phone. Mont had called him from the kitchen phone at the lodge. It seemed so impossible!

Josh rubbed his forehead, shook his head and thought the scenario through another time.

There were no tracks in the snow, he thought over and over again. It was almost like some angel had picked Kayla up and carried her to the lodge through the air, without touching the snow below them.

Yet Kayla insisted it was Mont who pulled her stretcher all the way from the site of the avalanche to the lodge.

He felt relieved knowing that Sparky's body had been brought back. Kayla had given them fairly good directions. He prayed she was equally accurate in her assessment of where they would find Mont.

The change in her demeanor and attitude toward Deity had astounded him. Kayla had such an incredible experience that it had changed her, for the better, forever. He was relieved that their children would one day learn from their mother to know God. He smiled as he thought of the possibilities this would open up to them. Intuitively he knew that Kayla would bless his own life because of what had happened to her on a lonely mountain slope in the Uintahs.

Within minutes the helicopter reached the bottom of the mountain where the foot of it rested in the quiet little valley known as Mountain Meadow. Not far from a small patch of forest, they spotted the boulder Kayla had pointed out earlier.

Ed maneuvered the helicopter back around while Tom and William studied the area with binoculars.

"I see a thermos," William said finally. "And I see some foot prints heading off into that stand of trees."

Ed flew the helicopter over the trees but they were too thick to see anything. He hovered around the patch so his brothers could focus on the perimeter.

After a few moments Tom said, "Nope. There are footprints going in, but none coming out."

"I'm going to put her down," said Ed.

"Careful!" warned Tom.

"We'll see if we can blow out an opening," Ed agreed.

He chose a spot not too far east of the trail where he hovered barely above the snow, allowing the propeller blades to move it around in circles away from them. After a few minutes he tested the spot by bumping it with the runners. The runners sank too deeply. Ed pulled up.

"Nope," said William. "It's too deep."

"I'll hover for you," Ed offered.

"Sure," agreed Will. "I'll go down. Tom, you man the basket."

"Will do," agreed Tom.

Ed considered. The last thing they needed up here was another accident. "Hurry up, then!" He instructed.

William fastened a belt to his waist and hooked it onto a karabiner on an electric pulley mounted in the helicopter. Tom lowered him to the ground and William released the karabiner.

William waded almost waist deep in snow until he reached the red thermos. He picked it up and noticed the Bar M brand etched into the bottom of it.

The packed snow around a small boulder indicated clearly that this was the spot where Mont had laid down beside Kayla, where they had slept until well after midnight.

William followed the tracks to the stand of thick Douglas fir trees. The snow had been crushed in spots by snow shoes, apparently the ones made by Mont at the avalanche site.

A short distance into the forest William found Mont. His body was on top of the deep snow, in a praying position. Will knelt beside the gentle giant and offered a prayer of his own. Then he took a radio out of his heavy coat pocket and pressed a button.

"Send down the basket, Tom" he said hoarsely. "Looks like Kayla was right. Mont and Pa are now partners in Heaven."

Tom attached the body-length basket to the winch and lowered it down to Will. Then Ed and Tom waited for Will to bring the body out.

"How long since you had your last drink?" Ed asked suddenly, taking Tom off guard.

"Since Wednesday night," came the clipped, tense remark.

"Forty-eight hours?"

"There about," said Tom defensively. "Why?"

"I made a promise to Josh," answered Ed, "that I wouldn't do anything until we found Kayla, Pa and Mont."

"What are you talking about?" asked Tom, pain evident on his face and in his eyes.

"I'm talking about Morning Sun," said Ed. "I want you to tell me what really happened that day."

"What?" Tom hedged.

"I'm asking you now," Ed explained, "because I have a helicopter to run, Tom. If I'd chosen to ask you when I had my hands free, I would have beaten you to a pulp first, and then asked questions. You're my brother, and God help me, I still love you. So I figured the only safe way you would have of telling me the truth is now, while my hands are too busy to wring it out of you."

Tom remained silent for a long time. He wrung his hands and paid no heed as tears slipped down his cheeks.

Soon they saw William dragging Mont's body out of the thicket of trees, as he prepared to place it into the basket.

Finally Tom confessed, "I was drunk and out of my mind with greed, Ed. I didn't mean it to happen. I went looking for the deed to the ranch, thinking I could forge Mont's signature and get all the money for it, but I couldn't find it. I got angry and drank myself into a stupor. The next day, when I finally came to, I thought it was all a nightmare. I kept thinking it was just a nightmare. I kept thinking it was Kayla I had attacked in a nightmare."

Ed exhaled raggedly. "Then it's a good thing Pa died up here. Because if the avalanche hadn't killed him, this news would have."

Tom's eyes, already filled with tears, produced so many that it dripped down his face and off his chin onto his gray parka. "I've been drinking ever since to bury the shame of what I've done."

"You're going to have to own up to it, Tom. You need to quit drinking now and set your life in order. If you don't, I fear you may never see Pa again."

Tom wept bitterly with these words. They clawed into his very soul as he realized Ed had said only the truth. "After we get Mont back, take me over to the Sheriff's office," he said finally. "I'll make a full confession."

Ed sighed heavily. He didn't know whether to feel relief or dismay. In his heart he felt the burden of what lay ahead for his family. It was a burden he didn't want to carry, but being the oldest son, he knew it would be on his shoulders now to help his family through the trials ahead of them.

"I know God wants me to forgive you, Tom," Ed whispered raggedly, "but it'll take some time. I hope you understand."

"I know," said Tom. "But not near as hard as it'll be for me to forgive myself."

For one brief moment Ed felt the exquisite relief one feels when, finally, they have approached an issue in a manner that enables relationships to grow, rather than disables. Of course his first instinct had been to rip Tom's legs off, but he knew that God had a better way. He'd been praying, ever since Josh told him about Tom, that he would find a better way. In his heart, he felt the divine and comforting sensation that he had.

Three days after surgery Kayla and Josh were married at the hospital where she would have to stay for another week, with exception of the double funeral tomorrow.

It isn't exactly like she envisioned her honeymoon, she thought to herself as she felt the tender rubbing against her right hand ease until Josh stopped rubbing it all together. She opened her eyes and looked at him tenderly. His head rested upon his free hand, on the bed, and he was sound asleep, while sitting in a chair next to her. Smiling at him, she realized he was definitely right. With Mont and Sparky both gone back to God, Kayla had little choice but to hire a nurse or marry him. She liked his second suggestion best.

Of course her wedding day was not supposed to have taken place in a hospital on the 28th of December, but it had.

The surprising thing had been her talk with Ed the night before. He'd asked Josh if he could speak with her in private so Josh had gone to the cafeteria with his parents to have supper. Ed pulled the chair up beside her bed and took her hand. He pulled it up to his lips and kissed it tenderly. "You know I love you, don't you?" he asked.

"Yes," she answered. "And I—"

"Big brothers are supposed to love their little sisters," he interrupted, giving her a tender expression that melted her heart.

"Yes," she agreed. "They are."

"I guess Josh told you we both watched the video."

"Yes." Kayla nodded.

"Dang, Kayla Dawn!" he drawled. "All these years of loving you and wishing I could hate you, only to find out I still love you, but it's still not like I thought I loved you. What a mess!"

She smiled. "We certainly had a lot to learn, didn't we?"

"Can you imagine if we'd married and had children, only to find out now that it was the wrong kind of love for marriage?" he asked.

"No, I'm glad we didn't go through with it," she agreed.

"I guess Josh told you about Tom?" Ed questioned.

"How is Morning Sun taking it?" she asked as she nodded in response.

"She doesn't want to press charges against him, but the sheriff thinks they will, anyway."

She tried to comfort Ed. "If Tom could give up the liquor and walk a straight path from here on, I think he could find some peace with what's happened. Morning Sun is delighted to have her baby and that should count for something."

"You've already forgiven him?" asked Ed in bewilderment.

"You forget," she said, "I've learned who the man upstairs really is. I turned my back on Him for almost twelve years, and He forgave me," she answered, surprised that she felt so strongly about it.

"I guess I can't be outdone by my little sister, can I?"

She smiled.

They talked for two hours before she had to take another pain pill. Josh had finally joined them after eating a hearty meal with his parents. The Clarks had gone back to the motel until the wedding tomorrow.

Of course, the Admiral was furious but Sarah had been able to smooth out the rough edges once again.

Right before Ed left he gave Kayla a kiss on the forehead. "I have a favor to ask," he said softly, staring into her dark brown eyes.

"What?" she asked.

"Let me give you away tomorrow. As your big brother, with both our Dads on the other side, I think I should."

Kayla looked at Josh quickly and saw a big grin spread across his face as he nodded. "Of course," she'd agreed.

And he did.

Kayla looked at the wedding band caressing the diamond on her left hand. She thought about the simple wedding that afternoon, Ed had pushed her into the hospital chapel in her wheel chair. Josh, sweet Josh, was waiting for her at the altar. Their wedding was simple and sweet.

Then she thought about her name. She rolled it around on her tongue several times, "Mrs. Joshua Bridger Clark. Kayla Dawn Allen Clark."

The past few days had certainly thrown some curves into her otherwise scientific life. She felt immediately grateful that Mont had given *one last gift* to her. He thought he had asked her to come home so that he could present her with KayDawn's gift. Little had he realized the greatest gift of all would come from himself. Mont had taught her more about the divinity of God that Holiday Season than he had ever hoped for, or dreamed possible. He'd been disappointed that she couldn't believe in God. He'd prayed for a miracle, for some way to show Kayla who God is and how much He loves her. Then Mont did what he had done all his life, he made the miracle happen.

Even that afternoon as she and Josh said, "I do," while Sarah cried and Bridger snarled (he had such a terrible time accepting itineraries contrary to his own), Mont had been on hand, teaching Kayla more each passing moment about her place in the eternal scheme of life.

Strange, Kayla thought, I spent a lifetime trying to learn about my mother and now I know her better in four days than I had in twenty-eight years. And yes, KayDawn Allen had attended Kayla's wedding just as surely as Mont and Sparky had. Kayla had felt their presence, but before she could even say so, Josh had whispered in her ear, "Your parents are here."

"So is Sparky," she'd whispered back.

It all seemed so perfect to her now. The eternal family unit was a doctrine she had been taught all her life. Yet only now had she begun to understand. It made so much sense, she reasoned, worrying why she had never been able to see this clearly before. It would be impossible for two people who love each other as much as she and Josh did, to be separated forever at death. Love carries on, beyond the grave. Parents are mindful of their children whether on this side of heaven, or on the other side.

And what about angels? Yes, angels are real people, but more likely than not, she realized, they are family. Parents watch over their off-spring from Heaven. It was only right that God should let them. Who else could love someone more than a family member could?

A lump of happiness filled her chest as she warmed to the inspiration of the spirit. Yes, Mont had given her a gift all right! He'd given her *one last gift* that would change her life forever.

The next day Kayla sat in a wheelchair at the chapel. Both her legs were wrapped in heavy bandages and splints. She wore a velvet blue dress and had her hair pulled up in a french twist. Sarah had styled it for her and Kayla was amazed at the talent of her new mother. Josh and Kayla had gone over to the church early so they would have plenty of time before the funeral began.

Kayla said goodbye to Mont and Sparky. Holding her father's hand, she whispered, "Thank you, Dad. You gave me back my faith." She closed her eyes and feasted upon the spirit for several minutes, basking in the love she felt from her parents and Sparky.

"Are you sure you want to stay for the funeral?" Josh asked after a long pause.

"They'd stay for mine," she insisted bravely. "Without them, I wouldn't be here."

"I know, sweetheart," Josh sighed. "But I don't want my wife taxing herself before the doctor even releases her from the hospital."

"I'll be fine," she insisted. "I've been through far worse times than today, remember."

He sighed and gave up trying to persuade her. He could see that her stubborn streak would, occasionally, get them into trouble. He chose to change the subject to something happier. "Thank you," he said softly. His voice filled her with deep tenderness. He kissed her nose.

"For what?" she asked.

"For marrying me yesterday," he grinned.

"Thank YOU!" she responded with a brief smile. "Though what you see that's so romantic about spending your wedding night in a hospital, holding my hand, I'll never know."

"Honeymoons can wait until you're well," he explained once again. "After what we've both been through, I may never let you out of my sight again."

"Wasn't that sweet of Ed," she asked, "to give me away like that?"

"Who would have thought?" was his response. "I guess he really does love you."

"Immensely!" she agreed. "I'm so glad he's realized the truth about our relationship."

"And Tom?" he asked. "What's the prognosis there?"

"I expect that he's going to get off easier than I'd thought. Maybe it's just as well, he's taking Sparky's death harder than any of us."

Kayla shook her head. "Ed told me that Sparky had an accidental death policy to split amongst the boys. He said Tom told him to put his share in a trust fund for Morning Sun's baby. That says something about Tom, doesn't it?"

"Yes, but his drinking?" Josh worried.

"That's not going to be a problem," came Tom's voice from behind them.

"Tom!" said Kayla, surprised to see him. Josh turned around and shook hands with Tom as he approached.

"I'm not staying for the funeral," Tom told her. "It's too hard, too many eyes, if you get my drift."

"I'm sorry, Tom," Kayla started.

"No, I'm glad it's out in the open," Tom admitted. "I was in a drunken stupor that day. I hardly even remember what happened. And since then I've tried to stay drunk so I wouldn't remember."

"What about Charlene?" asked Kayla.

"She won't answer my calls. I can't say as I blame her. What I did was wrong. I made a deal with the district attorney. I'll serve minimum time, pay all the baby's medical expenses and child support. I'm glad to do it. I just have one problem left and that's how to forgive myself." He looked at the floor dejectedly. "But I'm not going to drink anymore," he affirmed. "That's why I'm here, to tell Pa, to promise Pa I'm going to straighten out. I wish I'd told him earlier on, but maybe it's better this way. Maybe Pa couldn't have handled a challenge big as me."

"We'll give you some privacy," Josh suggested. He pushed Kayla's wheelchair, leading her carefully through the open double doors that led to the chapel.

When they were out of hearing range, Josh sat in a chair beside her. "Just think," he sighed, "twenty-five years from now, we'll be facing new trials with our own family. I expect we'll have our share of Toms and Eds and Wills..."

"How many children do you think we'll have?" she asked playfully.

"I don't know," came his response. "How many do you want?"

"Oh," smiled Kayla deliciously. "I want a whole meadow full of them."

Epilogue

Kayla looked up at the lodge one more time. It looked too vacant and empty to her, but that would soon change. Summer was here, and the end of a long pregnancy was just around the corner. She rubbed her well rounded belly absently and walked up the steps where she unlocked the screen door. Opening it wide, she put her overnight bag against it so it would stay open.

She stepped across the wide porch and waved at Ed as he rode toward her on his horse. The meadow was covered with a blanket of summer blossoms of every color.

"Howdy, Sis," said Ed with a broad smile. "Did you just get in?"

"Yes," she answered, giving him a big grin.

"Looks like you and Melanie will be racing to see who has their baby first," he observed, looking at her rounded stomach.

"Two more months," she said, rubbing her belly with pride.

"I guess she'll beat you then. She's due next month."

"I heard," Kayla smiled. "But it's okay. We'll wait our turn."

Josh carried a load of suitcases from the van and headed up the steps. "Good afternoon," Josh said.

Ed nodded. "You need any help with that, Josh?"

"No," Josh answered. "She promised to pack light this summer, and believe it or not, she did."

Ed laughed, nodded, and looked down the driveway, away from her.

"Did you get the house finished?" Kayla asked when she sensed Ed was ready to leave.

"That's where I'm headed," he answered. "Alyssa wants it ready by Saturday for the wedding, and I promised her it would be."

"We're so excited for you, Ed," said Kayla. "And we can't wait to meet Alyssa."

"Thanks," said Ed. "We made some improvements up at the cemetery, if you'd care to look," he announced. "Hope you both like it."

"We will," she assured him. "How's Tom?"

"He's been sober for thirty months now," said Ed, "and he's finally off probation. He met a sweet little filly from Texas territory who wants him to mosey on down there and manage her filling station while they get better acquainted."

"That's wonderful," said Kayla with a broad smile.

"I'd best get up there and get busy," said Ed. "Morning Sun came over last week and cleaned everything up. All the bedding is fresh."

"Spit and polish," laughed Kayla, "if I know Morning Sun."

"She'll be up for the wedding. She thought you might like to practice parenthood with her son, Matthew."

"Wonderful," exclaimed Kayla.

Ed nodded, then tugged the reigns to the right and clicked his heels. "Git up!" he barked. "See you later, Sis." His white stallion, Breeze, responded immediately by heading down the driveway and then left, up the mountain side.

"He looks happy," Josh observed, wrapping his arms around Kayla and resting them on her round belly.

"He does," she agreed. "And I'm so happy about Tom."

"I'm happy about you," he hugged her tight, then turned her around to face him. He squatted down until he was eye level with Kayla's round belly. "How are you two doing in there?" he asked. "You know you gave your Mom a rough time last night."

As if in response one of the unborn twins kicked and the movement was plainly obvious beneath Kayla's summer yellow smock.

They both laughed. Then Kayla took his hand and led him down the steps. "Come on," she giggled. "Let's go see what those boys did to the cemetery."

They wandered around the west side of the lodge, up the stone path, past the creek and the Spring House. Still farther they went, hiking until Kayla was winded and Josh had to pull her up the last few feet. "You're expecting your body to do more than it's able," Josh observed, watching her puff with difficulty.

"You're the one who asked for twins," she accused. "I told you I was perfectly happy to settle for one at a time, but no," she teased.

"We got a late start," he retorted. "We should have had one child last summer and one this summer. We're just making up for lost time."

She punched him playfully in the arm, "It's not my fault the doctor wanted us to wait an extra year for my legs to heal," she complained. "I was perfectly willing to start our family earlier."

"Twins!" he yelled aloud, "This is your daddy, loving your mommy!" He scooped her into his arms and twirled her around, watching her hair whisk behind her in soft, golden curls.

"I'm too heavy," she protested. "You'll hurt your back!"

"Oh!" he moaned as he gently put her down. "Maybe you're right!" He placed his hand on his back and bent over in a feeble gesture.

She looked at him curiously, worrying if she'd really hurt him. He stood up straight and gave her a big grin. "Not to worry, Lady Dawn," he whispered, pulling her close to him.

"Why do you keep calling me that, Bridger's Child?!!" she asked.

He kissed her hungrily. "Because you deserve it!" he grinned.

As they approached the cemetery, Kayla had no sense of fear or sadness. She knew exactly where her father was, and Sparky as well. She learned about Heaven long ago. So had Josh. "Do you think we should have told Ed about our going to the San Diego Temple last month?" she asked.

"No," he insisted. "He thinks we'll only be able to attend his reception Saturday. He has no idea we plan to attend his Temple wedding as well. It will be one of the best surprises we could give him."

"I hope you're right," said Kayla.

"When have I ever led you astray?" he questioned.

"Never," she agreed, as she kissed him.

As they drew nearer to the burial site of her beloved parents and Sparky, she grew silent. Sometimes she missed them all so much. She longed for Mont to rub her feet and talk to her, and it had been such a long time since she'd heard KayDawn sing. She thought about Sparky's whiskered smile and how she missed it!

Occasionally, when Josh found her in a contemplative mood, he took Mont's place and rubbed her feet while she poured out her feelings to him.

Josh had been good to her since they married at the hospital three days after her surgery. Poor Josh had spent the first year of their marriage playing nursemaid to her, and the next year trying to persuade her to follow doctor's orders and wait that much longer before they started making any babies. She smiled with all the sweet memories they had created together. The love she felt for him when they first married had only grown stronger with each passing moment.

Kayla walked toward the spot where Mont and Sparky were buried. An arch had been built that stretched from Sparky's headstone over to Mont's. Twelve feet tall, it was made out of hand-hewn logs and varnished thickly to last for years to come. Carved into the top part of the arch were the words: <u>Partners For Life—Partners Forever</u>.

Kayla smiled brightly. "What a beautiful gesture," she murmured.

Wild flowers of every mountain variety bloomed around the head stones, and Kayla knew she would never have to worry about the cemetery's care with Ed managing the ranch.

Looking below them, they could see the roof of Ed's new house in a little clearing on the mountain side northeast of the lodge. To the south they could see the great valley of the Bar M Ranch. Far to the southwest they could see for miles, as far as Porcupine Ridge and Mountain Meadow.

Kayla sat down on a patch of freshly mowed grass and pulled Josh down beside her.

He stretched out on his back and put his arms underneath his neck to support his head. "Have you thought any more about the names for our little boys?" he asked.

"Yes," she admitted.

"And?" he asked.

"And I think the names you chose will suit our sons perfectly!"

He gave her a broad smile.

"You mean it?" he asked.

"After all," she agreed, nodding her head. "If it weren't for each and every one of those four men, our sons could never be. It's perfectly appropriate that we name them Bridger Lamont and Joshua Sparky."

Josh leaned up on one elbow and used his other hand to bring her face right next to his. Kayla could feel his warm breath upon her lips as he whispered, "I love you, Mrs. Clark!"

She gave him a delicious smile as she replied, "I love you back!"

Sherry Ann Miller

A Brief Biography

Sherry Ann Miller, the daughter of Burke and Merlyn (Clark) Stone, grew up in Long Beach, California, Salt Lake City and Pleasant View, Utah.

After marrying her eternal sweetheart and best friend, Frank Miller, she devoted most of her life to raising their seven children in an active LDS environment, during which time she excelled in private and professional writing and college courses. She now resides in North Ogden City, Utah, with her husband.

Sherry has written and directed several musical productions for LDS Wards, Stakes, and North Ogden City. In addition, she continues to write latter-day fiction, a genre dear to her heart.

Involved in family history the past fourteen years, Sherry has gathered more than 25,000 family names for temple ordinances. She has written several family history books, a biography of her mother, and a collection of spiritual experiences that have occurred while serving her departed ancestors. Currently she is writing a biography of her father regarding his unique role during the 1963-1964 Presidential Campaign.

On the latter-day scene, Sherry has served in most ward positions available to women, as well as several stake assignments, that have enriched and influenced her life.

Sherry enjoys time spent with family and friends, especially her twenty grandchildren.

Other interests include sailing with her husband aboard the Shoosey-Q (a Cape Dory 36 ft. Cutter), fishing, marine biology, traveling, photography, reading, and crocheting.